Not Now but Now

A NOVEL BY
M.F.K. Fisher

NORTH POINT PRESS
SAN FRANCISCO
1982

First published by the Viking Press, Inc. in 1947;
Reprinted by arrangement with the author
and with Viking Press, Inc.
Printed in the United States of America
Library of Congress Catalogue Card Number:82-081499
ISBN:0-86547-072-3
SECOND PRINTING

For Donald Friede

THE nearest Jennie ever came to being untrue to Jennie was the night all four of them were staying with her. It was not just one of the people who adored her, not even two: they were all there, wary and jealous and demanding.

There was Paul, innocent at least in his assumption that he could ever have her for the simple reason that he wanted her. He made her bones yawn, which in itself was an affront to her inviolability: she hated the ignominy of being drawn to him just because he was young and teasing and clean to smell. It was like catching a head cold because somebody else had a head cold because somebody else had and somebody else. It paired sneezes and sexual pleasure as human indignities, which was a wrong mating indeed, as none knew better than Jennie.

Then sitting beside Paul in the oversized, oversoft chaise longue in the California patio was old Julia, less regal than usual tonight after a good share of the dinner bottles of Folle Blanche and Mountain Zinfandel, but still sounding like a spoiled character actress whenever she opened her handsome horsy face. She had come without quibble, as she always did when Jennie nodded. She was as much a worshiper as ever Paul or any other man could be, although it was reassuringly plain that she bowed down not to the small fine body of the woman but to her silky house, with its rooms always waxed, its windows sparkling out upon the still mountains, its kitchen fat. Julia took respite from her lonely, luxurious wait for senility in the warm homeliness of Jennie's house, as surely as young Paul felt strong and sure to have Jennie lean over him and let her breasts send out a little puff, a delicate gas, of her private smell. Each drank at her fountain, sucked from her what she could give.

And Sir Harry drank, sucked; Barbara too. All four of them lay there in the dark patio, the night Jennie almost betrayed herself, like queen ants being fed. They were immobile with content, too full of what she had given them, willy-nilly, to move more than they must in order to keep breathing. And as Jennie lay a little apart from them, looking dispassionately at the darker shapes of their couches and then at the gentle glimmer of light from the low house behind them, she asked herself which got the most from her.

Perhaps it was Barbara, because she was even more innocent than Paul, and such a state demands most and gets it, the way the youngest child in a family is coddled in spite of its harelip or its foul temper or its stinks. Barbara was well formed, of course, and her nature was sweet, and she smelled like new-mown meadowflowers because of her youth and the way she had been raised to groom herself, but God! how dull she was to Jennie, how deadly dull, and how tired poor Jennie was of being kind to her!

"Jennie is wonderful," the girl would say straight out in her breathless voice. "Ah, Jennie, I adore you, beautiful Jennie, so wise, so witty, so all that I'd one day be!"

And Jennie would smile and touch her lightly on her bare shimmering shoulder, and her bones would yawn, not as they did for Paul, but with an almost intolerable boredom for such love. Some time, she thought, she would like to whip Barbara with a little jeweled whip, in payment for the helpless kindness such adoration asked for. Meanwhile she smiled, touched, gave. . . .

It was easier with old Harry. He knew more than anyone in the world, except perhaps Jennie. He took what she had for him, like all the others, but it was resignedly, because he recognized at last that there could be no better. He had lived too long to grasp. Instead he came when Jennie asked him to; he let her brandy, her *côtelettes* Valmont, her perfume, flow without protest through his rugged, hoary frame. He felt her knowing fingers and the soft sheets of his bed with the same awareness, the same acceptance of their fleeting.

He was perhaps the best of them, Jennie thought as she listened to them all and knew in the summer night how they pulled at her, taking, asking so much, giving nothing. At least he was past any real assault, so that the two could meet unhampered on the battleground, knowing each other's weapons to be those of mind and jaded hunger rather than such sharp ones of lust and fright as Paul and old Julia and the girl could sport.

The talk went on in the soft darkness, soft dark talk without end or beginning. Jennie felt that she had not been listening to it but floating in it, not swimming through it but floating, for years, ten or a hundred even. She stood up quickly, and her chair scratched against the flat hillstones of the patio, and it stopped, except for old Harry, deaf old Harry, who still murmured lewd courtesies to Barbara.

Jennie could feel their eyes turned toward her, waiting.

She sighed, and then said like a hostess in a bad play, "Go on, go on. Forgive me. I'll be back. But don't say anything too wonderful. I'll be furious if you do, really furious."

Paul laughed a little. "Will you miss our gossip most, Jennie, or do you still like to pretend that all your guests are, by the very fact that they are your guests, wits or at least wags?"

Barbara stirred. "You're bitchy, Paul, worse than a woman. Jennie doesn't gossip," she said intensely. "Jennie, you don't gossip, ever! I never heard you gossip," she said as if she were the only one who had ever really heard Jennie speak at all.

Jennie laughed sparingly, tenderly. "Barbara is too young to be anything but merciful," she said, and touched the girl with a light hand.

"Or love is blind," Paul said.

Jennie felt angry, but only in part of herself. The rest was waiting, ready to escape from these well-bred people who talked so much. She would go to her room, read, lie in the dark, wait for capsules to put her to sleep.

Sir Harry, with the mysterious suddenness of deaf people, picked up Paul's sentence. "Love is never blind." He cleared his throat to signal a possible *bon mot*. They all waited. "That, if Bobs will forgive any play on words which may offend her incredibly young ears, that is a fallacy."

Julia laughed at once, to show that she at least had caught the carefully enunciated pun, to show that she was quick and worldly, a perfect guest. Barbara laughed a little too, as if in respect, the dutiful convent graduate following her elders and betters, the near-nun, near-sophisticate.

Jennie walked across to Harry's chair and leaned over it so that she knew he could smell the perfume on her skin, under the white lace and the little crystals that shone in the starlight. "You are a disgusting old lecher."

That was what he wanted her to say, in just that soft, laughing, excited way. She could feel him open out with happiness: there he sat, old yes, impotent probably, but with a plump, charming dowager near him, a nubile girl close by, good brandy to hand and a respectful young man to pour it, and Jennie, Jennie herself, bending over him.

Why should she not? Why should she be stingy, now at the last?

It was indeed the last, she knew suddenly. She was going far away, not a few feet, but far. She could live no more in this womb of chitchat, of dark cozy death. She must burst from it or die of weariness of all these people. They were killing her, sucking her breath from between her lips without feeding her as they sucked, so that she hungered with an ugly, painful hunger. She wanted life from them, but they gave back nothing to sustain her.

Old Harry—he took everything from her, good dinners and the glimmer of her crystals and the titillation of her half-offered body, genteel hostess-whore. And Julia filled up wealthy vacuum here, in Jennie's house so waxed and lovely, away from the smooth succession of luxury hotels so waxed and lovely but empty of Jennie and the charming, witty, waggish friends. She sent daisies and orchids and chocolates wrapped in tufted satin; the old man wrote exquisite bread-and-butter notes on crested paper; Jennie smiled, starving, and asked them to come again, soon, soon.

Barbara—how draining was her steady eagerness to be

loved, and her arrogance, no matter how innocent, in thinking that she ever would be by proud, pure Jennie!

And Paul the other innocent—Jennie hated him most, because he came the nearest, through accidents of chemistry and time, to her destruction.

She sighed again, relieved to feel herself able to be so apart; it would be good to leave thus coolly.

Sir Harry was already clearing his throat, prepared to splash off once more into his own little pond of vicarious venery.

"I'll be back soon, darlings," Jennie said, smiling into the darkness at her lie, and as she walked lightly away she let herself brush against Paul's arm, and knew that it rippled like a snake with shock at feeling her casual, remote flesh under her dress. It made her breath flow more easily, to have stopped his. Perhaps it would rouse him enough to exert himself a little toward Barbara, she thought with her own kind of primness. That would be good for them both, and more normal, two healthy young animals . . .

But what could it matter to her? Why should she continue to arrange such meaningless liaisons? What good did they do her? Her creatures lay back in the soft dark, lifeless, letting her feed and perfume and stroke. What did she get for it besides the knowledge that they were hers? As she walked swiftly through the silky perfection of her house she felt more and more outraged. If she were the kind of woman who permitted herself to cry she would cry now, tears bitter as alum. People took from her, took bread and her beauty and her fine sense of balance, and they gave her nothing but the involuntary narcosis of their gossip. She was sick of it, sick to death.

She stood in her room behind the thin, faintly moving silk of the curtains and let her tunic fall off and down and onto the floor. It was a sensation she loved, the slipping of the smooth fabric over her skin, the slow hissing of it as it went down, to lie there covering her feet, her legs rising like saplings from it, and then her small hips and the gentle roundness of her belly and her fine, pointed breasts. She attended to herself as if she were a trainer with a fine show-bitch: baths and feedings and exercise, all fit and proper. Then she enjoyed herself too, like the employer of the trainer of the show-bitch, and she felt proud ownership in all her own points, standing off to judge, coming close to caress.

There were the fit clothes for such a rich possession as herself. There were tunics for night, all made alike and full of art, sewn with little shining stones. Winters she wore black velvet trousers, quirkishly. Daytime she covered herself carefully from strangers, in the best way to make them desire her without knowing it, and on her feet she wore little slippers of snakeskin. Everything was nice.

Now she silently put things into a jewel case. She smiled to think of the trick she would play. She would go away. They would miss her, and suffer, but the house would run itself because of the momentum her mastery gave it, and Sir Harry would get his brandy as smoothly as if she were there, and Barbara would be desolate but soon consoled by ten minutes extra at her *prie-dieu* and an increasing tolerance for Paul's adept, inevitable nuzzlings. Julia would putter gently in the herb garden, pretending that no palace-hotel held rooms ready for her death. And Jennie would be free, quit of them and their discreet chatter, their well-fed banalities, the meaningless fact that they existed at all. She would break through the safe darkness, and come alive, and find people who would give her of themselves, not suck at her until she was hollow and dying. She would find generous people, as rich and full as healthy wet-nurses, to feed her and satisfy her without hurt.

She shivered, smoothed her hair for her little snakeskin skullcap, slipped her bare feet into the high-heeled shoes, and then stood silently behind the swaying curtains again, with no light to betray her, and listened to the four people out in the darkness.

They were still talking, on and on, afraid to stop. She could see them in the starlight, and in a tender gleam that came out from the many-windowed house, her house, which she kept polished and murmurous with comfort for them. She hated them. They were dolts, content to exist unborn, floating softly in the starlight. And they thought she would always be there, to nourish them on the bread and the wine of her flattery.

Old Harry sat back in the black shadow of the eucalyptus tree, and the signet ring on his hand, not liver-spotted in the nighttime, gleamed mischievously. "There's no doubt about it," he was saying, "our impenetrable Jennie—" He coughed, preparatory to heaven knows what genteel salacity.

Paul said roughly, "Our impenetrable and lovely Jennie, my dear Harry, is undoubtedly standing behind the flattering champagne-silk curtains in her bedroom, looking out at us and despising us for a group of people too well fed to be anything but mildly malicious about her. She keeps us drugged with comfort, the swine on her island who might otherwise do harm to her."

Jennie shivered suddenly. Truth had flicked like an adder's tongue into the facile chatter. Paul was too clever, she said in a moment ugly with fright. How had he guessed, young as he was, the reason for her careful generosity to them all? Was she to be betrayed finally by the very fact that he loved her to a point of bitterness and hate? It was impossible, she said. It was unfair, after all that she did to lull the four, drugging them with comfort, as he had drawled bitterly, hatefully . . .

"Yes, that's it," Paul went on in an excited way. "She keeps us quiet, clever Jennie! That's what I've been wanting to say, you know. Now I have, all right! It's like parachute school!" He laughed shortly. "When we were learning to jump."

In the patio and in the dim room the air was like the tunnel of a great ear, waiting. When Paul spoke again, in his new unweary voice, it was as if all the listeners puffed out their breath with relief of one kind or another, even Jennie.

"Our instructor told us about it, a marvelous trick really. When you jumped, you didn't pull the cord now, but *now*. You didn't pull it until you said once, very fast, 'Not now but *now!*' You see? It kept you from fouling the 'chute or anything like that. It gave you time, maybe a second and a half, but time to get free."

Jennie felt incredulous. Did he mean, this thin young man, this bitter lover, that he was free of her? How dare he? It was she who was about to flee from them, not he nor they who should want liberty.

"I finally said it," Paul continued with a relief that was almost smug, like a boy who has taken a dare. "Now why don't we for once forget the song of our private Circe, eh? Why don't we just this once tell what we know of her, why we're here? Let's see what it would do to Jennie!"

"Oh, I simply adore her," Barbara said in her light, dazzled, helpless way, and Julia said, "But don't we all, my dear, don't we all!" and Paul added with self-conscious sarcasm, "Yes, don't we all!" It sounded to Jennie in her dim silky room like an idiotic chorus, something in a dream.

Don't they all, don't they all, she mimicked ferociously. Nobody in the world loves Jennie. Inside herself it was as if she spat contemptuously, out through the thin curtains, through the motionless air, into the pool that lay without currents, without depth, over the treacherous people in the patio. Good-by, good-by, she said to them, rocking with merriment on the little waves that rippled out from the tiny splash of that invisible spittle. Good-by, she called, and she was laughing like a gargoyle . . .

I

One

IN 1938 there was a train that left Paris for the southeast
at a fairly good hour in the morning and reached Lausanne a little after teatime if you drank tea. You could go
to the station in time to get some bad coffee with milk and
good croissants in the strange little café on the platform,
which had trees in tubs in front of it as if it were out on
the street, and the high gray station roof of glass above it,
so that it always looked like rain but no rain could ever
fall there. The trains made a great hysterical noise of bumping and steaming, and there were one or two of them
being loaded with beautiful fruits and cheeses and vegetables, to get ready for lunch. You could watch them from
the pseudo-sidewalk of the café, between the sooty little
privet trees in green boxes, which made it a café instead of
merely part of the platform, and the food was exciting,
so that already you looked forward to eating it. That would
be near Dijon, gastronomical center of the world, the people from Dijon called it. You would not be eating anything
particularly fine, gastronomically, but it would be fresh
and amusing, and at the end of the meal there would be
a great tray of fat cherries bordered with banks of green
almonds, perhaps, and always little cream cheeses that
tasted better on trains than anywhere else. Dijon would
stop and then slide by, and you would head through the

Côte-d'Or vineyards toward Vallorbes and Switzerland.

That morning train was the one Jennie took, one day in June. She felt gay and fresh and free, with a deliberate and cold freedom, from everything that had happened to her. She was about thirty, with a small delightful figure and a skin like cream, and her simple dress and her little slippers and skullcap of green snakeskin were as delightful as she. She had poured one glass of the café's best brandy into her coffee, and as she walked down to the car where her seat was reserved she could feel the liquor warm and encouraging in her stomach and her knees. She stopped at the book wagon and bought a paper copy of *Les Enfants Terribles* by Jean Cocteau; it would be fun to read it again, or to hold it before her eyes if there were ugly people in the compartment with her.

It was empty when she got there. An old porter, wheezing almost tangible red wine and garlic, was lifting her jewel case onto the rack. She had a window seat of course, facing forward, so that, as always happened, she got the porter to change it to the opposite one. She loved to ride backward, so why should she not? He smiled, wheezed, and went cheerfully off with her good tip and her smile. She always tipped well and smiled to the people she tipped. She could afford both extravagances and enjoyed them, so why not?

A few people stamped past the closed door of her little glass room—peered in and hesitated when they saw it was Jennie and then went on. She felt almost safe: it was time to start, and still she was alone. She hated people near her when she traveled. When she was an old lady she would rent all six seats, she decided, and save herself this pre-voyage worry about being confined with boring or dis-agreeable or smelly humans.

The train was already moving smoothly past the harried cooks around the door of the Cannes Express dining-car on the next track when a man came into her compartment. She did not look at him, nor let her face change, nor, in truth, feel anything but a small prick of exasperation before she shrugged. It was too bad, but it had happened: there was nothing she could do about it, so she would forget it. When she felt like it she would look, and then start cutting the pages of her book with the cardboard cutter tucked into it. At least there were no children. And she was there, she, Jennie, alone and full of amusement at her escape. She was free from everything that had so long irked her, kept her floating lifeless in a soft dark prison. The light on the houses was beautiful, sharp, clear, as if she had never seen it before, and there was a thin delicious feeling all about her, like champagne, like being born, perhaps.

The man was sitting opposite her, bending forward with such concern that she could no longer ignore him. She turned away resignedly from the window.

He was tall and heavy, with a full grayish face and pale eyes, an unhealthy burgher who had once perhaps been dashing. At least he would not bother her: he was com-pletely ordinary. She looked impassively at him, knowing that the full stare from her large gray eyes, set wide apart and fantastically lashed with black, would frighten him. It amused her to see him draw back sharply, and then redden a little on his flabby cheeks and his high crinkled forehead. The trick always worked. Men were always disconcerted by it. Men were stupid. She kept on staring at him, not rudely, but passively, and the silence that amused her was, she knew, increasingly embarrassing to him. But why should she help him? She was comfortable, even enjoying herself in a mild way. There was plenty of time. She let her eyes widen a little more.

"If Madame will forgive me," he said finally, with a pleasant middle-class accent, a heavy voice.

"Certainly, Monsieur."

"A thousand pardons, but I notice that Madame has stupidly been given the wrong seat. All ladies prefer to ride facing the engine, to avert any possible touch of faintness. May I not have the pleasure of changing places with Madame?"

Jennie looked at him a little longer, without blinking, so that he reddened even more. He was an interfering dolt, and now she would hurt him, as he deserved. She said, without letting interest or disinterest, pleasure or displeasure, show on her face or in her voice, "Thank you, Monsieur. I prefer to ride backward."

She turned to the window, not bothering to pretend to read her book. The man disappeared from her world, ant under an unconscious heel.

The country was coming, more and more of it, through the clusters of neat, repulsive villas. There were farms, with fine gray horses pulling the earth up straight behind them, and tendered wheatfields splattered with blood-scarlet poppies, and hydrangeas blooming blue and pink and sturdy in the windows of the little houses of the crossing-guards. Jennie thought that she had never seen such a stout freshness anywhere, such a rich promise from the land. It was a part of her own new feeling of rebirth, so that she seemed to be humming silently with all the bees, flying through the sweet air with any meadowlark at all. She closed her eyes, smiling.

When she opened them it was deliberately into the look of the man across from her, as she had known it would be. He flushed again and slid his own rather small pale gaze past her and out the window.

For a time she read. The book was amusing still, perverse in such a catlike malicious way—it must be horrid to have a brother, but if Jennie had ever had one she might have liked it if he and she had been Cocteau's siblings.

She took a ticket for the second service of luncheon and noticed that the man did too, with hesitation that said he really preferred the first. When she went to the water closet, he stood up with surprising grace for his bulk and slid back the compartment door for her. She thanked him gravely, and he bowed without speaking.

When she came back, apparently no different in her smooth soft elegance, but with new lipstick on and her nose powdered for her private aplomb, she put one toe under the cushion on her seat and swung up to the rack and down again with her little jewel case before the man could help her. He leaped to his feet, and Jennie brushed against him in spite of herself as she stepped down.

"But Madame should have asked me," he protested, and his voice sounded truly concerned and hurt, as if she had touched the inner vanity in him, the male core, instead of just the part that made him do what he had been taught to do: be attentive, be courteous, be discreet . . .

Jennie thanked him. "I am used to traveling alone," she said without any pretense of ambiguity, and she sat down and opened the little case and took her gold flask from it. Unconcernedly she flipped up the top and tipped her head back for a full fine swallow of the brandy.

When everything was in place again, she held out the jewel case to the man. She smiled dazzlingly, trustingly, at him, like a pleased child, and he took it as if he had been struck, put it carefully above her on the rack, and then sat down in a heavy tired way, without looking at her.

Jennie was grateful to him for reacting so typically to her: it made her feel powerful and sure. She was like a basket full of ripe plump strawberries, with one more just this instant added on the top.

She leaned forward, her lips parted. The man did not turn his head toward her. "Did you ever see the country more beautiful?" she asked warmly.

He looked up, openly startled, and then made his face stiff. Jennie liked that. After all, she had hurt him and rebuffed him, and she liked him for being cold now: it proved that he was not such a lumpish man as he appeared to be. She smiled at him, and when she said again, in her correct, rather singsong French, which could have been spoken by a Swede, an unusually linguistic Englishwoman, or even an American, "The country, isn't it exquisite in June?" he smiled back at her. First it was with his eyes, which did not then seem pale or flat. Next his gray sagging face lifted itself in gaiety and relief. Indeed, he suddenly sent out such a gust of grateful friendliness that Jennie almost drew back, alarmed for her next few hours of yearned-for isolation. But she was very sure of herself, and if this man proved as dull as she expected, she could easily stun him again into weariness and silence.

"I have never seen it so beautiful," he said thoughtfully. He leaned forward, at ease now, as if they were old acquaintances discussing a rather weighty but not pressing problem. "Last year it was lovely, true, but this year there is a kind of richness about it that I have never felt before. It is in a way as if I had never seen it, as if this were the first time."

"But that's the way I feel too," Jennie cried, and her heart beat happily. "It's as if I had just been born into it!"

"Full-fledged," he said, smiling.

Jennie spoke little during the next two hours or so, but she smiled and frowned so prettily, and let her creamy face fall into such open sympathy at the man's words, that he did not realize, then or ever, how much of a monologue was their opening conversation. Part of her mind went on watching the sliding countryside, planning new clothes, thinking with glee of her foxy disappearance from the old life. And part of it found what Monsieur Jeannetôt said extremely interesting, in rather the same way that she would have found a banal and hackneyed novel absorbing on an otherwise unbearably dull voyage. She let the pages turn casually, reading and yet not reading, mildly held by the thread of plot. There was no suspense, because the story had been written so many times before. But the characters, underneath their bourgeois behavior, held a certain piquancy for her, a kind of subevident decay.

He was an electrical engineer, one of the best in Switzerland, he said without any smirk or fuss. He was well-to-do. But—and here Jennie knew that he was going to tell her that his wife was an invalid—his wife was an invalid, and had been for many years. Their life was very quiet.

Inevitably he managed to imply, perhaps even a little sooner than Jennie knew he would, that his home life was far from satisfying. That meant, she knew, that he either had a mistress, or wished he had, or was at least wondering why he had not. It meant that he was beginning to be alarmed at the flight of time and to wonder if it were too late. It meant that she was making him wonder, she, Jennie.

He had a son and a daughter. He talked a great deal about them, and there was a kind of bewildered anguish in his heavy voice and in the way he kept wiping his palms with his fine white handkerchief as he spoke of their lives. Jennie had heard that tone, seen that gesture or others more helpless still, from loving fathers everywhere. It was their own fault, to have been stupid enough to conceive in the first place, and then to have let themselves believe that children might still bring joy and happiness. What a cruel joke that was! And what dupes they!

Young Jeannetôt was just back from the French colonies, spoiled, feverish, with a little Algerian half-breed tagging after him, wanting marriage of all things. She was good to look at, the father said, and here Jennie saw that he was jealous of his son's rights over her. But marriage! It had sent Madame into one nervous crisis after another, so that Paul rarely came home any more, but spent all his time with his Petit' Chose, the Little Thing he had brought back from Algiers with him, living God knows how on his allowance and what his mother gave him secretly, dancing at the Palace, not working . . .

Jeannetôt slapped his hands together in disgust. He looked out the window, too angry suddenly to go on. Jennie knew he was thinking of his own younger years, years full of hard, sober work, of two young promising children, of a gradual rise, better apartments, all as it should be for a Swiss engineer. What a dolt he was!

"Tell me about your daughter," she said gently, and she let her hand light for a second on his thick, well-clothed knee. He turned back apologetically to her, and his eyes were a little moist with gratitude and self-pity.

"What is there about you, Madame, that makes me talk this way? It is not my habit, I assure you. Forgive me, and forget my silly confidences!"

"No, no," Jennie protested, her voice full of the understanding and compassion she knew he now expected. She was completely amused: this was all part of the unreal staginess of her flight. Instead of a book it was now high comedy, written and rehearsed so that it unfolded too smoothly ever to be stopped. Every line was there, every puppet in place. The scenery was consummately designed and lighted. And the audience—ah, who but Jennie?—the audience was tight with anticipation, with eagerness to be entertained, with tolerance. "Talk more," she commanded sweetly. "Tell me of your daughter, Monsieur Jeannetôt."

He looked at her for a minute, and his eyes dried, and he tossed back his head with a hard, mocking snort of laughter. "Hah!" he said. "Now, there's a case for you!"

Jennie relaxed in her comfortable gently rocking seat. She thought vaguely of another swig of brandy, but decided there would be too many complications. They were past Avallon. Lunch would be soon. She'd order a Byrrh first: it was always so good on trains, like the cream cheeses and the Cointreau afterward, sweet, sticky, horrible stuff anywhere in the world but there, and there a part of the intricate immobility of shooting across Europe with grace. Thus Jeannetôt was perfect. He lured her, and in what was almost a kindly way he interested her. Papa Jean, she thought mockingly, dear old puzzled family man, kindly clown Papa Jean . . .

He was talking about Léonie. She smiled trustingly at him, and nodded and frowned, and although so much of her was not there, a great deal was. What she heard she tucked away, just as she would unconsciously have remembered the details of a dull novel or a hackneyed play.

"Of course Léonie is a few years older than Paul," he was saying heavily, painfully, as if he were reading from a letter he himself had written after much thought, but had never meant to make public. "That may perhaps explain her—her troubles. Paul has always been a happier kind of person, very insouciant and teasing and thoughtless. And then there is the question of religion. Her mother is believing and very devout. I myself, I must confess to you, am agnostic, and have always been so. But Madame Jeannetôt—as I say, she is devout. Indeed, at certain times . . ."

Jennie knew that he was telling her that the Church was a part of their marital pleasures, and that the Cross was a sword between them on the bed, and that when his wife was full of monthly pain she knelt more easily than ever to confess her sins. The lines were written: the puppet was jerking neatly on cue. She sighed in sympathy, without looking at him. He would go on.

"Yes," he said, "Léonie was raised according to her dear mother's wishes, and I cannot help feeling, although of course I have no right to say so, that it might have been better for her to have left the convent a little sooner. Léonie has never been beautiful—"

"Oh," Jennie said in soft protest, "anything young and fresh is beautiful."

Jeannetôt looked at her instead of going on, and for a second annoyed her by stepping out of his part. He should have reminded her that his daughter was not young. Instead he looked at her. She was soon reassured, for she knew that he would say the alternate line, the other possible one.

"Yes, that is true," he said, and he looked on at her heavily, with courteous sincerity. You are very beautiful, he was saying.

Jennie smiled at him, a little withdrawn to remind him that they were, theoretically at least, strangers, and then she said, "But Léonie? Is she not beautiful?"

"No. No, I regret to admit. When she was about eighteen, that is when she should have left the Sisters. But now she is past twenty-five, past the age."

"The age?"

"That is, she is not interesting to the young men we can introduce her to, men in my office, friends of Paul's. They all find her too serious. She has let herself grow sallow, and she seldom goes to the beauty salons for her hair, her nails. Instead"—and in his voice was an impotent curse—"she goes down to St. Jacques and falls on her knees and sucks in the incense. Then she comes home, locks her door, weeps."

He looked at his hands and wiped them carefully with his handkerchief. He was leaning forward slackly, swaying with the train, like an old clown. "Children are sometimes very disturbing," he said.

Jennie thought, Oh no! No, he can't be going to say those lines too! She felt a little hysterical, as if she might laugh in his face. If he told her that they were still worth all the suffering they caused their parents, she would. She shrugged a little and let her eyes fall away from his grayish face.

"I have never been a mother," she murmured as softly as she could against the noise of the train. Then, before he could say, "Ah, Madame, there is no joy to compare with that of motherhood!" she asked eagerly, "But Léonie with the Little Thing? What is the situation there?"

He did not answer, but smiled grudgingly, as if he were remembering things he should not smile to remember.

"I am indiscreet," Jennie said. "I ask impertinent questions."

"Not at all. My God, I have never met such a magically intuitive, sensitive confidante in my life, Madame! My own indiscretion astounds me. How could I, how dared I, thus unburden myself to you, a complete stranger?"

"But I do not feel like one."

"No. No, you are not. You are a part of this whole exquisite day, so full of rebirth . . ." He looked at the rich land flashing by. "We are almost at Dijon. When the train stops, will you be charitable enough to join me at lunch? We are two cars away from the restaurant. It is easier to walk then."

His knuckles were white, Jennie saw. She did not want to eat with him. She wanted to be alone, to look unhindered at the lusty or mincing or suspicious or jolly manners of the people all about her. She wanted to be silent, to be alone and enjoying it, not pitted against the world, as she drank the crude *apéritif*, ate the crude *hors-d'oeuvres* and then the simple crude fresh food on its great trays held skillfully over and around her as the train hurtled through Burgundy. She loved eating alone on trains. She looked again at Jeannetôt's tired burghermaster face and then at his hands, which he surely did not know were thus tightly, whitely clenched before her. She smiled and said she would be very glad to join him at his table, and it was not until she was smoothing her hair in the gritty water closet that she realized that this was the first time in her life she had ever accepted such an invitation from a stranger, an ordinary picked-up traveling man on a train.

She grinned at herself in the jumpy mirror. Freedom had gone to her head for fair! She would be as careful as a nun at a carnival, would Jennie!

Two

IT WAS a pleasant meal. They sat opposite two other human beings whose age and sex Jennie could not have told a half-hour later, two courteous zeros who bowed as she sat down, wiped their silver on their napkins, and bowed as they left. Jeannetôt was more entertaining than she had expected, and they discussed with liveliness the strange subject of the scarcity of graveyard space in Switzerland. He, as an electrical engineer, thought not only that the state should forbid any burial except by cremation, but that it should build a series of federal furnaces. He had worked out a system that would, within a few burnings, start generating enough electricity in a cumulative pile to out-do any fast-running river, enough after, say, ten funerals to light a whole city for ten hours. Jennie was amused by him and pleased by the way his lumpish face lightened as he talked and by the complete lack of ghoulishness in his scientific interest in cadavers. She decided he was worth talking to, listening to.

He asked her permission to order a large bottle of the best red Bordeaux on the list, and they lifted their glasses solemnly to Burgundy as they slipped from the station in Dijon. Bordeaux traveled better, they agreed. They both liked Burgundies better, they added without haste. They would not drink them every day, they said comfortably, but for festivals and holidays and the high flavors of such feastings, what was better? This was good too, they said, touching glasses; for a railroad claret it was not bad at all.

When the bills were being made out Jennie said, "Mine is separate, please." Jeannetôt frowned politely. She smiled at him. "You are the first man I have ever permitted to dine with me in a train," she said. "I've enjoyed your wine so much. I thank you for it. But it's a matter of principle with me to pay for my own meal."

He smiled back at her, with a little bow, and she knew that she had moved wisely. It was not that she would have hesitated to move any other way that pleased her: it was that by now she liked this man and was interested in making him enjoy her. The fact itself interested her. Certainly he was the dull solid businessman he had first seemed to be, and yet by now the warmth of his eyes and the astonishing latent gaiety in his face were biting at her consciousness of him.

Back in the compartment they sat across from each other as before, but between them and the two other people who had got on at Dijon (or were they the zeros from the dining table?) there was a wall built of sudden compatibility. They sipped a little brandy, she straight from her flask and he from a tiny silver drinking cup he produced gleefully from his pocket. They said almost nothing. Then Jennie put her head back against the stiff crocheted tidy with PLM on it and closed her eyes. She knew that Jeannetôt would watch her as she dozed, and it did not bother her at all, because she was as sure of him as if he were a dressed trussed hare lying ready to be sold upon a marble slab, and she the one to sell him. He was a good man in his way, and he had made her day amusing, and it would be fine to see the last of him, him and his small gallantries, his wine, his silly tears.

When she looked up, her eyes clear as pond water, they were in the hilly country, nearing the border. She loved it there, so rocky, with far peeps into pretty valleys, and the air thinner. She watched Jeannetôt, reading hungrily at her book, cutting its crumbling cheap paper as he read. He scanned the pages expertly, his face impassive and his eyes so alive that it seemed as if each one were a brain by itself. She liked that. She felt that he was an intelligent man, one who had gone flabby along with his body. She wished idly that she had known him when he was twenty-five, not fiftyish.

He looked up easily at her, as if sure she would still be there for him to enjoy, unabashed by her gray gaze, and when he saw her awake and watching him, he clapped the book shut and almost stood up in his confusion. For a few seconds he was the flushed bourgeois she had dismissed from her mind in the Paris suburbs. Then they both smiled, and he sat back.

"I hope you don't mind," he said, holding out the book to her.

"Keep it. I've already read it, years ago."

"It is good. I am shamefully ignorant of everything but technical writing. My wife—I find myself exasperated by her extremely uncatholic taste for Catholic literature. And what an appropriate title for me to study—*Les Enfants Terribles!*"

He laughed a little, unwillingly. Jennie knew that his easy conversation of lunchtime was over. He would talk now about the children, his typical banal common children, with their silly little frustrations and amours. She settled herself into the corner of her seat, her soft green slippers tucked under her, and let herself consider the exciting prospect of being alone, free, beautiful, unhampered by any obligations except to her own body and bones, her own imperious fastidious belly and bowels. Where would she sleep that night? She would have to buy more clothes in the morning, and perhaps some luggage. Geneva would be best. She would lie on smooth Swiss sheets, and eat honey on her breakfast roll, and watch the lake and the paddle-steamers . . .

"My poor daughter's crises do not come often," Jeannetôt was saying in a low pained voice. "I have put her under the care of the best doctors we have. Twice in the past year my poor Léonie has been in their private hospitals. When she has come home she has seemed almost happy again. But it never lasts. Now they are trying injections. She is much worse since all this trouble about Paul."

"But surely," Jennie said as if she cared, "surely he is old enough now to take care of himself! Why do you worry?"

"Ah, I know. But he was sickly and spoiled when he was little. Everyone spoiled him because he was so gay and so handsome. He is still. He was intelligent, much more so than I, but he always failed his examinations. Then Algeria—I gave him his head there, because I remembered how I'd wanted to live in a foreign country when I was young. And now he comes back with a Little Thing off the streets, a little female with the brains of a sparrow and the damned tenacity of a surgeon's leech. I see him everywhere with her. It is the scandal of Lausanne. At home his mother speaks of nothing but Paul, as if it were all my fault. And Léonie weeps and faints. *Les enfants terribles,* my dear Madame!"

He tossed the book down beside him, mockingly, and let his hands hang between his knees, tired clown again.

Jennie was a little bored, but not enough to do more about it than ask, "Why don't you send Léonie away?"

He looked at her in a strange, cynical fashion. "Madame, perhaps I should explain the intricate ties that bind a neurasthenic convent girl to her own town, her own confessor. Or would I offend your religious susceptibilities?"

Jennie laughed. "Not mine, Monsieur. I have one religion—if any. There is me. And there is nothing. At least, that is as far as I have guessed, up to now."

He looked a little taken aback before he nodded. "Perhaps you are right. At least it is something to have surmised that much. I myself, I have always thought that if I acted honestly and did my best—but now I doubt that too. Where is there any reward for being a respectable husband and father?"

Jennie felt mirthful and excited, as she had earlier, before he became a pleasant table companion and was simply an actor in this old play rewritten and restaged to ease her train ennui. Now he was reading his lines again, timing them skillfully, as unsuspecting as all earnest mountebanks must be that what he said had ever been said before. He was back on the stage.

"I see my colleagues, men almost as successful as I, leading their lives as if they were irresponsible youngsters, as if they were Paul's age. Their wives are neglected, wronged. And yet they look like healthy women and full of animation when I meet them. What a contrast they are to my own poor companion! Their children make good marriages—they even accept their fathers' mistresses socially in some cases . . ."

Yes, Jennie thought, he is definitely considering the obvious pleasures of infidelity before it is too late! He is trying not to say to himself that if his son can do it, he still can too. Poor clown! How easy it would be, she thought casually, to give him a really fine fat holiday from all his cautious ways. Perhaps she could talk a little more to him before Geneva, and goad him to take the Little Thing away from Paul! She felt highly amused, and looked with solemnity out the window until she was sure her eyes would not betray her.

Then they were at the border. There was a long wait: some trouble with two thin little men in kaftans and bowler hats, who were trying to take a rug into Switzerland. They spoke only Polish. One of them stood silently weeping. The other wept too, and screamed and wrung his delicate hands, as tiny and bleached as a pickled frog's. Jennie watched, frowning a little with distaste for their abandon. She moved away from them, her own simple luggage already inspected, and drank a glass of beer at the station restaurant. It was good to be alone. She would have dinner served in her room that night, perhaps on her balcony, unless the lake breeze blew too coolly. In the morning she would shop. She loved the clothes in Geneva, such a mixture: Bavarian ski suits for the English, English tweeds and pullovers for the French, French scarves and dainty silver purses and little nonsensities for the fat Germans. She might go to see the consul and hear all the gossip about people she had left behind her . . .

"Why didn't you wait for me, my dear lady?" Jeannetôt's implication that there was any reason why she should annoyed her almost to the point of snubbing him again, but when she looked up over her last swallow of beer at his eager eyes, the surprising youthfulness underneath his flabby graying skin, she could only smile at him.

"I wanted to be alone," she said candidly. "I am used to it. I told you that this morning. Do you remember?"

"There is only one thing I can say—it's not right! It's against the laws of nature!"

"Others have thought so too," she said, and they were laughing at their foolishness. "But here I am. And now do we have time for you to drink a beer with me?"

"No," he said. "Unfortunately for me, but fortunately for my digestion and my waistline, we do not."

"You could have ordered one of those bottles of lemonade," she said as they went toward the train. "I've always wanted to see someone drink it. I'm sure it's ghastly."

"On the contrary. I often enjoy it. It is very good on hot walks in the country on Sundays, slightly acidulous and highly carbonated."

How pompous he was! No wonder his daughter had hysterics, his wife megrims, his son a succulent Little Thing. No wonder he was lonely. Was it too late for him after all? Jennie hoped not, in an easy uncaring way.

As they got into the train she saw the two little black-gowned refugees again. One was half lying against his companion's shoulder, his mouth open like a dead child's. They and the station slid past the window. Perhaps they had been arrested. It was too bad, Jennie thought. They should stay in their own countries, all those thin pale people . . . although Poland was not a pretty homeland for the Jews, she'd heard. But they should at least know better than to travel with rare rugs over their shoulders, delaying trains and making trouble . . .

In the compartment she felt upset and sat looking remotely out of the window at the craggy hills of the borderland. It annoyed her not to have now any of the morning's excitement. She always felt this way in the afternoon on trains. Perhaps the English were right to insist on pots of bad tea and slabs of cake in the dining-car, no matter what country they sped across. She leaned forward impulsively.

"Monsieur Jeannetôt," she said, "let's go see if there is any of that lemonade in bottles! On the train, I mean."

He smiled delightedly at her and stood up.

"We'll drink one bottle," she said, and all her happiness was back again, as if the swiftness of the train had wiped from her spirits the remembrance of the refugees, of Jeannetôt's sententiousness, of whatever it was that for a few minutes had been treacherous. "That will give me plenty of time to collect myself before I get off."

He stood as still as a tree, as if the train could not possibly make him sway and jiggle. "Get off?" he asked.

"Certainly," Jennie said, and as she stood close beside him in the narrow aisle between the seats she looked up at him with her wide gray eyes.

He was still immobile, in a way that suddenly excited her so that she wanted to touch him, to test her power to break what it was that held him thus. She wanted to embrace him. She drew back, still looking up at him, and as she looked she remembered how free she was, how far now from the past. She was Jennie, looking for people who could give to her, not take and take. Jeannetôt could give. He was brimming with eagerness to give, to give as he had never known it possible . . . Jennie could teach him how.

She smiled a small polite smile as she answered. "Certainly," she said. "At Lausanne. I'm staying at the Palace."

Three

BY FIVE o'clock the next afternoon she was inexpressibly bored, and cross too. The day had seemed endless. If she had only bought a pretty little watch in one of the souvenir stores, Jennie thought wryly, she would have been the perfect tourist, killing time between trains.

She sat now on the terrace at Ouchy-Lausanne, watching the silly gulls swoop and cry and the silly people toss crumbs at them along the quai, drinking her tea like a proper lady, dribbling her stiff brown honey on her toast so neatly, so sweetly. God, how dull it was! The slanting sun twinkled in a well-bred way upon the orderly lake, and behind Jennie in the teashop three decayed gentle-women sawed expertly at "Tales from the Vienna Woods" on their stringed instruments, with the youngest doubling on a bird whistle when the score called for it. Tweet tweet tweet, she went, embarrassed to the top of her graying head. Murmurmurmur went all the English people above the tweets and the sound of their own relentless chews and swallows.

Well, what had she expected, Jennie asked herself savagely—hampers of red roses with her breakfast tray, protestations of undying passion before lunch, lovers' flight to Lake Como with her demitasse? She had acted stupidly, like a gauche schoolgirl, and that was what irked her so, and she sat turning the little goads round and round in the raw wound to her self-respect. It was intolerable that she, Jennie the inviolate, had let herself be so clumsy.

She paid her bill impatiently and sped from the place. The tram up to the city crept like a toad. Halfway there she swung down to the cobbles. She could feel the other passengers staring back at her as they ground on upward.

She walked swiftly, past the little stores all on a slant on the steep hill, their windows palely lighted in the summery twilight, their sausages and baby clothes and carefully iced cakes a kind of respectable soporific to her too wakeful nerves. By the time she turned the corner to the hotel door she was breathless and no longer angry, except in a remote, scornful way, as she might have been toward a long dead and almost forgotten family scapegoat, the kind whose small sins soon became a ridiculous and faintly affectionate legend. Yes, once Jennie, drunk with freedom, got off a train with a fat burgher and sat waiting in a fat-burgher-town for him to say he loved her, so that she could laugh at him and go on. But he never said it, not he; he left her politely, from his taxi, at the hotel door; and there Jennie was, feeling like a fatuous ninny, until suddenly she came to her cool, intelligent, proud senses and got on the train again and went away from that fat-burgher-town.

She walked straight to the desk in the lobby. A tea-dance orchestra sounded faintly, teasingly, through the endless marble pillars and the aspidistras. She would have the concierge call the station for her. What train was the best and the soonest, going south or west or east? She must have first class in a *wagon-lit*. No, she would sit up, third class. She would put her head in its little skullcap upon the nearest shoulder and sleep peacefully, going far away.

Jeannetôt stood at the long desk. She bowed politely to him and he to her, and he raised his stiff wintery hat to her and stood holding it while Jennie took her key and a letter from the clerk.

"I have just left that for you, dear lady," Jeannetôt said. "Until very soon, let us hope, until very soon." And he bowed and hurried away.

Jennie went to her room without speaking to the concierge. She would read the letter, pack her things peacefully, go to the station and eat a good dinner in the first-class dining-room, take any train anywhere.

What an uncouth man, Jeannetôt! How it would ease her to give him one final hurt! She would go away and forget him, but he would be there in Lausanne for the rest of his life, wondering.

"Madame," the letter said. "I beg you to forgive my writing in the place of my wife, unhappily indisposed. She presents her compliments and the assurance that as soon as possible she will be happy to send cards, awaiting the pleasure of making your acquaintance. Meanwhile, may I have the great honor of introducing my daughter Léonie to you over a cup of tea or an ice tomorrow at 4:45 at the Tea Salon St. Martin. Please accept, dear Madame, my most respectful salutations. Emile Jeannetôt."

Jennie burst out laughing, so spontaneously and loudly in the emptiness of her big room that she looked around, feeling foolish. This was wonderful! Never had she imagined anything so amusing, so completely in character. The stolid arrogance of the man! Who else in the world would dare issue such a royal order to Jennie, *Jennie*, to appear to eat at a certain hour, a certain place, to enjoy the favors of his sallow-faced daughter, simply because he had been spoken to on a train? Oh, poor Jeannetôt!

Gaily she dressed in thin wool shot with silver, bought that morning near the Palace, perfect for the hour of the cocktail, the sales-duchess had assured her, infinitely more perfect for the tea dancing. But when she got downstairs the orchestra was silent, and there was a pre-dinner hush everywhere. She shrugged and walked light as thistledown along the dim corridors to the bar.

As she pushed open the heavy door, so soundproof that it made her feel as if she were sneaking into the sanctum sanctorum of a Piccadilly club, two people stood aside for her, and she knew in the first second of her cool glance at them that they were Paul Jeannetôt and his Petit' Chose. He was tall and sulky and well dressed in the inevitable brown tweed jacket and gray Oxford-bags that all young stylish Europeans believed was English-style. She was tiny and as toothsome as a piece of molded almond paste, deeply tinted, soon to be mustached. They looked furious.

Jennie ordered a dry Martini. There were two or three couples sitting at the low tables, and she sat easily by herself at the bar, watching the man behind it and remembering him at every good hotel bar she had ever drunk in, on every good ship. He would be named Duval and be called Harry. She felt comfortable and at home, and amused at her certainty that young Jeannetôt would soon be back, which he was, and alone, which he was.

He stood scowling near the door for a minute, quarrel still heavy on his face, and then he said, "Another, Harry," to Duval. The first half of the Scotch and soda he drank in one swallow, and then he swirled the rest slowly in his glass and looked down into it, and his expression lightened so that it was merely sulky, not furious. When he was twenty-three years older and twenty-three kilos heavier, Jennie saw, he would look almost like his father, except for his dark un-Swiss eyes.

She waited to see if he would have another drink. When

he did, she said casually to Duval, "That is the younger Monsieur Jeannetôt at the end of the bar, isn't it?"

The man nodded, his face as bland and dead as a croupier's. "Yes, Madame," he said in a way that told her he recognized that she would behave herself, that she might be a whore but she was also a lady. "The Martini was as it should be?"

"Perfect, of course," Jennie smiled at him, to thank him for his completely Duvalish estimation of her.

"Shall I inform Monsieur Jeannetôt that Madame wishes to speak to him?"

Jennie shook her head. The bar was empty now. She would give herself the pleasure of being misunderstood for a second by the young man waiting so unsuspectingly a few steps away from her. "No, thank you. I shall surprise him," she murmured to Duval, who permitted himself an almost invisible smile and turned his back upon his last two customers.

Jennie looked candidly at Paul as she stepped to his side, her full glass steady in her smooth silver glove. He started, and then looked back at her with polite cynicism and an obvious but restrained smirk of flattered manhood on his face. Before he could bow to her and make the second move in what was plainly a pick-up, she asked, "You are Paul Jeannetôt, are you not?"

He was startled, and became at once the well-bred family scion. He bowed as if she were his grandmother's long-lost second cousin. Jennie smiled to herself, murmuring implications that she was an old friend of his father's, that many many years had passed, that he resembled dear Emile so startlingly . . .

Paul smiled incredulously at the fact that she could possibly have known his father long ago, and she approved of his recognition of her untarnishable beauty. She sat on the stool beside him and saw his young tired face grow merry and mischievous, the way yesterday Emile's old tireder one had done, because of her magic. Power sang in her bones, and when she had finished her drink and paid Duval and told Jeannetôt's son that she was having tea with his sister the next day, she walked from the room like an empress who has just sealed her enemy's death sentence.

Four

AT FIRST Léonie was just as anyone who had heard Jeannetôt's confessions in the train would expect, a tall pale girl with nails bitten to the quick and a bad hat. She made conversation as if she were still in the convent parlor, called down from her studying by the Sister Superior to meet a correctly introduced relative. She leaned forward with an artificial interest in everything Jennie said, her eyes flatly bright, her head tipped a little to show her politeness.

It was easy. Jennie went to work on her like a chess master disposing of an important but unfrightening adversary in a tournament. She was as good with women as with men when it seemed wise, and Léonie unfolded innocently in the wily sunshine of her attentions.

It was the same with Jeannetôt. Plainly, he thought as he saw his daughter lose her first strained air, as she talked more easily and smiled without putting one hand nervously against her mouth, this was what she needed, a little more fun, a little gaiety. He pressed jam and iced cakes upon the two women and beamed with a kind of relieved smugness at them through the smoky hubbub of the smart tearoom. Yes, Léonie needed companionship . . .

Jennie could have laughed in his face, his sagging tired face. She looked coldly at him from behind her own smooth smiling creamy one. What had made her think, ever in her life, that he was still capable of gaiety? It was too late for him now. But Paul? Someday Paul would be old. Before he was she would see how gay he could be, see what the father might once have been.

"But I feel lost here," she was saying with a hint of gallant pathos that she found revolting and very funny. "I am used to being alone, as your father knows, but I must admit that Lausanne frightens me a little bit. Where are the good shops? Where do you go for—for gloves, that sort of thing?"

"Léonie, my dear," Jeannetôt said, heavily inspired, "what about your mother's glovemaker? Why don't you make a rendezvous with Madame, if she will permit, and take her to some of those little places all you women know about?"

He sat back contentedly behind his empty parfait glass, convinced, from his expression, that he had brought off a complex coup. Jennie gazed happily at him: he was perfect.

She glanced at Léonie. The girl looked eagerly back at her for a minute and then dropped her eyes. They were good eyes, blue like her father's but large, and promising of depths to them if ever they could grow less restless. "If

Madame would enjoy that," she murmured in her immature way.

"Oh, but I would," Jennie said, smiling with wide-eyed candor. "I must probably move on soon, and I do need decent things again. Tomorrow? Tomorrow morning?"

Léonie started to assent and then withdrew. "Not tomorrow," she said, and she rolled crumbs nervously about on the glass-topped table under her long white fingers with the unpleasantly blunted tips.

Jeannetôt stirred irascibly in his chair. "Why not? Why not, Léonie?"

She straightened herself and looked coldly at him. "Tomorrow is Paul's saint's day," she said in a flat voice.

"But, my dear girl, you haven't even nodded to him for a month, for God's sake, so what of it?" Jeannetôt spoke with a kind of repressed frustrated fury, quite forgetful of his guest's supposed ignorance of the family troubles.

Jennie sat watching the two of them silently, the discreet stranger.

Léonie leaned forward, stiff as wood, her cheeks suddenly an ugly spotted red. "That is why I shall pray for him," she said, her voice flatter than before. "But I cannot believe, dear Papa, that this is at all interesting to Madame. Thank you, Madame, I am completely at your services after I have come from Mass at noon."

Jennie smiled. "I am delighted," she said, as if there had been no interruption to their girlish planning. "Shall we say two o'clock then? Or will you join me for lunch?"

"Tomorrow is not a day of celebration for me."

Jennie heard Léonie's father let out a kind of puff of annoyance, as if he had been tapped on the solar plexus.

She did not look at him, but answered in a warm understanding voice, "Of course, of course. It is good of you to bother with me. Let us say three o'clock then. And now, before I must hurry away, may I smoke just one cigarette?"

Jeannetôt fussed confusedly with his lighter, and Jennie gave Léonie time from behind the screen of smoke to compose herself. The girl had more self-control than her father had hinted at, at least in public. Jennie watched the white line fade from around her lips, and her fingers calm themselves a little on the tabletop. What a fuss! *Les enfants terribles*, Jeannetôt had said. Were all thwarted sisters as obviously jealous of their handsome brothers and their handsome brothers' little half-breed tarts? It would be interesting to find out.

As Jeannetôt paid the bill Jennie said confidingly, intimately, to Léonie, "I have so enjoyed this! You are a darling to bother with me. I really look forward to tomorrow."

Léonie flushed, this time becomingly, and smiled a little, so that fleeting as a comet Jennie saw her brother in her, her father even, a gay spirit, before she was the proper young lady making a proper speech again. And as Jennie stood up, with apologies and thanks, and walked alone past all the little tables covered with cakes and fashionable elbows, she knew that Léonie was watching her with a new excitement, that Jeannetôt was watching her with an old, almost forgotten one. His was less important than the girl's. Jennie smiled to admit it and then hurried a little: she must win a bet made with herself that Paul Jeannetôt would be at the Palace bar—alone.

Five

IT WAS not until after dinner that Jennie saw how things were with her about Paul.

She sat in a quiet, soft, smoky corner of the big *brasserie*, listening to the well-fed murmur of French and English and Swiss-German, watching the old men hide behind newspapers and chessboards, and the young ones, the Lausanne blades, prowl and investigate with their wise eyes as they sat in groups waiting for digestion to yield place to possible copulation. It was a big fat place, full of people like it, dressed even in June in heavily opulent clothes. Jennie had eaten slowly, a fastidious, gluttonous meal, and drunk a small bottle of metallic red wine from the Valais. She felt good inside.

She had found Paul charming that afternoon. He was polished the way more youths should be, so that in spite of his obvious youngness he seemed at ease in the world, not driven to mask his inevitable gaucheries with cynicism as would a like boy from England or America. It was not only that he was experienced sexually, Jennie felt: his whole attitude toward life was more balanced, more able to evaluate properly. Or perhaps she appreciated him mainly because he was rather like her? That was amusing.

They had had two drinks together and talked as casually as if they were old friends. He spoke English well, but it was hard for him to say her name—Djai-nee. "Call me Jeanne," she said, but he frowned quickly. "I hate the name," he said. "Jeanne, Jeannetôt—no, I love Jennie. Let me call you that."

Later he said, looking at her as they touched fresh glasses, "I have a little friend who should be here now, sitting where you are sitting."

"I saw her with you yesterday."

"Yes. She hated you."

"It looked, there in the doorway," Jennie said lightly, "as if she hated you too."

"No, she is mad for me. She is wonderful, very exotic. I owe a great deal to her, to what she's taught me. But she's beginning to drive me crazy. There are scenes—my God! And then my family! Has my father said anything to you? Have you seen my mother? I never go home any more."

Jennie hesitated and then shrugged. "Tea was—interesting, shall I say? I found your sister—"

Paul leaned close to her, his face savage. "That female! She repels me, do you hear? She is insane, that girl!"

"Oh, Paul!" There was an infinity of compassionate reproach in Jennie's voice. She watched the boy swirl his highball, his face gradually clearing, and finally she said, "Léonie and I are going on a delightfully feminine jaunt tomorrow at three . . ."

"Yes," he said politely, "that will be very nice for you."

He sounded like his father, setting the womenfolk into little paths of behavior, quite unconscious of Jennie's mocking voice. She sipped her drink and then went on as if he had not betrayed himself, ". . . at three, after she comes from hearing a special Mass for you."

Paul put his glass down so hard on the bar that Harry-

Duval glanced veiledly at him. "What?" He was really shouting at her, although his voice did not rise above the muted clatter in the hotel bar, filled with a dozen countries' wastrels and spies. "A Mass? My God!"

Jennie kept on looking at him, a faint smile in her wide eyes, while his face showed nakedly his anger and bewilderment and exasperation. He looked up at her. "Women!" he said slowly, and then they both laughed, their shoulders touching, like mischievous, sexless children with a secret.

That had been delightful, Jennie remembered as she sat watching the fat people in the *brasserie* without seeing them, hearing their middle-class fat voices without listening. It was long since she had felt so young and lightsome. Paul was charming. More young men should be like him. Was that a sign, she wondered mockingly, of her increasing years? She thought in an idle, full way of the foolish, the stupid, the crazed old women she had watched everywhere, pecking like vultures at their pretty-boys.

Paul and Petit' Chose walked with the sureness of known customers through the little wicker tables on the lighted terrace and into the *brasserie*. He was tall, easier in his clothes than most Europeans of his class, with deep shadows in his eyepits from the lights overhead. She, ah, Jennie thought, she looks very much like me—if I were an Algerian half-breed! They walked across the first part of the restaurant and to a corner table reserved for them, the waiter smiling and pulling out his order book in their wake. And as they walked, Jennie's little smooth slender hand tightened around her coffee cup until from the whiteness of her knuckles one might have thought to see it crumble to bloody dust, and the bones in her fine body went hollow with an ominous yawning, and inside her some-thing shaped like a screw turned once, from her throat down down into the most hidden vital part of her. Desire stopped her heart. Her breath was stopped too for a moment.

Finally she ordered good brandy and drank half of it very fast, like a cold hunter with his first swig of bourbon. So that is the way it is, she thought. Jennie, my girl, poor Jennie!

While she waited for the bill she powdered her nose, a thing she seldom did in public places. Finally she permitted herself the possible agony of looking once across the room at Paul. The light came down cruelly on all the flesh-covered skulls between her and him in the big place, but there against the wall he sat, smiling, young and pale, his dark eyes looking carelessly about as the girl talked close to him. Could he ever really look like his father, Jennie wondered . . . his eyes were so deep and dark, the brows above them so finely drawn . . . The screw started heavy and murderous and slow inside her. She stood up perforce. She must walk slowly to the door, and then up the summery street to the hotel, and then she must let herself alone alone alone into her room alone.

Halfway across the room Jennie and Paul looked at each other. She smiled politely at him, and he half rose, half bowed, and then sat down again.

His expression was the most truly boyish thing she had yet seen about him, a mixture of pride at being recognized by a woman every man in the room was eyeing, and smug-ness at being there at all but especially with a desirable little piece plainly his mistress, and resignation at having to sit down again to a well-ordered meal soon to be interrupted by a new variation of an increasingly domestic and familiar quarrel.

Jennie smiled a little more, in spite of herself, and found her eyes full on the eyes of Petit' Chose. They were, like something in a cheap movie script, blazing, and the girl's artfully molded white silk bosom was lifting up and down so rightly for the scene that the handsome emerald pin upon it tossed like a leaf on a disturbed duck puddle. All this could not possibly be real, Jennie said with a relief partly scornful. It was like cool air to her though: she felt sure of herself again and quite untroubled by what blissful sickness she might feel when next she looked at Paul.

She strode through the door and across the terrace, serene and powerful.

Six

SHE lay in bed until almost noon, reading editorials in the pile of Swiss dailies she had ordered with her breakfast: "The Chocolate, Its Place in 19th Century Society," "Interesting Anecdotes Concerning George Sand," "Influence of the Hot Jazz on American Youth." . . .

She wet her forefinger and picked up all the little crumbs from her tray and ate them one by one, and she looked across the lake toward Evian and tried to remember a system for winning at roulette that she had once used.

She managed, thus resolutely, not to think about Paul. As she had told herself the night before, it was foolish to risk sleeplessness and a tired face and possibly worse, and what good would it do her at all? She had taken two pills, and so well disciplined a woman was she that not one dream dared intrude.

As she dressed, she decided to walk down to Ouchy for lunch. She would eat fillets of perch and drink rather a lot of white wine, to make her insouciant of the afternoon's dreary rendezvous with that stick Léonie, that smug sallow bitch . . .

Jennie mistrusted people who professed churchly faith: she had never felt it herself, and therefore she concluded that it could not possibly be anything but hypocritical. When she heard a person say that religion or the Church or God was a haven in time of suffering, she almost laughed aloud with scorn, thinking of the many dreadful things that had assailed her, and of her own strength to stand straight, unpropped, unbandaged by any priestly ministrations. People were weak fools. Léonie Jeannetôt was worse than that, a neurasthenic one. What need could she possibly have for God, young as she was and rich?

At the desk Jennie's hand began to tremble a little when she found a note, not addressed by Jeannetôt, obviously not by a woman. She went slowly into the discreet little writing-room off the lobby.

It was from Paul, and it said that he was in black despair because he would not be at the Palace bar that evening, and that it was her fault because she had looked too beautiful to a little thing, Little Thing, the night before. "Do you understand, Jennie the mysterious, adorable Jennie?" it asked.

Jennie tore it across. It was a schoolboy note. She shrugged and put the scraps in her purse. The Jeannetôt men were alike in assuming that she was waiting to meet them when and where they wished, bold, arrogant school-boys.

By the time she met Léonie she was free from her morning's deliberate emptiness and her irritation. Lunch had been good. The lake had sparkled, and the air and the thin white wine had gone into her together, like the perfume from two meadowflowers growing from one seed. The people around her, elegant and easy in their summer clothes, had confirmed her own elegance and ease.

Léonie looked drabber than ever, sitting with her ankles crossed properly below her black dress in the lobby, but her face seemed younger, almost as if she had washed some spiritual dust from it during the night. She stood up eagerly, and "No, no!" she cried when Jennie said without much air of apology that she knew she was very late. "Nonono! It has been fun sitting here—such types, all so sophisticated! I used to come here to the winter balls a little, but I have given that up, all of it."

It gave you up, Jennie said coldly, silently, and she looked with distaste at the girl's pale mouth, at the little hairs that grew across the bridge of her nose above her large nervous eyes. It would be amusing, perhaps, to take her in hand.

"Madame!" Léonie said eagerly.

Jennie interrupted. "Call me Jennie, my dear," she commanded, hoping that she sounded like an old family friend, the kind who boasts of being a real companion to the younger generation.

"Oh! Oh, may I? I'd love to. Jennie, the most marvelous luck! Today Papa gave me a hundred francs!"

God, this is dull, Jennie said to Jennie. I don't think I

can stomach it. Aloud she said, "How wonderful! But Léonie, don't you have your own money? Forgive me for being indiscreet, but . . ."

The girl's face stiffened, and she looked away. "Of course I have my allowance," she said finally. "But Papa—I love my father, but he has no understanding of what I owe to my parish, to all the dreadful hardships in the mission field, to the good Sisters. When he finds that I have spent my allowance on all that he flies into a rage and cuts it down. Mama helps me, but then I hate to upset her. Poor Mama has such nervous attacks when she knows that Papa has misunderstood again. Jennie," she said very low, biting with a kind of hunger at her thumbnail so that to Jennie she sounded horridly like a girl wolfing chocolate or bread, "my father is an agnostic, a professed agnostic!"

Jennie felt like asking what about Paul, what was he, what kind of disbelieving monster further to torture his self-righteous sister? How ridiculous the whole thing was! She put her hand on Léonie's arm and shook it gently. "Come along," she said. "A hundred francs! What on earth shall we do with it all?"

Léonie knew good places to go, little rooms up dark stairs, rooms filled with incredibly fine lingerie, handkerchiefs like cobwebs, racks of silky leather for gloves, bolts of Lyon silks. Jennie ordered drunkenly, watching her companion gradually grow tipsy too. They each bought a hat, and Jennie made Léonie order two simple dresses, the clear color of hyacinths and lake water.

"Oh, this is such fun," the girl cried over and over, and her eyes were beautiful. "Darling Jennie, where did you come from? It is like magic, the way you make me feel!"

Jennie was firm: no teashop. She walked Léonie with little protest into the quiet bar of the hotel and ordered vermouth and soda. For a minute or two convent training revived itself; then the soft chairs, the polite omnipresent Duval, most of all Jennie's obvious ease, loosened the chill oil of propriety in the joints, and Léonie sat back, relaxed and excited.

"What time is the cocktail hour, Jennie?" she finally asked naïvely.

"Pretty soon. Why?"

"I must go before then. I don't want—that is, maybe you know about Paul. Maybe Papa told you. Paul will probably be here."

"But what of that?" Jennie asked. "I should like to meet him if he is as sweet as you are. It would be so gay, the three of us here!"

"But Jennie!" Léonie put a finger into her mouth and drew up her lip, like a rabbit about to nibble a carrot. Then she took it out again, looking nervously around the almost empty room. She leaned closer. "Paul wouldn't be alone! Oh, no, not Paul! He has a little friend! He has a mistress, right here in Lausanne, and he goes everywhere with her, and it is breaking our dear mother's heart! But does he care?"

She stood up. "I must go, Jennie," she said rapidly. "I will not, I absolutely refuse, to meet Paul here. I refuse!"

"But my dear," Jennie said in a quiet voice that she hoped would shame Léonie a little, "how do you know you will meet him here? Can't we sit peacefully and finish our drinks? Why should your brother's wild oats spoil our tête-à-tête? Aren't you treating him as if he were a naughty little boy?"

By this time the two of them were almost at the door. Jennie glanced at Duval and made a sign that she would pay him later. She followed Léonie into the dim corridor that went past the restrooms into the lobby. When they were almost at the end of it the girl turned, her face wild and pale.

"Jennie, will you ever forgive me?" Her voice was hysterical. "You've been so wonderful. It was so rude of me to impose our family disgrace on you. How can I ever apologize? You've been so darling . . ."

Jennie touched her hand. "Call me soon," she said gently. "I want to see you very soon again."

Léonie suddenly, awkwardly, bent down and kissed Jennie's cheek. "You are so understanding! It's like magic, what you do," she whispered, and she hurried out through the open door into the sloped street.

Jennie turned back and went into the restroom and rubbed a little perfume from her pocket vial on the spot where she still felt the girl's lips: she loathed being touched without invitation, especially by women.

She drank a Martini quickly. The bar was filling, and for a capricious second she considered staying there, to see if Paul came, and then to smile sweetly at him and Petit' Chose. But she went sedately to the desk instead and asked for her key.

"There is a gentleman waiting for Madame in the small writing-room," the concierge said. "I took the liberty of informing him that Madame might be returning soon."

"Thank you."

She felt a quick flutter of triumph. But when she went into the room, it was Emile, the father not the son, who stood up heavily to meet her.

Seven

"GOOD EVENING," she said. "You were waiting for me?" Jeannetôt bowed without speaking. They stood for what seemed a long time, and then Jennie with a little sigh sat down on one of the forbidding gold chairs. She decided to let him speak next, but when he silently took his handkerchief from his pocket and began to wipe his palms with it, she asked impatiently again, "You were waiting? You wished to see me?"

At the same moment he blurted, "Madame, I—" and they looked mutely again at each other.

The light was soft, but even so his face seemed months older than it had yesterday, years older than in the train. He had been suffering.

Jennie smiled at him, not too warmly but not quite as artificially as she felt like doing. "Monsieur Jeannetôt, it is so nice to see you again! I have really been lonely. Your little Léonie has been so sweet to take pity on me. We just parted."

"That is why I stopped by," he said, and his voice rasped as if he had not used it for a long time. He cleared his throat nervously. "I wanted to thank you."

"But for what?"

"Ah, surely you must know! It is like magic, the way

the child turned overnight from a sour old maid to her sweet self again! This morning she looked like a girl, a dear girl."

Jennie laughed a little mockingly. "Yes, she showed me your bounty. And let me assure you, we spent it all, and more too. I made her order two frocks. And she charged gloves and some extremely pretty underwear to you."

He smiled back at her, and his eyes were almost merry suddenly. "Good," he said. "That is good, as it should be. You are a sorceress, Madame."

"I am tired of that word Madame," Jennie said in a speculative way, as if she were considering much more than the word itself. "Madame. Léonie is calling me Jennie now. Why not you? I am after all an established old friend of the family—of half of it at least! Perhaps some day I'll have the pleasure of meeting the other half?"

"My poor wife," Jeannetôt said automatically, his voice hushed. "Poor lady! How she would enjoy you!"

"And your son Paul—I look forward to meeting him, the other *enfant terrible.*"

He shrugged. "As for that—if he ever behaves himself, the young fool! He's not been home for weeks. He writes his mother occasional little notes, thanking her for her checks no doubt. We meet now and then on the street, and when his Little Thing is hanging on his arm he at least has the grace not to recognize me. No, I think he is too occupied even to meet so wonderful a person as you— Jennie."

It seemed as if the name, newborn on his lips, tore suddenly at all his training, everything he had learned in fifty years about how to behave in public, or even in private.

He groaned and put his head into his hands so that she could not see his face. "Jennie," he said over and over, as if each time he were tearing a piece of his own flesh from himself.

"Someone may come," she remarked coldly at last. "This is part of the hotel lobby." She stood up and walked to the wide window, and through trees saw the darkening lake.

In a minute he stood beside her, but she did not look at him. His breathing was all right, she noticed.

"Madame—"

"I am still Jennie."

"Ah, Jennie then. My dear Jennie, I shan't ask you to forgive me. You know too much to bother with that. You know that I did not come here like a stupid schoolboy to thank you for bewitching my daughter. That was—"

"A schoolboy's lie?"

"Of course. And you know the other lie. My wife knows nothing about you. She did not present her compliments and promise to send her cards. She cannot ask you to her monthly at home—oh, yes, she still manages to calm her nerves enough to keep up that amenity!—she cannot ask you because, my dear Jennie, she does not know that you exist. Léonie agrees not to disturb her just now. Léonie gives me a chance to see you. Léonie is my dupe. I have lied about you from the first, Jennie. It is because I cannot bear to share you with anyone. Yesterday, in the tearoom with my own daughter, I suffered like a—"

"A schoolboy?"

"You're a little cruel. No, I suffered as I never suffered before in my life, even when I was younger and hotter-blooded, Jennie. You've bewitched me too. Poor Léonie! But at least you cannot make her feel like this! Jennie, what have you done to us?"

He did not move to touch her, and as they stood in the dusk Jennie felt, to her astonishment, the same wave of desire for him that she had known in the train, the same almost frightened sense of his own ferocious hunger, so tightly held. And all the time she heard, as if it were a play she listened to, their stilted little speeches, and she watched their bowings and low curtseyings. It was fantastic. She had seldom enjoyed anything so much and at the same moment been conscious of such a need for caution. Jennie must not be hurt . . .

"Since I first saw you, sitting there backward in the train, unlike other women, unlike all women, I have been half mad, Jennie. I want to give you everything I possess. I want to marry you. But I have a family, a devoted wife who has sacrificed her very health for my sake. I have an important position in Swiss engineering. Before long I shall be the dean of it, the dean! You came too late, Jennie. I am too old and too careful and timid to take you with me to a far place, to make you a princess."

Jeannetôt went on talking in his odd rasping voice, almost without expression. Jennie looked up curiously at him, because she knew he would not see her do it: he was in a kind of trance. She felt more strongly than ever before the desire to caress him and embrace him, and always with it the consciousness of how completely fatuous he was sounding. His words came out as if wrenched from him past his unwilling throat, and they were banal and dully strung together and quite inappropriate to the summer dusk, to the perfection of the woman Jennie who half listened.

I suppose I must call him Emile, she was thinking. What a shopkeeper's name! Paul, that is different. And in thirty years could I say, if I were here, that Paul too was a stout soul-thin shopkeeper? Yes, she said, yes.

"Emile," she whispered. She could see him shudder a little. "Emile, all this is so strange. It seems to have nothing to do with the passage of time. It is almost as if we were still on the train, with the countryside so fresh and dreamlike and newborn. And you must go now."

He sighed sharply and turned toward the door. "Do you know what it means," he asked without reproach, "for a man of my age and of my upbringing to talk as I have just done?"

He stopped his slow heavy walk and without looking at her said, "Jennie, there is just one thing. For the love of God stay here a little longer. I must know that you are here. If you went now it would be the end for me, the end completely. Give me a few more days, to get used to what has happened to me. Help me that much."

"Of course. Poor, poor Emile! I promise you. We can lunch together perhaps."

"No. People would gossip."

"Even if Léonie came too?" Jennie could not help being malicious that much.

"I must think of my dear wife. And of you," he added so hastily that it was not even awkward. "You I must not hurt, Jennie. Only stay."

"I promise, Emile. And now good night." She went swiftly away and into the lighted lobby, and he stood not watching her for once.

Eight

THE way Jennie broke her word was unfortunate, and later she regretted it mainly because it was against her principles to say she would do anything she did not do. It was a pity for Jeannetôt too, she admitted.

At about nine that night she fled her room. She would get a sandwich in a discreet corner of the bar, she said, and then inside she bowed mockingly to herself to admit that she must go to the bar for something much simpler than food. If he was there with Petit' Chose she would not even speak, she said; she would not nod. She would eat slowly, and drink one glass of ale, and go to her room, and hope to God that the yawning in her bones would stop, to let her sleep, and the dead-tired voice of Jeannetôt, and his immobility, leave her in peace and not gnaw at her. I cannot quite confess that Paul is almost young enough to be my son, she said sardonically, but at least Emile could be my father. Ah, poor Jennie, she said, with as much dispassion as a dog trainer consoling his best bitch in her seasonal woe, Jennie must take care.

Paul was there, alone at the bar. He looked exhausted and very drunk.

Duval left his two night-helpers working and came to take her order at the little table she chose in a far corner.

"I am tired," she said simply, looking up at him as if he were her nurse, her confidant.

"Let me fix you a double eggnog, Madame," he said. "No food. No cocktail." He turned away without waiting for her to agree and then added, his eyes lowered, "Monsieur Jeannetôt has been here, I think waiting for Madame, since perhaps five. Shall I tell him Madame has come? He seems a little . . ."

"So I saw as I came in. No, thank you, Duval. The eggnog will be perfect."

Jennie felt small and light as she sat waiting. She was tired in a pleasant way, as if she were a child again waiting to be lulled and bathed and soothed into the darkness. She pulled her feet up under her and let her head in its little skullcap fall back against the soft leather of the chair. Duval was wonderful, prescient. And when the drink came she held the glass childishly in both hands and drank from it in many little sips, feeling the sweet foam upon her upper lip and the infinitesimal gravel of the grated nutmeg.

"You look like a child, Jennie," Paul said far above her. "May I sit down?" He almost fell into the low chair across from hers. "Dreadfully sorry, but quite tight. Suppose I should eat. Dreadful."

"Oh, stop talking like a phony Englishman," Jennie said haughtily. Then she laughed to see him look at her so amazedly, his face clearing as if she had slapped it with a cold cloth. "What on earth did you get drunk for?"

"I don't know. I had to come here. I had to see you. You kept on being late."

"But, you damned fool, you sent me the note that you wouldn't be here."

"Yes," he said slowly. "So I did. But then I felt sure that you would, that you would feel how much I needed you to come."

They sat looking at each other, and Jennie felt growing in her such excitement, such an intolerable, horrendous turning of the screw, as she was sure she'd never known before. She sipped at the eggnog, her knuckles white on the glass, to keep from fainting or being sick. She was horrified, thus to find herself love-sick, caught with a boy too drunk even to focus his eyes properly on her across the little table. It was ignominious.

"Jennie," he said at last, "I see you know. You feel as I do, Jennie. I love you, Jennie. I am dying."

They stood up, he fairly steadily, and walked from the crowded room without a glance anywhere. In Jennie's rooms Paul said, "Let me alone for half an hour," and without another word went into her bath and shut the door gently.

He left before dawn. Jennie turned like a cat and found him gone, and then turned again and slept until the mid-morning sun streaked through the tall shutters. She lay flat as a shadow for a few minutes, her flesh over the fine singing bones like a mold made of cream, of satin, of the fumes of a long-gone brandy. She rang for breakfast and then went into the bathroom.

Her tray was ready when she came out, and she looked voluptuously at the large white envelope on it and made herself wait to open it until she had drunk the hot milky coffee, eaten both rolls, both pats of butter, one marked with a plump bee and the other with a cow.

She was surprised, but in a remote way too amused to be angry, when she saw that it was her bill, made out with

Swiss thoroughness and with unusual dispatch, since even the eggnog was added at the bottom.

Jennie, she thought, crossing her legs under the cherry-colored satin robe on the chaise longue, Jennie bounced from the Palace!

She got up after a time, packed her clothes, and summoned the maid and valet for their tips in a kind of laughing dream. It was about noon when she paid the bill, solemnly as a judge, to the solemnly agreeable concierge. And after she had tipped him too, and asked him to send all her new fine luggage to the station to be checked, she strolled into the bar.

"Good morning, Duval," she said pleasantly, and then when he as pleasantly answered her, she knew with a shout of silent laughter that it was he, of course, who had told the management about Paul. Dear Duval! "The eggnog was a lifesaver," she said with a frank smile. "I shall miss such delicious attentions."

"Madame is leaving?"

"Unfortunately. Almost at once."

"Ah? Madame too will be missed."

"Thank you, Duval. And in case I am unable to say, 'Until we meet again,' before I go—" and Jennie gave him a folded bill. He bowed, put it in his pocket with the unmistakable look on his dead face of an old-timer who is telling through his fingertips what the amount is, and then bowed again.

"One last dry Martini?" he asked.

"Thank you. Monsieur Jeannetôt will be here soon." Jennie hoped that she was right. How could she get in touch with him, except, strange sardonic thought, through

Léonie? Or Emile? Ah, Emile—she had promised him not to go . . .

"May I join you, dear Madame?" Paul asked.

"Of course." She watched him slide onto the bar stool beside her, and saw Duval double the gin in his little crystal mixer. "How nice . . ."

Nine

THEY went up away from Lac Léman, through vineyards and then high meadows white with narcissus blossoms, and stayed in a village hotel for four days. At night they could hear the many voices of the cowbells making a slow song from all the slopes, and could see the stiff white linen curtains over their window move in and out in the light from the one street lamp below. They walked up into the little forests above the village, across fields knee-deep with a hundred different kinds of flowers, and then came back to eat languorous long meals in the hotel's dining-room: trout, crayfish, thick cream stirred with kirsch for their wild strawberries. They sat drinking white wine from thick glasses in the café downstairs, listening to the black-smocked men and playing double solitaire. Mostly they stayed in bed, sleeping, not talking much, drinking a little, making love.

The second day, while Paul went down to the desk for cigarettes, Jennie wrote a gentle note to Emile. "I could not stay," it said. "Forgive me, my dear. I was too disturbed, for you and perhaps even for myself. I ran away from you. I shall come back soon."

The maid took it to the post-box. Jennie felt better for having been so thoughtful and so generous of herself, and when Paul came back it seemed to her that she had never been happier.

On the way down toward the lake again Paul talked for the first time of Petit' Chose. Jennie hardly listened to him: the clear June air streamed past them so sweetly, she felt so voluptuously tired, so keenly alive. And it was Paul's affair, not hers. He must arrange it for himself.

"It's the end, of course. We've known it would happen before long. The quarrels have been horrible. But it will almost kill her, poor little thing. She wants to stay near me, she says, even when I marry." He laughed shortly. "Can you imagine Lausanne society if I kept her here for the rest of my life?"

"But you'll have a mistress anyway. Why not her?"

"But Jennie! She is—it's hard to say without sounding foolish—she's part of my being a bachelor, that's the trouble! If I kept her on here after I married and had children, people would think I was completely stodgy and stupid and couldn't even find myself a new, more mature woman!"

Jennie laughed delightedly. "You mean that Lausanne would criticize you, not for having a mistress, but for having an outmoded one?"

"Exactly," Paul agreed seriously, and then they both laughed until they felt dizzy, and they stopped and drank tea and ate more strawberries and cream at an inn among the vineyards. They were trying not to get to Lausanne, they both knew. They sat for a long time on the little terrace, listening to the heavy-shoed workers climb up the slopes between the vines, watching the far lake darken. Finally the lights of Evian, across the purple waters on the shore of France, flickered and twinkled palely in the twilight. Jennie and Paul stood up without words and went to his car like people moving in a dream.

In Lausanne he took her to a hotel down the street from the Palace. It was large, pleasant, middle-class, with the big *brasserie* downstairs where Jennie had eaten alone and watched Petit' Chose's bosom heaving at her across the room.

"This is perfectly respectable," Paul said half teasingly, "except, my dear Jennie, there is no Duval here to keep one eye on his customers' extracurricular activities. That makes it somewhat more popular among the gay blades of the town."

"We shall miss him," Jennie murmured. "Perhaps we might drop in for a Martini with him now and then?"

But Paul was not really listening to her. His dark eyes looked strained and nervous suddenly, almost like Léonie's blue ones, and Jennie knew that he was thinking of the return to his apartment, of the scene, the tears. Would Petit' Chose threaten to kill herself? Probably, and Paul too.

"Be careful," she said lightly. "You are quite important to me. The Algerians are hot-tempered, aren't they?"

Paul looked soberly at her and then smiled. "Oh, that," he said. "I can take care of that. Why, she's even tinier than you!"

Jennie felt like weeping suddenly with anger at his

blandly comparing her to that overstuffed little half-breed with a nascent mustache. She was tired. She held out her hand to him and thanked him for having her bags brought into the hotel. "Good-by . . . until soon . . . good-by," she said, the old family friend.

"Good-by, dear Jennie," he said impersonally, kissing her hand with automatic politeness.

She watched him, slender and graceful, walk away from her. For a minute she wished that she had let tears show in her eyes, to puzzle and disturb him. Then she turned with a sense of release, of freedom, to the little arrangements at the hotel desk.

She liked her room. It was completely Swiss: practical, solid, comfortable, without any of the faded elegancies of the Palace. It made her feel anonymous. She thought of all the well-fed travelers, people like Emile Jeannetôt, who had slept here and gone on respectably to the next stop and the next, unworried by poverty or passion.

After she had bathed luxuriously (the wash basin and pitcher of hot water at the village hotel had been fun, but now she threw extra crystals of perfume into her deep tub as if she were saying a deliberate good-by to all that adventure), she walked through the *brasserie* and engaged the same table she had sat at before, and then went out into the cooling street.

There were several letters for her at the Palace. As the concierge handed them to her, he asked politely, "Has Madame a forwarding address?"

She looked easily at him. "Not yet."

"Perhaps," he said, his face as impervious and dead as Duval's, as a croupier's, as a good concierge's, "it would be convenient for Madame to call for her correspondence at General Delivery?"

Jennie almost laughed aloud at his insolence, so completely a part of him and his world hatred, his well-trained loathing of the people he must bow to, the sores he must cover discreetly, the graves he must dig every day there behind his desk. She admired him for daring to be thus insulting to her, to suggest that she go where all the other whores went for their mail, General Delivery at the main post office, General Delivery where she would stand in line with the rest of them, and guess their prices, as she waited for her bills and love letters, by the way they smelled and combed their back hair.

"Thank you," she said gravely. "That will not be necessary. I may perhaps call here once more, and shall appreciate your keeping any possible message for me."

He bowed over her tip without looking at her and wished her good night.

Jennie would have liked to drink champagne, but she decided against it as not circumspect for herself alone in the town's favorite *brasserie*. She did not really notice the average amount of stares and speculations that always seethed about her; indeed, she admitted that their absence would bother her much more than could they. But there was no point in drawing undue attention to herself if she planned to be there long, and to dine often with Paul and drink with him and talk with him, all of which she did, most firmly, plan to do.

She wondered vaguely how he was progressing in his farewell to the Little Thing, and then permitted herself the luxury of a large rare steak with watercress and a bottle of Chambertin 1929, all fine and heavy and dark after the delicate trout and the thin wines of the past few days. When she was through, and had eaten a bit of cheese with the last glass of her wine, she propped her letters efficiently against the little silver coffee pot and opened them slowly, enjoyably.

They were from Emile, except for two short notes from his daughter. His were easy to read, alike in their anxiety for her, their stiff anguish at her flight. The last one, written after he had heard from her, thanked her formally and then went all trembling and wild. "You cannot call me here," it said. "My wife is prostrate . . . more trouble with Paul again. But I must know, Jennie, I must know, when you return to Lausanne. Can you not call Léonie? Can you not pretend some reason or other or anything? God, Jennie, I cannot live . . ."

Jennie felt disgusted, faintly annoyed. She would telephone to him tomorrow at his office or send a note there. He was impertinent to suggest anything else. She disliked this breaking down of all his dignity.

Léonie had written, on her part, a somewhat gushing but agreeable note thanking her for the gay afternoon and saying how sorry she was to have ended it so abruptly. She had been unwell the past year, she said, and grew tired easily. But when, ah, when could they meet again? At the end she said, "Dearest Jennie, you can never know what meeting you has meant to me. It has given me new strength in all this tedious trouble we are going through about my brother and about poor Mama's health. Since you came I feel happy inside. Until soon, until very soon, your devoted friend, Léonie."

Jennie tore it across and laid it on the little pile with the father's, for the waiter to take away. The last note from the daughter, she felt, would be the most interesting, the fitting finale to this well-assorted little family correspondence. She opened it pleasurably.

"Darling Jennie, wonderful friend, forgive my haste. I must see you. You in all the world may be able to advise me. I feel so terribly alone, and you are so wise and experienced. Paul has disappeared! My mother is under opiates with shock. Papa whispered to me this morning that you are out of town. I implore you to telephone me as soon as you return. I feel quite desperate. I have never seen poor Papa so unnerved by anything Paul has done before. What an ungrateful son! How my heart bleeds for my dear parents! The world is so ugly that I understand now why the good Sisters leave it. Perhaps I do have a real vocation, Jennie. Dearest friend, I pray that you return soon, soon. Léonie."

Jennie added the torn note to the others. The whole business seemed ridiculous to her, undignified. Why should any normal human being make such a fuss over the casual absence for a few days of a young man who after all had spent many months away, who was openly leading his own life in his own apartment? She shrugged. Families! She hated them.

The headwaiter bent over her table: she was wanted on the telephone. She paid her bill leisurely and walked with only faint curiosity into the lobby. Almost before Paul could speak she said coldly, "I am not used to being called from public places to answer the phone."

He did not answer for a minute. "I'm terribly sorry,

Jennie," he said then. His voice was faint and high. "I am calling from the police station."

Jennie waited and then said, "Well?"

"She has disappeared, Jennie. No note, nothing. God knows what she may have done with herself. She left two days ago. The police know nothing. They say they will help me."

Jennie heard his voice crack a little. "I'm sorry, Paul," she said slowly. "But what do you expect me to do about it? Why do you call me about it?"

There was no answer.

"Of course if I happen to see your—your little friend, I'll let you know. I am quite sure I'd recognize her."

"Jennie," Paul asked flatly, "may I come? May I see you for a minute? May I at least join you downstairs for a drink? Ten minutes. Five minutes, Jennie!"

"Oh, Paul, I'm truly sorry, my dear! But I am desperately tired. Not tonight." Then she said slowly, childishly, "Good night, Paul," and put the receiver down on its cradle before he could answer.

Almost at once she felt a little ashamed. But how could she call him back? It would be silly to try to find him at the police station, and which one, in which quarter of the town? Her annoyance at his bothering her about another woman melted: poor Paul, so young! But he would probably have a drink or two and go back to the apartment and get a good night's sleep. He should be thankful not to have his half-breed female storming at him and making scenes and screaming. He was probably as tired as Jennie, poor Jennie . . .

She left word not to be disturbed and went sleepily to

her room. The bed was turned down, and beside it was a fluffy white mat which said, in pretty blue, *Bon Soir* . . . *Bonne Nuit.* "Good night," Jennie said to herself, and was asleep.

Ten

SHE called the Jeannetôt house a little before noon. A maid answered, and then Léonie, breathless and hushed. She sounded almost tremulous when she heard it was Jennie, as if she were going to weep. At first she said "Nonono" in a shocked way when Jennie asked her to come downtown for lunch; her mother was desperately ill, she said.

"But, my dear, there are nurses surely," Jennie said patiently, thinking how true it was that martyrdom upon a family altar increased in proportion to the lack of beauty in the martyr. Very few really pretty girls have ever devoted themselves to an ailing parent, she said coldly to herself, listening to Léonie's fluttering assurances that yes, yes, of course the dear Sisters were there night and day so wonderful so calm—

"Then don't be a little ninny," Jennie said in a gay, chiding, sympathetic way that amused as much as it disgusted her. "You must give yourself some relaxation, my dear. Would you like to walk down to Ouchy? Just tell me where you want to lunch with me. Perhaps a quiet tearoom?"

Léonie fluttered a bit more and then asked if perhaps she might just see Jennie for a little while in her rooms at the Palace. Jennie grinned, remembering the neat plain bed, the oak dresser, the two straight chairs upstairs, wondering what Léonie would think of a lady living above a *brasserie*.

They agreed finally to meet at a highly respectable restaurant halfway between the two hotels. Jennie started toward the elevator and then turned back to telephone Emile, as he had begged in his letter. She thought better of it: he would be emotional. She would let him lunch first.

Léonie looked paler than ever, and when Jennie asked her gently where her new hat was, she appeared horrified at the suggestion that she could wear anything but her old black uniform while her mother lay ill at home. Jennie resolved to be patient, but she felt a rising wave of boredom and revulsion even in the face of the girl's obvious happiness to see her. She insisted on sherry before their soup, and Léonie relaxed almost magically as she sipped it.

"Jennie darling," she said, stretching her thin hand with its blunt, gnawed fingertips across the table impulsively, so that Jennie had at least to pat it a little instead of pressing it tenderly as Léonie plainly longed for, instead of pushing it away as she herself wished to do, "Jennie, I hate to seem so distracted. I wanted our first meeting after you came back to be wonderful and gay, the way it should be for anyone like you."

The girl is developing a delayed convent crush on me, Jennie thought a little wryly. A pity she is not more attractive. Jennie felt sudden depression seize her, as it always did when she was caught with another human who was ugly or malformed or dreary. She longed to get up and hurry from the restaurant, away from Léonie's wild blue eyes and her shy pale-lipped smile. She drank her sherry quickly and ordered another for each of them.

"I am tired a little," she said. "My trip was boring—nothing but business. And now, my dear, I am so sorry about your mother, about all your worries. Tell me! Tell me how you knew your naughty brother was gone if he doesn't live with you."

"Oh, Jennie, it was dreadful! I have never seen poor Mama so upset. That little—Paul's little friend came to the house, forced her way in. She had a letter Mama had sent to Paul by messenger that morning, with money in it. She tore it up, yelling and crying, and threw the pieces straight at Mama, and said horrible things. I ran in when I heard the noise. It was awful. The maids were listening in the hall and wouldn't go away. Mama was almost fainting, covering her ears, and this creature was screaming that Paul had a new friend and that he had run away with her. I got her away, and we called the doctor, and Mama's confessor came . . ."

She talked fast, eating the luncheon food as if she were starved, so that crumbs caught on her lips. Jennie watched, and made little sympathetic cries and shrugs, and loathed her. Léonie could not stop. She repeated herself. She said over and over that the maids had kept listening.

Jennie ordered dessert and a bottle of chilled sweetish wine with it. Perhaps that would calm Léonie a little. At least it would be a diversion.

When they had almost finished, and the room was beginning to empty, so that Léonie's voice sounded more loudly in it, Jennie looked away from her flushed face to the doorway. Emile Jeannetôt was standing there, and as if he might fall, stiff as a tree. His eyes were as deep-sunken as Paul's almost, but Jennie knew he was staring at her. Perhaps I should marry him, she thought dispassionately, as she felt again the strange lust his immobility gave her. Of course he would insist on the proper wait after his wife died . . .

She raised her hand, not smiling but letting her face show warm and delighted at the sight of him. But he turned like a tree on its root, unwillingly, wrenchingly, and was gone from the room.

"That was your father," she interrupted.

Léonie stopped as if gagged and stared crazily at her and then around the room. There was some chocolate on her lips. She put her hand to her mouth and chewed first at one nail and then another in little ferocious snaps. Finally she said, "Papa?"

"Yes. Papa."

"Oh, Jennie, what shall I do? What will become of us? Paul is killing us all!"

Jennie waited for a minute and then asked in a casual, chatty voice, "Don't you think, my dear Léonie, that you are making some new peccadillo of your brother's much too important? Why should the fact that Paul has cast off one mistress for another throw three mature, intelligent people like you and your parents into such a frantic state?"

Léonie looked helplessly at her. "But I don't think you understand," she said, trying hard to make her voice as calm as Jennie's. "We were upset about the other girl. It was horribly embarrassing to have Paul bring home a colored woman, which is what she is, from the colonies. We had always been very close, a close family, and then suddenly we couldn't invite him to dinners with our old friends, things like that. And he was seen everywhere here with her, and in Geneva, and people would even see them in Berne and Paris and ask us about it all. But we grew used to it, in a way, at least poor Mama and Papa did. But this is different. Now Paul should be settling down. He should finish the work for his degree, and go into Papa's office, and make a good marriage. Mama was preparing him for that, so wisely, with her wonderful letters. Papa was less tolerant—he used to see Paul and that girl in cafés, and it always upset him."

"And how about you?"

Léonie drank thirstily at her wine, not looking anywhere. "Ah, how about me?" She shrugged. "I thought of other things. I went more often to church. That was a wonderful comfort. It kept me from being lonely."

The place was almost empty now. Jennie caught the eye of a politely yawning waitress, and paid the check, and they sat silently finishing the last cold, perfumed swallows of the wine. Jennie pulled on her gloves.

"It is a pity then," she said, "that this new woman has appeared, isn't it? All your plans for Paul's life are really upset, aren't they? It may not be just a youthful affair this time. And how does your father feel about it?"

"He is like a madman. I never saw him so wild. He does not sleep. It is like his coming here, and then leaving, not speaking to us. He is not responsible, Jennie." She suddenly began to cry, harshly, without any coquetry of hidden eyes or muffled, bitten sobs.

Jennie stood up. She felt the waitress looking curiously at them. "Come on, Léonie," she said. She almost pushed the girl out of her chair and toward the door. "Come to my room. It is near here. This is foolish. Try to control yourself."

Léonie stumbled along blindly, making rasping sounds, her hands stiff at her sides. Jennie felt almost overwhelmed with boredom and embarrassment, but still she had to seem tender. She put both the handbags through one arm and half led, half supported the girl down steps and into the street. When they got inside the hotel Léonie asked in a loud, suspicious voice, "But where are you taking me? Where are we?" and then went off again into wilder sobs.

"My friend is not well," Jennie said unnecessarily to the old elevator man.

He clicked his tongue in sympathy. "A nervous crisis? A shock? Shall I send for one of the maids? Would Madame wish some brandy perhaps?"

"Oh, you are so nice," Jennie sighed, as Léonie's ugly noises grew uglier. "Yes, please have the headwaiter send up brandy, and soon, soon!"

"At once," he said, bowing them out of his cage. "It is perhaps only the time of the month, Madame, if I may speak as a family man. Do not worry. There is nothing like brandy."

No, nothing like brandy, Jennie thought gratefully, full of love for the little old man. She needed some. It upset her to see such lack of dignity. While she waited for it she made Léonie lie down on the bed and laid her poor stiff hat neatly on the starched mat of the dresser. The girl drank a swallow of the spirits when they came and then went off worse than ever, crying out "Paul! Paul!" as if she were in pain. Jennie sat by the window, sipping gratefully after her first fat swallow. Women were fools, she knew, but she had never heard such an unmitigated one as this. It was as if she were in love.

"Tell me what Paul is like, my dear," she said after one of Léonie's fits of sobbing.

Léonie stopped sharply, and Jennie knew, although she could not bring herself to look, that the girl was staring at her. "Paul?" Her voice was high and wavering. Then she giggled a little. "Paul is very attractive," she said.

Jennie sipped slowly at the fine hot brandy. "Has he always had affairs like this?"

Léonie sat up on the bed and then fell back again, talking between her sobs. "Oh, he was such a darling little boy! I am five years older. He was like my child almost. All my girl friends adored him. We used to play house with him. And then they all fell in love with him, all, all!"

"Did you ever see him—kissing them?"

Léonie breathed shudderingly. "No, Jennie! No, of course not," she cried out. "But I know he did. I know he kissed them, just the way he kissed his Petit' Chose, the way he is kissing that new woman now. Jennie, tell me, tell me, darling Jennie—" She twisted on the bed, so that brandy spilled and ran down across her and onto the blue coverlet.

"Tell you what?"

"Jennie, I read what I can find, and one of the maids brings me magazines, secret ones—but what is it like to be kissed, I mean the way Paul kisses that woman now, the new one?"

Jennie went slowly to the side of the bed and stood looking at the tousled girl who moaned there, eyes closed, face wild and crooked, everything out of focus. It was revolting. She put her empty glass carefully down on the night table. "I can tell you, Léonie," she said. Her voice was cold and heavy like a sword blade. "I can tell you."

The girl lay without breathing, her eyes open again and fixed on Jennie's face bent over her.

"I know about kissing, Léonie, the kind you mean, because for four days now your brother Paul and I—"

Léonie cried out once, like a woman in labor.

"Yes," Jennie went on. She felt hideously powerful. She was getting revenge for all the boredom and disgust this female had inflicted on her, for the way Paul had slashed at her by going back to look for Petit' Chose, for Emile's passionate pother, and for the way he humbled her with his fat-burgher immobility. "Yes," she said softly. "Four days and three nights, and then, of course, one other night —but I shan't tell you any more, Léonie. You must learn the rest for yourself, from your secret magazines. Or from your mother maybe."

She watched Léonie's eyes dart more and more frenziedly about the room and wondered what would happen next. She hoped it would not be screaming.

"Paul, Paul," the girl muttered, her teeth clenched. She stiffened on the bed, a look of almost ecstatic horror budding in her. "Where did you bring me?"

Jennie rang the bell beside the bed, three times, then three, then three, as Léonie bent her head back farther and farther, so that she lay arched sideways in a way that made her thin body beautiful. Her breathing was very heavy, and her eyes were closed, and suddenly she was unconscious.

A kind fat maid with discreet curiosity in every fold of her came to sit by the poor young lady, and Jennie went unhurriedly down to telephone. It was hard to get through to Emile. It made him seem more important a man than Jennie had thought him to be.

"Emile," she said close to the mouthpiece, "you must listen to me. This is Jennie, you know. Listen." She waited. "Are you there?" she asked sharply.

His voice sounded high and faint and ridiculous, like Paul's last night from the police station. "Yes, I am here. Yes, Jennie."

"Emile, I am terribly sorry, but Léonie is ill. She is here with me. She felt ill at lunch, and she is in my room now." Jennie told where she was, and her room number, into the echoing voicelessness of the telephone, and waited, and finally said urgently, softly, "Emile! What shall I do? I am completely alone, and frightened."

"What does Léonie look like?"

"It's like epilepsy I think, but it isn't that. It's a kind of hysterics. She has fainted, but her breathing is very heavy. She cried a lot."

She heard the man sigh. He sounded exhausted. "It is one of her attacks, Jennie. I was afraid of it. Don't you be afraid. Cover her warmly, and I'll send for her. I'll send nurses from the clinic she was in last time. How long have you been in that hotel, Jennie?"

She was speechless with surprise and then anger. His voice had not changed at all between his fatherly arrangements and the colossal impertinence of his last question. Schoolboy, she thought furiously. And why should she be

kind and lie to him? "Since last night, Emile," she said
softly.

"It is no place for you."

"The Palace was dreadfully stuffy."

He finally said, "I shall come with the attendants, Jennie.
It is a form of hysterics, yes."

Upstairs Léonie looked less stiff, and her mouth had
fallen open a little. The maid had already tucked a soft
coverlet over her and sat placidly now beside the bed.

"My poor little friend," Jennie whispered. "She has had
a great shock. How can I thank you, Madame?"

"But, Madame, it is nothing! Let me stay here a little
longer. There is no danger, but . . ."

Jennie touched her shoulder gratefully and went to the
window. Midafternoon sun streamed in, and she turned
the blinds softly, to make things less harshly neat and
clear in the room. She tiptoed with the two empty brandy
glasses to her closet. Then she sat in one of the hard chairs,
her face smooth and bland as cream in the half light.

It was perhaps an hour before the people came for
Léonie, who still lay in a heavy trance. A huge silent man
with a child's look picked her up gently in his arms. The
nun with him, after making efficient notes in a book as to
pulse and respiration and such, nodded brusquely and
followed him out of the room. Jeannetôt, standing with
great dignity at the door, said dully as his poor daughter
was carried past him, "I shall follow you, Sister."

"All my thanks," Jennie said to the kind maid, who had
stood palpitating with curiosity and delight. "I shall thank
you more practically later."

"Ah, it was nothing, nothing to do for Madame who is always so generous," the maid said with automatic, not quite servile, not quite mocking, good nature, and she ducked from the room.

"I am sorry, Jennie," Emile said.

"No, no! It is I who am sorry. Poor girl!"

"This is happening more often."

"Emile," Jennie said, and there was pity in her voice, "why don't you send her away, to the Midi perhaps, away from all the illness at home and her brother and all that? It is what she needs."

"We've tried, Jennie." Then he cried out, as if saying her name were too much again, "Jennie! What have you done, my God? What have you done to me? I must see you—" He still stood by the open door, so that anyone in the hall could hear the nakedness in his voice.

"Not here, Emile," and Jennie looked distastefully around the austere room, at the rumpled bed. "We can't talk here. Later. How long will you be at the clinic?"

"Half an hour perhaps. They know me by now."

"Can we talk downstairs then?"

He shook his head fiercely. "Not in public. People— there would be talk."

Ah, fat burgher, Jennie thought scornfully. Finally she said, "There is no place then, unless perhaps the little writing-room at the Palace, where we met before. If that would not be—would not disturb you too much?"

"You are good, Jennie, an angel! Do you remember that too, how cruelly I once upset you there? And you forgive me!" He shook his big head from side to side, and his eyes were very blue and grateful.

"At five then?"

"At five." He bowed gravely and closed the door behind him with a careful click.

Jennie sighed, and stretched this way and that with relief. Then she went into the bathroom, turned on the tap full force, and emptied the rest of her box of perfumed salts into the seething greenish water. What a disgusting experience! People were so thoughtless, so selfish. She shuddered and resolutely put the sound of Léonie's rasping sobs, the sight of chocolate upon blubbering lips, from the front part of her mind.

Eleven

BUT before she was undressed even, she was disturbed again. The old cricket of an elevator man knocked and knocked, and when she finally heard him he told her that she must come down to the telephone. It was urgent, he said, bowing and darting back into the cage.

Jennie turned off the roaring water, straightened her hair, and went downstairs to the office desk. For a minute it sounded as if whoever was on the wire had given up waiting. Then Paul answered her icily patient voice.

"This is most embarrassing," she said, and could have fallen to the floor for wanting to see him, feel him beside her, hear the many-voiced cowbells on the summer mountainsides. "Where are you? Where have you been?"

"Jennie darling, I've longed to talk with you. I called about noontime—"

"I forgot to ask for messages," she said. She wanted to call him her dearest love, to ask him if he missed her, if he wanted her. But the clerk stood impassively at the desk. She could hear waiters arguing behind a screen at the end of the hall. From the open door into the *brasserie* came the sound of slapping feet and slow midafternoon voices. *Paul*, she wanted to cry out, with all of Léonie's agony and more. "Where have you been?" she asked again.

"Geneva. Jennie, it's been ghastly. I spent all morning in the morgue."

For a minute she could say nothing. She was completely flabbergasted by him. How dared he, how dared he, call her down from her room to tell her about hunting for his Petit' Chose? She almost gasped with a kind of naïve wonder at his stupidity.

"She wasn't there, Jennie. I'm in Lausanne again. The police in Sion have called. I'll go down there tonight, on the chance—Jennie, can you hear?"

"Paul, did you love her?" Jennie was unconscious now of the desk clerk, uncaring. She wanted to know the answer, that was all.

He said in a minute, "Jennie, I can't talk now. It isn't a question of love. But she was so good to me. She gave me so much and asked nothing. I'm in a café. I can't talk now."

"Did you really love her?"

"Jennie, what's the matter with you? No, I didn't love her. But God in heaven, look what I did to her!"

"Paul," Jennie said finally, "can you meet me for a few minutes before you go to Sion? When do you go?"

"I should leave by six. Jennie, let me come afterwards. I'll be back by midnight. It will be better."

"No. Meet me in the little writing-room just before six, Paul, the one down the corridor from the bar at the Palace. I'll be free by then. I simply want to see you for a minute, to tell you that I understand about her, that I'm so dreadfully sad." Her voice caught. She was shaking with rage.

"Darling," he said gratefully, "last night you frightened me. Now it is different. Yes, I can be there. Maybe we can have one good Martini, Harry's best, eh? God knows I need it. Jennie, have you ever been in a morgue?"

"Paul, don't. I'll wait for you." She hung up before he could add more to his histrionics and hurried upstairs. The bath would be ruined . . .

Twelve

JENNIE was late, which annoyed her very much indeed: she disliked women who told lies and women who were late anywhere at all. It seemed to her that the Jeannetôts deliberately made her do many things she prided herself on not doing: break promises, not keep appointments. It was annoying.

She had bathed slowly and then fallen across the fresh bed as if stunned by all the wretched, ugly things that had happened that day, and then the churchbells were ringing everywhere through the open windows of the town, and it was far past five. She dressed as fast as she could, and saw that she looked smoothly windblown under her cap, and that her fresh gloves matched the soft leather of her little slippers. Up the hill to the Palace she hurried, but judiciously, so as not to seem too breathless. In the lobby she nodded casually to the concierge. He called something after her, but she sped on softly over the elegant carpets and the marble and stopped, like a bird, like a sea gull landing on a rotten orange, just outside the door to the writing-room.

She could hear Jeannetôt and Paul talking. That was too bad, she thought. She had not really meant them to meet, not consciously. How stupid of Emile to wait, of Paul to be earlier than he had said. It was not she who had broken her word, but the men.

". . . everything you could," Paul was saying excitedly. "You and Mama have always disapproved. Why couldn't you treat me the way other people treat their sons—let me alone a while?"

"And have you drag your little half-breed all over Switzerland with our blessings? What do you think it has done to your mother? And what of Léonie? Why do you suppose she has these religious fits of hers?"

Paul laughed sharply. "Religious! What she needs—"

"That's enough. Hold your tongue, Paul. At least there's one decent child in my family."

"And what has driven her half crazy?"

"Ah!" The father sounded impotent, like a tired clown. "You have no pity at your age, have you? Do you care what is happening to us at home?"

"Of course I care, Papa." For a minute Paul sounded

loving and soft. Then he asked angrily, "And do you care about me, about what is happening to me?"

"Of course. But unfortunately, my dear chap, we know. We happen to know all about your latest flight from reality with another beautiful whore—"

"Shut up," Paul shouted. "Don't dare say that, you damned old fool! What do you know about it? She is a lady, everything you and Mama wish I would marry. She's—"

"So that's why you sneak off with her, eh, and break your mother's heart, and drive us half mad with worry? She's a lady, eh, for four days and nights! Wouldn't your paid mistress answer the purpose?"

In the dim corridor Jennie pressed her hands nervously against her mouth. Her heart pounded hard, hurting her. How could they talk so? How ugly they sounded! She did not dare look in at them, for fear of the faces she would see, the beastly ravening faces. How could people be so horrible?

"My paid mistress, as you so genteelly put it," Paul said viciously, "happens to have yielded place to an old friend of yours, a companion at tea lately of my holier-than-thou sister."

In the thick silence Jennie knew that no footstep could be as loud as her own heart. She was appalled by the raw words, the feeling that what was being said had no skin on it, nothing to cover decently the bloody, brutal flesh. Why did the big hotel not stop and listen? Why did not someone come to end all this beastly talk, this shouting and snarling? She felt as if she were floating in a dark ugly pool, too deep for ripples, and she too small to get to the surface. She was drowning, drowning. These selfish people were killing her with their dark words. They thought of nothing, ever, but their own selves. They sucked at her and fed themselves from her beauty and her generosity . . .

In the room Emile Jeannetôt finally spoke, in a way not speech, a word that was not a word, as if he were a tree learning. "Jennie!" he cried loudly.

She shivered to hear her name thus mouthed. Everyone would hear . . .

"I'll kill you," Emile cried out again, and she looked wildly around her. She could hear people coming, the concierge probably, the doorman . . .

There was one more terrible sound, sobbing and wrenching, and then Paul said, like a weary old man, with great compassion, "Ah, my father! You too?" His voice was low. By then servants were running.

Jennie walked through them as if unconcerned, her feet in their soft little slippers skimming the fine floors. How they talked, what fusses they made, all the people everywhere! She hated them did Jennie. Good-by, good-by, she called. Good-by, all you clowns! I hate you, with your selfish gabble, with your thoughts all for your own puny, stupid lives. You can't hurt me though. I am free of you, escaped once more from your dark pool. Jennie is free . . .

II

One

IN 1847 there was a passenger-and-freight train that left for London early in the afternoon every day and covered the seventy-five miles in a little under four hours unless the load was heavy and the wind was against the nose of the handsome steam engine. It stopped several times, the first half of the trip, in little country stations surrounded by rolling hedgebound fields, and the guard unlocked the doors, and people clambered up and into the roomy coaches and spread their baskets and bundles amply about them on the wooden seats. But toward London there were no stops, and the speed seemed frightening as the mighty vehicle puffed stolidly past waving children and the thinner meadows and into the first tentative ugly suburbs.

The passengers sat stiffly, unspeaking. Gentlemen read their newspapers or pulled the brims of their high hats down and pretended to think, and the ladies and women who were not holding children watched the whirling landscape, read religious tracts, or patted eau de Cologne upon their temples, according to their proclivities and stations in life. Occasionally a tea basket was produced, but for the most part the voyagers stayed themselves with nibbled biscuits and lozenges until their arrival, famished, at Euston Station about six o'clock, well past the dinner hour for all but the most elegant.

That was the train Jennie took, one day in March. She should have known better: the air grew steadily more difficult to breathe, and even when she pressed her forehead surreptitiously against the cold windowpane, her sickened eyes could not see much beyond the rain streaks. She was sure she would not be ill: the surgeon had said she would not. She must get to London, that was all. Once there, she would soon feel strong and untarnishable again, her own fortress against what might bow down other weaker females. Once away from the jouncing, vibrating torture of the train her back would not pain her so, and she would be able to recall that in the greening meadows wee lambs lay passively beside their mothers, and that the hedges were blooming and blossoming. She would be able to know again that she was free, Jennie was free, not menaced as she had been until this morning.

She hardly noticed that the train had stopped until they were sliding away from the station and she heard the large woman next to her say, "Last stop, you hear me?" to her little boy.

"Yes, Ma." He kicked one foot shyly, his eyes fixed on the bobbing tassel at the top of his shiny black buttoned boot.

"There'll be no help for it, you hear me? You'll have to contain yourself like a man," his mother went on in a low ominous way. "We're locked in now. The stationmaster locked us in, and now if you want to you'll have to wait until London, that's all, like a man. You hear me?"

"Yes, Ma," he said, looking small and anguished, as if already he recognized a prick of necessity within him.

Jennie closed her eyes. She felt stranger than before.

There was no denying it. Where one red-hot knife had lain on her back an hour ago, ten hissed now, and it was as if something had broken inside her, below her tight lacings. But it would not be long, two hours more perhaps, and then she would be in London, free Jennie.

When she next saw anything, the little boy was leaning around his mother, gazing at her as if she were a cat perhaps, or even another little boy. She looked back at him. He smiled faintly and disappeared without hurry, and all she could see was his little boot tassel kicking gently to the wheels' tune.

There was a countrywoman across the way, eating a meat pasty unashamedly in the presence of the strictly unobserving gentlefolk behind their fans and papers. She broke it open as if it were a ripe peach, deftly, so that the partly congealed gravy in it stayed as if in two rich cups, and she put one half and then the other into the red cave between her teeth. Her mouth looked gigantic to Jennie. Her teeth were like white tombstones. When she closed her full fat lips there was a dimple deep as a well in either cheek. When she put out her tongue for one crumb yet untasted on her chin, it was like a lion's, rough and flexible.

Jennie stared hard at her, while she felt whatever had broken inside her rush down. How undignified, her mind cried out as she slipped moaning to the littered floor. How ignominious to be a woman!

When next she was Jennie, she looked up to a ring of other women's faces, curious, strangely gentle behind their curiosity. They bent over her, and she saw slowly that they had spread out their wide skirts so that there were no men anywhere, so that she was in a kind of tent, a stockade, of velvet and fine wool and unruffled homely spun-goods.

Beside her the countrywoman kneeled, and she was ripping her own clean white petticoat into strips and deftly making Jennie nice again. It would be a hard job, Jennie saw wryly, with a kind of light-headed interest in the whole bloody business. She closed her eyes, not in pain, but because of her annoyance at this thing. She was helpless: then let these people do what they could for her. She must be right again before London.

The strong smell of salts and *eau de toilette* faded before a wave of musky *millefleurs* that almost literally pushed a hole in the circle of women, and a firm beautiful voice asked brusquely, "Well, how is the girl now? Better, eh?"

Jennie looked up into an old woman's face, a long heavy face, like that of a small-eyed horse, elaborately painted beneath a monstrous traveling turban topped with black cock feathers. The eyes looked straight back at her, knowing everything, without curiosity or censure. Jennie closed her own wide black-edged ones, wondering with a teasing scorn of herself why she felt timid and not merely faint.

"Can you set her to rights?" The old lady turned sharply toward the woman who knelt beside Jennie, and her voice softened as she saw what kindliness there was in the way things had been done. "You're a good soul," she said. "What is your name?"

"Mrs. Cairns, Madam, and I'm sure any human body would do as much for a poor young lady took so sudden."

Her questioner made a noncommittal sound behind her large teeth and then prodded Jennie very gently with the toe of her heavy silk slipper.

"Will you be able to walk, Miss?"

Jennie forced herself to look into the small knowing eyes. "Yes, Madam," she said weakly.

"Friends are meeting you?"

"I am alone, Madam."

"I shall take you in my brougham then," the old lady stated with regal simplicity. "And you, Mrs. Cairns, you remember the address on this card, and, when you can, you come to see me about that good underskirt you used. These trains—if people protested it, perhaps we might be given something more than the comfort of brute-kine, some privacy for accidents like this, at least a basin of water . . ."

Jennie heard the voice talk on, with a forceful abruptness in all its words, and she felt the respecting, shocked attitude of the other women, and knew that behind their papers at the end of the car the gentlemen were listening uncomfortably, above the smell of blood, to such unladylike and open references to physical urgencies from such an obvious lady. It would be good to have a carriage to sit in for a little while. She felt as empty as a cast-off adder's skin, and as light. She dozed, not minding the grind of the wheels beneath her.

The train was slowing, stopping. Mrs. Cairns and another woman helped her to stand, and after one cool look at her traveling cloak the old lady covered it with her own tent-like pelisse and unconcernedly folded a shawl from her baskets about her thick shoulders. Jennie felt hideously unclean, piteously befouled, like a sick cat, and hung her head weakly to think of walking through the station, she, proud, meticulous Jennie, in stained clothes hidden beneath a stranger's rich outmoded wrappings.

"Come, girl," and the old lady shook her gently by the shoulder. "This will soon be over. And you kind people, we thank you. Mrs. Cairns, we shall be happy to see you at your convenience."

Jennie raised her head as the guard unlocked the door and relatively fresh beautiful air flowed almost tangibly against her face.

She heard the little boy, still well hidden somewhere among the skirts, ask in a clear voice, "Is the pretty princess well now?"

It made her feel strong again. Without a glance behind her she followed the old lady down into the arms of a strong, uniformed coachman, onto the platform, and then walked between him and a pageboy with a green silk cockade in his hat, leaning on their arms unquestioningly.

The brougham was smart, she saw, dark green, the color of the cockade, and two fine bays stamped and tossed their heads impatiently while a street lounger held them. It was good to sit down again. Jennie put her head back against the cushions for a minute and then sat up primly and touched the curls on either cheek.

"I am Mrs. Collinswood, Mrs. Julia Collinswood," the firm beautiful voice said from beside her.

"Yes, Madam," Jennie said, looking down at her black cloth gloves. "I am very grateful to you."

"Are you in trouble—that is, anything more onerous than meets the eye? Are you fleeing from a jealous lover or a raging father or any other such romantic situation? Because I do not care to embroil myself, Miss. I am far from the procuress I might well seem at this point in our relationship."

"No, Madam. I am quite free from any entanglements."

"You are a fool to try to travel so soon. When was your operation?"

"This morning, Madam."

Mrs. Collinswood snorted impatiently, very much like one of her bays. "Do you have a place to go? You need rest and care."

"No, Madam," Jennie said impersonally, as if she were discussing a third person. "I am sure a place can be found." Jennie can always find a place, she said proudly to herself, undaunted by even such bedragglement as shamed her now. "If I may keep Madam's cloak until tomorrow . . ."

There was no answer for a minute or so, and Jennie let herself float on a dark sea of weak delight at the comfort of the brougham, the smoothness of its springs against the London streets, the intoxicating smell of richness and luxury and Mrs. Collinswood's musk.

"How old are you, Miss? About thirty? You don't look it, even today, which must have been a somewhat distressing one."

Jennie finally turned her head full toward her questioner, a large mocking blur in the dimness of the carriage. She felt an almost unconscious relief that the small cool eyes, which were, she knew, focused upon her, were invisible. They seemed to assail her tottering dignity in an uncomfortable way.

"It is useless to question your respectability," the voice went on. "You obviously have none. But your manners are good, and you have the fingernails of a self-caring person. Unless you wish otherwise, I shall take you home with me, and in a day or two we can decide your next move. My own respectability," the voice went on dryly, "can, I suspect, be vouched for by my coachman if you have doubts of it."

The blur that was Mrs. Collinswood turned away again. Jennie sighed, full of a light triumph under the musky cloak. Jennie, ah Jennie, she said to herself, as her head fell back peacefully once more against the soft cushions, nothing can hurt you, my girl, pretty princess . . .

There was a great to-do, a bustling with lights and the smell of fresh wood-wax, and Mrs. Collinswood was saying, "Have Mrs. Spackle help this young person into a good bed by herself in one of the maids' rooms, with a bath and hot milk and brandy. Two egg yolks . . ."

She felt herself being carried high into a warm fine house.

Two

IT WAS a week before Jennie left her room, and many months before she stopped sleeping there, high under the eaves, and moved to the spacious alcove of Mrs. Collinswood's bedchamber. The first week was the most important time: it was then that she made all her plans and decisions for the next fifty, so that there was really nothing more to do but watch them take shape as she willed.

The first problem, she realized the night of her arrival, was Mrs. Spackle.

Her head felt clear and cool as she lay in her hard narrow bed after the bath. She looked swiftly at the little room in the candlelight, while the two maids who had silently cared for her went away with her bundled clothing, and she knew that few London servants had white walls and proper linen and a window in their rooms, and that it was less Mrs. Collinswood's doing than the housekeeper's. Mrs. Spackle ruled this world then, and while Jennie was in it she would rule Jennie too. The idea was a challenge. Jennie lay motionless, pulling into one strong core all her power to meet this woman, to judge her rightly.

One of the maids was back, breathing heavily from the innumerable flights of stairs, to fuss once more over straightening Jennie's sheets.

"There now, my dearie," she said. "Smooth down your front hair a bit more. She's coming, and she'll want everything tidy. She's bringing you something to put heart in you, all right!"

That I don't need, Jennie thought sardonically. Courage is all I have left, but it I have in plenty. It's information I lack here, and that will soon be remedied.

She smoothed her hair dutifully and then asked in a soft voice, "What is your name? Mine is Jennie."

The woman smiled down at her. "I'm Betsy Vaughn, Vaughn here because I'm first chambermaid, but you call me Betsy, now do! I'd like that. Poor little Jennie! Will you be staying, do you think? We can use another girl upstairs. You be sweet now to Old Spack, and you'll be staying."

She spoke in a low hurried way, and Jennie could feel great loneliness in her, perhaps for some child left behind, perhaps for an affection impossible in this household. She made herself smaller than ever in her bed and looked up empty-eyed and candid as she touched the older woman's wide warm hand.

"I'd like to stay," she whispered, and she smiled to herself, thinking how easy it had been: the despotic old lady on the train, the rich brougham gleaming in the station lights, the smell of musky *millefleurs*, and her own sense now of cleanness and freedom. Of course she'd stay! The great house was new mystery to her, and it and all it held waited to be known, solved, plumbed. Surely she deserved whatever good she might find, after the blackness that had driven her to London. She would make new friends, find new humans to love her and understand her and be kind to her. She would nevermore need lend herself to the stupidity and selfishness of ordinary creatures. She was almost trembling with amusement and excitement. She closed her eyes and bit back the smile that tickled at her mouth. Of course she'd stay!

"Are you feeling bad again, my dearie? But here comes Old Spack!" Beside her Betsy stood stiff and proper. Jennie heard the door open. Then Betsy said respectfully, "Good evening, Ma'am. This is Jennie, Ma'am."

Jennie made her eyes blank as she opened them, so that there should be no shadow of her inner gaiety, and her hands lay limp alongside her little body, not betraying the core of perceptiveness that she had summoned to meet this new ruler.

Mrs. Spackle was not old, not, that is, the way Mrs. Collinswood was old behind her mask of French unguents and perfumes. Mrs. Spackle might even have been about Jennie's age, or Betsy's, but it was the way she held herself inside her skin, the way she covered that skin with vigorous respectability, that made her seem like a grandmother. She was fairly tall, and her hair was combed down flatly over her ears, as if to point out its even graying, and her neck seemed to rise like the end of an iron rod from the stern blackness of her shoulders. Her sleeves were barely full and almost covered her hands, and her skirt fell straight to the floor without a sign of stylish belling outward, of generosity. Her black eyebrows, Jennie saw in the next second, went straight over eyes that were large and beautiful, and to anyone who had ever known passion, her mouth was a betrayal, shocking almost, held sternly but unsuccessfully to deny itself. Mrs. Spackle had great force about her.

She put a tall mug down upon the table with a click and then stood looking at Jennie with her large white hands folded, nearly hidden in their black sleeves, over her waist. Finally she asked, in a pleasant voice that was as impersonal as water, "Do you feel better now, Jennie?"

"Oh, thank you, Ma'am," Jennie said weakly, imitating as best she could the respectful breathlessness of Betsy Vaughn, with a kind of vocal curtsey in each syllable. "I've given you such trouble!"

"Tonight you must rest well," Mrs. Spackle went on imperturbably. "When you are stronger we can talk. Madam tells me that perhaps you may wish to stay on here. I shall discuss it with Mr. Spackle. Drink your brandy and milk while it is still well mixed. Good night."

Jennie felt her breath go out in a little puff as the door closed. Betsy was watching her, and she let herself smile one-thousandth of the amusement that was in her.

Betsy grinned. "How do you like Old Spack, eh?"

"But Betsy, she said Mr. Spackle! Who is Mr. Spackle?" Betsy leaned closer, her broad face shining with delighted friendliness. "Who is he? Mr. Spackle, my dearie, is the butler here, Madam's right-hand man so to speak. Mr. Spackle is Mrs. Spackle's Christian husband!" And here Betsy snickered close against Jennie's ear, "Or so Madam thinks!"

Jennie lay still as a cat.

In a few seconds Betsy drew back. "Now don't go thinking I've a nasty tongue," she said in an affronted voice, and she smoothed down her big white apron and looked proudly into a dark corner, hurt and suspicious.

"Oh, Betsy," Jennie said warmly. She held out her hand and pulled the woman toward her. She must have her completely, keep her an ally. "Betsy, you've been so good to me tonight!"

"There then! I don't want you thinking things. The other girls don't know it. I'm no gossip. But you're not the same as them, that I saw the first minute you were lying here, my dearie. I have my own ideas about the Spackles, but I keep them to myself all right! But what am I doing, chattering here? You drink this now, and just remember that Betsy is your friend."

She took a good swig from the mug as she handed it to Jennie. "That's Madam's own brandy, all right, not the kitchen bottle," she said, licking her lips happily. "Madam likes you, my dearie!"

After she went, Jennie turned the mug around so that her mouth would not fall where the big woman's had been. She sipped pleasurably at the warming punch, her disdain at being the confidante of a loud-breathing chambermaid gradually fading before the realization that for as long as she wanted she could be wrapped about in the warm cloak of her secret and nourished on its fine bread. Betsy had given her the weapon, clumsy Betsy, and she, Jennie the adroit, Jennie the knowledgeful, would use it as she thought best . . . and when . . . and where . . .

She turned over carefully in her narrow bed, and it and the room and the whole great London house were hers.

Three

B Y THE end of the week Jennie was twitching to be up and out of her tiny cell. She felt completely alive again.

Betsy was hers, a great loving girl who washed her as gently as if she were a baby, and brushed her fine hair voluptuously into bobbing curls on either cheek. Betsy sat in the little room whenever she was free, near the window, with her sewing: she was cutting down one of her own coarse snowy night-robes for Jennie, and she sang a little and talked, happier than she had been for many a year, she said.

Daily Mrs. Spackle climbed the long stairs, and stood unruffled in the doorway behind her folded hands to ask one or two quiet questions and look once or twice toward Jennie, but not at her, with her large eyes, and then left again. As her steps faded firmly away, Jennie always let out her breath in a merry little puff, and if Betsy were there they grinned at each other.

Jennie was careful though, not to ask anything more about the household. Instead she let Betsy talk as she willed. It seemed less common that way, less as if she were gossiping with a servant girl. And from the things Betsy said, she and the other maids who stopped in now and then to chat in a kind, curious way with the newcomer, Jennie knew all she needed to by the time she dressed herself carefully in her clean plaid traveling costume and sat waiting to go downstairs for the first time.

She knew that everyone liked Mr. Spackle. He was a kind man, they said, strict enough, but still not hard like his wife. They didn't envy him, they said, living with Old Spack: she was a terror for work, and perhaps in the privacy of the butler's apartment she was a scold as well, for all of her calm ways. He was a human being: not that he took liberties like some men they could mention in even grander houses, but Old Spack was a fair stick, and in bed too, they could wager—and here Jennie would drop her eyes and let her mouth grow cold, and the girls would stop giggling and soon leave her. She did not care that they found her full of airs and a bit above herself as long as great Betsy was safely hers. They could not possibly either hurt or help her.

She heard light firm steps coming to her door and was sure that it would be Mrs. Collinswood's maid Melanie, who had finally decided to show herself, instead of Mr. Spackle, to escort her to her first interview downstairs. She hoped so: she was curious to see the aloof Frenchwoman mainly because nobody seemed either to know or care anything about her. The staff of servants was incurious, as if she were a part of the gentry, like the old Madam or one of her company.

But when the door opened it was a tall very fat man, Mr. Spackle surely, who stood there. He balanced himself, as if he were a cloud or a dancer, on his handsome little feet in their fine pumps, and his legs swelled up monumentally from the silk stockings into his great firm thighs and then into the convolutions of his ponderous airy body in its dark green richness of livery, to the thoughtful majesty of his head. When he raised one of his gloved hands in silent beckoning, Jennie stood up as if God Himself had called her, and sped across the room in her little soft slippers with her eyes fixed in awe upon his face. When they were almost to meet in the door, then he smiled. It was a good smile, fuller of dignity than Betsy's of course, but with the same generosity of spirit in it.

Jennie looked up candidly at him, feeling like one of the lesser cherubim in an Italian painting.

"Let us go down," he said in a somewhat high vibrant voice. "Madam is waiting in her morning-room. You may take my arm, Jennie, in case you are not fully yourself again."

It was exactly as if they were in a play, Jennie thought as they stepped and turned their way carefully down all the stairs, down into lighter, softer carpets, sweeter smells, with the sound of his voice still throbbing in her head. She leaned with wan discretion upon the great warm pillar of his arm. When finally she saw through a window that they were on the first floor above the street, she stopped and let her head droop for a second. Then she looked up into his face from her wide-spaced gray eyes so thickly fringed with black.

"Mr. Spackle," she said softly when she had caught her breath, "I am frightened."

"Nonsense," he said gently. "Madam is—Madam is the finest of God's creatures—that is, with Mrs. Spackle. Everything is arranged if you wish to stay. I have spoken with Madam."

"Oh, fortunate woman that I am!" Jennie murmured rapturously, princess in a Christmas pantomime, one little hand on her heart. She stood with her head bowed for a moment and then looked up again into the great benevolent face.

"But I am destitute," she whispered. "My costumes—this is all I possess, Mr. Spackle, this poor traveling robe, and what the good Vaughn has lent me." She shrugged a little and almost smiled. "Vaughn and I are not modeled in the same form."

Mr. Spackle's arm shook with an inaudible chuckle of agreement under her tingling fingers, and she knew that in his mind's eye coarse Betsy stood like a mountain beside her own small exquisite image.

"Mrs. Spackle will, of course, attend to all that," he said far above her. "I have only the accounts to settle in that department."

"Ah!" Jennie pounced as delicately as a tigress. The wait had been long. "Then, Mr. Spackle, may I come to you when I need help, when there is anything that troubles me too desperately about my monetary, that is, my financial —oh, I feel so completely alone!"

The arm propelled her gently down the long corridor.

Their feet made no sound on the roses of the carpet. It seemed to Jennie that her heart stopped beating until at last she heard the butler say impassively into the rich air above her, "Of course, Miss. I shall be glad to assist you when necessary with whatever advice is essential to you. Of course."

They were at the door. Jennie let both hands fall prettily down into the fullness of her rustling skirt and kicked with unthinking skill at the flounces of her petticoats to make her robe stand out bell-like about her. Soon, soon now, she would have a crinoline, she promised herself.

A thin dark woman let them in. Ah, she wore one, stiff and modish under her fine black silk! Jennie hated her with a tiny unimportant hate, like a gnat's bite.

The room was large and beautiful, with sunlight streaming through gauze curtains onto the green and gold and white and all the picture frames and bird cages of lacquer and the roses everywhere. Jennie skimmed across the floor and made a low curtsey, full of gratitude and grace, before Mrs. Collinswood.

"Get up, girl," the old lady said dryly.

Four

THE most significant things in Jennie's progress of the next few months were her increasing friendliness with Melanie Groscoeur and the evolution of her wardrobe. One was a part of the other, of course, being a part of Jennie herself.

She had been put to work at once at light duties in the linen room, where all the maids who could hold a needle decently sat stitching and resting when they could. By now she was used to Old Spack's silent, staring inspections of her, and she smiled easily up at the dour woman from the sheets and towels which seemed to lie heavier and heavier each day across her knees. But she sewed beautifully, like a fairy, Betsy Vaughn said in a possessive proud way, and soon she was mending Mrs. Collinswood's own exquisite underthings, which the French maid herself would bring and entrust to none but Jennie.

The cobwebby linens and soft laces, like balm to Jennie's fingers, were pepper in her heart, and she sat smiling and listening to the chatter around her in a black rage of hatred for the chemises and white cotton drawers and guimpes she herself must wear, coarse things cut down from what the other maids did not need, garments as solid and thick as the skins they were meant to cover, never Jennie's.

As for her robes, she could not bear to think of them. It was not because they were altered hand-me-downs: that would have been a *contretemps*, but bearable. They had all, all—and Jennie's skin crept with revulsion—belonged to Mrs. Spackle! There was a fine dark green wool, the Collinswood green, for church and such, for the rare days when she walked through the spring-filled streets with Betsy or, later, Melanie. There were two heavy white calicoes sprigged with little gray roses, which made Jennie's gray eyes as sweet as a kitten's, while her blood churned with anger. There was, richest insult, a fine black dress of silk crepe for times when she might be called downstairs to help Melanie or a guest.

Jennie fitted the costumes to her little body, and stood with gratitude fair on her creamy face while pins were stuck in everywhere over her tight stays and great swags of the material were cut out to transform her into a shadow of the unsmiling queen of the household. How she loathed everything about herself in those respectable husks! It would have been much easier on her pride, she knew, to wear something of Betsy's, heavier green wool, thicker calico, no silkiness. And she fretted inwardly, souring herself on her own acid, until she could hardly bear to look at Old Spack. When she heard that measured, uncritical, unwarm voice, she wanted to throw down the lingerie she worked on and press her little hands on the corkscrews over her ears. When she had to bob her head and say "Yes Ma'am No Ma'am," she felt her lips stretch into a death grin of resentment. Old Spack was so big, so calm, so utterly not Jennie.

It was quite easy to stay longer each time Jennie took Mrs. Collinswood's mended things back to the second floor. The old lady was usually writing, some book or other the maids said, in her morning-room, or away, or with friends in one of the many mysterious chambers of the great house. Jennie soon knew her way through the little back door into the bedroom. She knew how to knock softly, so that Melanie would hear her from the alcove where she sat sewing or reading.

The two women would greet each other with warmth, but not smiling, and then often sit down together while Melanie finished a hand of solitaire. Jennie could feel her anger and outrage fade from her like fog in the musky comfort of the apartment. She would stick out her feet, invisible under her petticoats, and let her spine fit once again into a soft little chair that became it more than the hard high-backed bench in the linen room.

They began to speak French together, and gradually Melanie told her a little of her fellow refugees in London. Jennie was much less interested in their liberal hopes to rid their country of Louis-Philippe than in the loot they brought with them as they fled: painted court fans on long sticks of ebony and gold, tiny velvet muffs sewn with mirrors no bigger than a pinhead, whole night-robes made of lace . . .

Finally Melanie brought something to show from a friend's trunk. Jennie's throat dried with a kind of anguish when she saw it: a *canezou* of pale green organdy, with long full sleeves embroidered in silver roses, and three sloping capelike ruffles that fell over her shoulders as kissingly as if they had been sewn only for her. There was a belt just cut to her waist, to hold down the front tabs of the little costume. Ah, with that to wear, Jennie in her gray-sprigged calico would be a pretty princess, not a sour queen's shadow any more!

Melanie, looking sideways at her cards, considered. Then she said that she was sure Jennie could buy it—dearly of course, but it was brought but a month ago from Paris . . .

It did not take long for debt to ride high between the two women, and, strangely, it seemed to strengthen their friendliness, so that when they met in the alcove they kissed tenderly, and then they sat with their arms wound about one another's little waist, while they talked of shawls from Persia and Chinese silk and the jeweled fringe reported in *The Standard* that day upon a great soprano's costume of the night before. Now and then Jennie would say, as she unwrapped the tissue paper from a tiny pair of silk slippers with soft kidskin toes or a pair of mittens embroidered all over with forget-me-nots, "But my angel, I must owe you so much! Great heavens, what a ninny I am! If my fellow chambermaids"—and the two would laugh sardonic tinkles—"if they but knew what was hidden in my little attic room!"

And Melanie would look sideways and stop her protestations with a soft kiss, and Jennie would skim to her room with one more exquisite prize hidden tantalizingly in the folds of Mrs. Spackle's cut-down robe.

Melanie grew moody with the summertime and told Jennie she must have money. Things were going hard with her poor friends, she said. Prices were rising in France, and there was terrible unrest, and she must help more and more liberals and republicans to prepare themselves when she passed through Paris with Madam on the way to Wiesbaden. Jennie cut off her dull moping: it was easy to cheer the thin dark woman with a coin or two, and then a gentle caress on her flat cheek, a little kiss.

And it was even easier, thank God above, to get money from Mr. Spackle. Jennie could not count by now the times she had gone quietly to his office and watched him while he benignly marked in his ledger and then handed her another advance on her quarterly wage. When the wage was due she collapsed, as she knew she should, to learn that there was nothing for her at all. Mr. Spackle, as she knew he would, begged her in his throbbing high voice not to weep, not to worry herself. When he gave her a florin, she let herself touch his great gloved hand, and rejoiced to see him flinch.

Hot weather turned the street mud into cloddy dust, and all of Mrs. Collinswood's world and all the maids and valets and pageboys and couriers and cooks who kept it running left London. The great houses, old Julia's among them, were dim and quiet, while their owners bathed and sipped noxious tonics in the smartly inaccessible spas of the Continent. The maids trooped back to their villages, to help with the hop-picking and such, and to breathe and kiss again like human beings in the freedom of the star-lit hedgerows.

"Come home with me, my dearie," Betsy urged her princess one last time as she tied up the bonnet strings under her firm round chin. "You've grown thin as a needle. You'll be too much alone here. I don't like it for you. Come along with me, and let my old mum fill you out with plum-duff and cream!"

But Jennie could barely wait to be alone, to be free from all the dull chatter of the other maids, the sight of their honest hands and faces. "No, no," she said gently to Betsy.

"No, Ma'am, thank you," she said to Mrs. Spackle with a little shrug. "I am used to being alone, and of course there are ways I can be useful here. Mademoiselle Groscoeur has asked me to inspect all of the Madam's autumn costumes and underthings. I shall be quite happy, thank you, Ma'am."

Mrs. Spackle looked searchingly at her as she tied the strings of her sternly becoming traveling bonnet under the white cliff of her chin. She sighed sharply. "You are a strange girl, Jennie," she said as she turned away. "I have tried . . ."

"Yes, thank you, Ma'am," Jennie said in a humble, mocking way. "You and Mr. Spackle have been most kind to me. I am sure I do not know what might have befallen me."

Mrs. Spackle did not reply, but went almost unwillingly from the room and down to the waiting carriage.

With every one of her slow steps Jennie felt lighter, happier. The house was hers. There were two or three maids left, to cook and dust. Mr. Spackle would be there now and then. But the books, the great dim rooms, the cupboards and the drawers, even Melanie's soft bed in the alcove off old Julia's bedroom, were for Jennie.

She ran to her room, and in a fever of delight put on her new black satin slippers with the yellow lacings, over a pair of fine net stockings, and fresh petticoats, and an underskirt dead-heavy with lacy ruffles, and a freshly laundered dress, Mrs. Spackle's hated calico for sure, but now, today, this very afternoon, to be made right with the delicious *canezou* upon its shoulders!

Jennie laid it out upon her bed, the fragile filmy pale green thing. In the light from the attic window the little silver roses on its sleeves gleamed sweetly at her, and the three descending capes invited.

She made her cheek curls discreetly loose and then put on her new bonnet, the one of gray silk faced with little yellow bows that she and wheezing Betsy had sewed on by candlelight. She slipped her arms carefully into the full gauzy sleeves of the *canezou*, and pulled its tabs down across her round little bosom, and then fastened the silver stitchings of the belt around her waist, tiny as a bee's. Ah Jennie, she cried in a kind of pain.

She went in a slow, light, voluptuous way down through the stillness of the house. At the little back door into old Julia's chambers, Melanie's door, she paused, tapped mockingly, then walked on, smiling. In the music room she stood beside a gold piano, covered but for its legs, and her head tilted as if she were listening, and she swung her little gray silk bag to a far-remembered rhythm from it, from another . . .

She sped silently past the servants' dining-room. Inside she could hear the girls who were left laughing and clattering their teacups. Perhaps, she thought with scorn, they feel free too, in their own way. What could they really know of it? Poor dolts, she thought, and forgot them.

The door opened easily for her. A little late-afternoon wind lifted the top capelet of her *canezou* softly against her cheek, and she smiled again to think of how she had always gone through the tradesmen's entrance with big Betsy, or with the Frenchwoman, and how now she was alone.

It was at that moment, when the smile lifted her lips properly, not in a death grin of hateful, mocking gratitude, but sweet and fresh as cream, and the green cloud of the capelet touched itself against the corkscrews on her cheek, it was then that Mr. Spackle strode like walking marble, unreally light and dancing marble, around the corner of the mews and to the areaway. It was then that he saw Jennie.

He looked odd in a hat, and when he swept the tall black silk funnel off and down, Jennie saw with an astonishment only half laughing that his fine white brow was actually marked by it, as if he were an ordinary man.

"Ah, Mr. Spackle," she said warmly, but with her eyes correctly lowered, "you have caught me."

"Caught you, Jennie?" He was breathing heavily, as if he had been running, as if, perhaps, he were upset.

"I thought everyone was gone," she said. "I was going to walk once around the square. The air is so delightful now, and with all the gentry gone I thought a chambermaid might venture . . ."

"I have just seen Mrs. Spackle onto the train," he said. "She was much disturbed about leaving you here without some pleasant female companion, Jennie."

God eternally damn it, Jennie cried out, will the old bitch not leave me any peace? Then she touched the *canezou*, and knew how it transformed Old Spack's calico, and she smiled up at Mr. Spackle. "I am used to that," she said softly. "I am like a street cat—yes, do not protest, dear Mr. Spackle! And you have all fed me on cream. But I have known other less—less pleasant nourishment."

She let her head droop, so that only a soft curl or two showed from under her bonnet. She heard Mr. Spackle shift his great body uneasily on his tiny dancer's feet.

"May I not accompany you on your little promenade?" he asked very gently.

She put her hand without a word upon his arm, and the two of them floated, genteel shadows, out into the shadows of the genteel, dimming square. Jennie felt a surge of what was almost gratitude to poor sallow Melanie Groscoeur, for the net stockings, the laces and silks, the pale green *canezou* that made this possible for her.

Five

IN THE next weeks it grew quite proper for the two of them to walk out into the cooling streets together; to sit in his little parlor while he read Tom Paine and Byron in his high vibrant voice, and she leaned her head back in Old Spack's chair and watched him posturing in the lamplight. Perhaps the maids giggled about it, but Jennie felt innocent and happy because it was so obvious that he did.

When he went down to the country she drifted about the house, relieved to be alone, but anxious still to see how soon he would return, how soon flee the bucolic companionship of his dour wife. Each time he came back more eagerly, it was plain to see, but with not a word to say about it. Then the little walks would be resumed, the evenings' conversations.

Jennie pleased him by her knowingness of all the problems of French liberals, which she had tucked away subconsciously in a brain seemingly fuller of Melanie's luxurious scavengings than of her murmured fear for the scavenged. He, in turn, puzzled her more than she had ever known she could be by his attitude toward old Julia Collinswood.

She knew about passion, and even, in a vicarious way, about the affection that can exist between children and parents, or two men or two women. But the obvious feelings of deep respect and devotion and tenderness that the butler felt for his mistress were inexplicable to her, and they nagged at her inherent wariness. Something must be wrong, she would tell herself as she went up to her room at night: it was odd, it was unnatural, for a man in his middle years to feel this mixture of emotions for an old woman, and an old woman who hired him to work for her. He should despise her, at least a little. But he worshiped her. When he talked of her his great noble face softened, and his voice throbbed with a kind of doting admiration for her mind, for her wit, for the books she read and made him read, for her attitude toward men and birds and human boundaries. It was crazy, Jennie thought. It piqued and worried her, because it was beyond her, and she kept it as far back as she could in the maze of her pragmatic little mind.

One night Mr. Spackle, oddly ill at ease, presented her with a thick small book, bound in worn wine-colored leather stamped with gold. It was his mother's once, he murmured. Mrs. Felicia Hemans' works were perhaps not so highly estimated now, but might he read a few of the finest to her, and then dare ask her to keep this volume for her own private inspiration? He patted a handkerchief nervously over his monumental forehead as Jennie stood holding the present without speaking.

Finally she looked up at him, and her wide gray eyes, at no small cost to herself, were brimming. "Mr. Spackle," she whispered, and then looked away. And for two or three evenings he intoned enthusiastically while she bit back the yawns, and longed for her silent attic, and finally permitted herself the satisfaction of a little scene to end it.

"A flower its leaves and odors cast
    On a swift rolling wave,"

he read, one long white finger pressing down the gilt-edged page. Then he looked significantly at her. Yes, yes, she cried out impatiently, I am the flower! I have understood that far, you great honey-voiced dolt!

> "Th' unheeding torrent darkly pass'd,
> And back no treasure gave.
> Oh, heart of love!"

He cleared his throat, and then repeated,

> "Oh! heart of love!
> Waste not thy precious dower!
> Turn to thine only home above,
> Be not like that lost flower!
> Not like that flower!"

There was a stifling silence. Jennie knew that he was looking beseechingly at her. He meant it! He meant that she was a helpless flower, she, Jennie! There was no other alternative to her abysmal amusement: she burst into sobs and fled.

The next night, to her relief, there was no mention of her maidenly and apparently successful show of emotion. Mr. Spackle talked about labor reforms and then read "The Song of the Shirt":

> "With fingers weary and worn,
> With eyelids heavy and red,
> A woman sat in unwomanly rags
> Plying her needle and thread . . ."

"Stitch! Stitch! Stitch!" he intoned, flickering his eyes meaningfully at her as she sat across the lamplit table from him. "Stitch!"

Jennie made her face compassionate.

"O men, with sisters dear!
O men, with mothers and wives!
It is not linen you're wearing out,
But human creatures' lives!"

As she bade him good night he picked up from the table a white tissue-wrapped package that had driven her almost frantic since her first sight of it, and with a little bow he said, "My dear Miss Jennie, will you permit a foolish old man to give you this little frippery? It is much more suited to your years than an outmoded book of verse, and to your pretty head than my world-sick musings."

Jennie gasped, and for the second night fled to her room, this time trembling with triumphant excitement instead of repressed hysterical laughter, the package held against her as if it were a babe.

He had bought her a little sunshade with a hinged handle so that it could stand upright like a flower above her head or tilt this way or that when and if she ever rode in her carriage in the Park. It was made of dove-gray satin, with pleated scallops of rose satin and tulle all about it, a dainty cloud, and sewn everywhere among the pleats were tiny crystals. It was like the Queen's—Victoria, not Old Spack—but so much lovelier!

Beneath its flowerlike shade Jennie thought of the housekeeper's face, and fell helpless with laughter on her bed. Then she took off all her clothes and put on her best slippers of white silk embroidered with gold stars, and the *canezou* over her pearly, sloping shoulders, and she skimmed up and down her room with the little parasol held now this way, now that, above her loosened hair.

The next night there was a fan for her, and the next a pair of long delicate pink gloves of kidskin, and so it was every night except when Mr. Spackle returned from the country and brought perhaps a basket of strawberries or a pot of cream for poor lonely Jennie, always with his wife's good wishes.

Jennie borrowed some money from him, to buy a proper little trunk to hide her things in, and almost never heard again in her dreams the awful voice of Mr. Spackle, louder than real and hideously vibrant, that had haunted her sleep the night he gave her the wee sunshade:

O men with sisters dear! Stitch! Stitch! Stitch!

. . . unwomanly rags . . .
. . . eyelids heavy and red

It is not linen you're wearing out, it is not
satin it is not *mousseline de soie* it is not
unwomanly rags stitch stitch with fingers weary
and worn it is not
heavy and red
O men, with sisters dear!

O sisters dear!

Six

THE great house shone like one of the gold-and-lacquer cages in Mrs. Collinswood's sitting-room, and the birds were back from the aviary in the country, and Betsy Vaughn and all the other maids from their summer's assignations. There was a new cockade for the pageboy's tall silk hat, and even a new pageboy to match it.

Mrs. Spackle worked like a madwoman, and three days after the end of her holidays looked as dourly worn as ever. Then a telegram came from Paris: Melanie Groscoeur must stay there for a little longer, and the old Madam would return alone.

Jennie thought that she had never heard such a ridiculous pother. The Spackles acted as if a valuable idiot child had got loose. Surely Mrs. Collinswood could take care of herself? Had she not been alone the day Jennie first met her? But she was an old lady, they felt, not meant to travel unaided, even with her advanced ideas of social equalities and the goodness of man . . . Bosh, Jennie said to herself, at last openly resentful of this long-faced dowager with the mocking little eyes, so strangely, deeply loved.

Mr. Spackle himself rode down to meet the channel boat, armed with shawls, a little wicker tea basket, and the latest newspapers, and while he was gone Jennie went with his wife into Mrs. Collinswood's apartment. They looked in every drawer to find it tidy, and at the piles of cloudy underwear tied with soft wide ribbons—unfit, unseemly, for a selfish old lady, Jennie thought bitterly; in the cupboards and closets at the rich rows of cloaks and capes, the racks hung with brilliant velvets and artful, giddy ruchings— disgusting, Jennie thought wryly, to spend so much time and money hiding an old body instead of revealing a young pretty one. The winter furs were ready, and there were at least a dozen new bonnets and turbans, high piles of exotism to wave over such a tired face.

Mrs. Spackle sighed and sat down for a minute on the edge of a chair. Fatigue had loosened the gray-black hair about her face, and her mouth looked soft and sweet. When Jennie stood before her, covering with creaminess the antagonistic envy that bit at her, the older woman smiled.

"You have been a great help," she said gently. "Now heat the shovel, and we'll leave the rooms until we hear the carriage stopping."

Jennie kneeled before the coal grate, holding the brass shovel just above the rosiness, listening mazily to Old Spack. What had happened to the skinny Melanie, she wondered, to let her desert the idolized Collinswood? Would she return at all? What new stitched beauties would she bring, stuffed in amongst her boring pamphlets about liberty?

"It was a good summer," Old Spack was saying softly, in a way Jennie had never heard her speak before. "But it was long. And lonely. And you, Jennie? Was it long for you? Here," she interrupted herself, "it's hot enough."

Jennie held out the shovel, and the housekeeper dropped essence on it from a little bottle, and the air filled with the heaviness of musk and *millefleurs*, everywhere, under the fat chairs, under the chaises longues and the tables, as Jennie skimmed lightly about, poking it here and there, with care, into the air. It was exciting. She felt happier than for days, than since the end of her summer freedom.

"I worried about you," Old Spack went on, still in a kind of dream in the warm, scented room. "I should have asked Mr. Spackle—he could have taken you for a little promenade occasionally. That would have broken the long days."

"Yes, Ma'am," Jennie murmured, and she gingerly lifted a chair ruffle and poked the steaming shovel under it, and rolled mocking laughter in her mind. "You're very kind, Ma'am." She wished the stupid woman would stop talking. She wanted to be alone in this dim silkiness, this opulence of coal fire, brocade, scent . . .

"Jennie!" Old Spack spoke more clearly, as if she recognized the spell they both were under and must break through. "I have discussed with Mr. Spackle the possibility that perhaps you may be able to assist me here, in the Madam's own rooms, while Groscoeur is absent."

There was a long silence between the two women. Embers settled shushingly in the grate, and from the morning-room came the sound of a drowsy cockatoo cracking a sunflower seed.

How well it is going, Jennie thought. This big ugly creature believes she is telling me some news, when I knew this must happen months ago. I knew it! She thought of the summer nights she had spent in Melanie's alcove, sitting in Melanie's soft little sewing chair, lying delightedly awake in the bed, the devoted maid, ever-conscious of her

< 127 >

mistress's faintest call, the faithful, indispensable Jennie, more a friend than a servant, designing old Julia's peignoirs, ordering her meals, nursing her, hearing the will read: And to Jennie I do bequeath . . .

"Oh, Ma'am," she whispered, "if I but felt myself worthy . . ."

"Of course you are!" Old Spack stood up briskly. "I never make a mistake in my girls, Jennie. I've watched you. And Mr. Spackle tells me good things of your seemly actions this past summer. It will mean some new costumes, of course. You have been very patient, waiting for them in my old ones. And better wages too! I shall be glad to go with you to Madam's own *dentellerie* one afternoon, to help you choose a little lace for your best frock."

Jennie smiled and blushed and fluttered. Ah, how blind they all are, she thought with a kind of benignant scornfulness.

"I shall sleep with Madam, of course, until she is well rested from her travels," Old Spack went on, as she gave a last skillful stare at the order everywhere, and headed for the little door into the back hall, with Jennie soundlessly behind her, the queen's shadow. "Then"—and she turned and smiled with a pleased, almost gay look—"then perhaps you, dear little Jennie, can stay here with Mrs. Collinswood! Think of that!"

"I shall be very happy, Ma'am," Jennie answered tonelessly, properly, and Old Spack's face settled into impassive dourness again, with a kind of regret about the small full lips.

"You will not be needed again tonight, Jennie," she said. "Go have your supper, and I shall speak to you in the morning if the Madam has agreed with Mr. Spackle's suggestion."

"Yes, Ma'am." Jennie knew triumphantly that she had hurt, had baffled once more. Old Spack would go off now feeling that she had made a fool of herself in some way. Jennie's eyes were wide and candid. "Oh, you are always so good to me," she said breathlessly, shyly, and she hurried away, shaking with amusement.

Seven

BY THE time Melanie came back (and she looked thinner and yellower than ever, Jennie saw coolly), Mrs. Collinswood was used to being without her. "Send Jennie down," she would say to the Frenchwoman. "You go rest, Melanie. You look tired. Let Jennie do my hair."

She would say, "Jennie, you may read what Spec says in this issue of *Punch*. I like to hear his satire in your naïve voice."

Once she looked sharply at Jennie in the mirror in front of them. "My friend Mr. Spackle says you have a brain," she said. "Do you plan to do anything with it?"

"Alas, Madam," and Jennie let one hand fall light as a crumb upon her breast, "Mr. Spackle is too charitable. Does a lost flower"—and she searched quickly for a line from one of the poems he had read to her—"does a lost flower tossed on the rolling waves of life have brains?"

Mrs. Collinswood tipped back the tall yellow feathers of her turban in a rich laugh. Then she stopped, looked once more with her little mocking eyes at the reflection of Jennie in the glass, and said speculatively, "Yes. Yes, sometimes it does. Ring for Melanie, please."

What Melanie had brought with her from Paris, Jennie found slowly through the autumn, was even more wonderful than she had let herself dream. One time the Frenchwoman would show her a filmy nightdress sewn with miniscule bows of turquoise and coral satin, and the next she would produce miraculously from her little trunk a muff, round and soft as a kitten, made of sable and black velvet. There were black lace stockings lined with silk the color of flushed ivory, of Jennie's legs. There was a shawl so fine it slipped through the little gold ring Melanie wore always on her right hand. There were handkerchiefs and feather roses . . .

Jennie bought them all and paid her friend with everything that Mr. Spackle silently advanced her. But it was not enough. Sometimes Groscoeur would weep and tremble, and her voice would shrill out alarmingly. Then Jennie, in the butler's office, would weep too, and talk like a child of the silk and feathers and the ruffled falbalas, until he stood up as if in pain and thrust what coins and notes he had into her hand and pushed her through the door.

"Here, here," she would say to Melanie, and the poor sallow woman would kiss her passionately and murmur through the kisses of how ghastly Paris was, how poor. It was almost time, she would whisper, for an uprising so terrible—there would be revolution surely, and she was helping. Jennie would divert her, charmingly, to assuage her own boredom at such talk. It was easy to please with a caress, and now and then a golden coin.

One bitter day near Christmas, in the warm linen room odorous of beeswax and starch and lavender, Jennie sat stitching lazily. Betsy stood near her, and her thick pink hands moved with marvelous skill among a heap of muslin ruffles with her little iron, click, snap, flip, over and over along the bottoms of a dozen pantalets and petticoats.

"My old mum will make a pudding big as your head," she said happily, "and post it up to us. We'll treat all the other girls. Maybe we can get a drop of spirits for it! What's a Christmas pudding without it's lighted? And what do you think, my dearie, would the Spackles step in too for a few minutes and a smell of it, do you think?"

Flippety, snap, click, the hot curved iron whizzed among the ruffles. Jennie shrugged and smiled. Dear God, she thought, how dull and red-faced I shall grow here, giggling with chambermaids over a dram of tavern rum on a country pudding! But Betsy was useful, to do her ironing always: never had Madam been so pleased with her ruffles as since Jennie took charge of them.

Melanie Groscoeur stood in the doorway. "I must speak to you," she said curtly in French, not looking at either of the women.

Jennie put her mending neatly on the big table. "I'll be back soon," she whispered to Betsy in an intimate way that made the big woman flush with delight.

In the hall she asked coldly, "How dare you summon me like that before a servant, Groscoeur?"

Melanie gripped her arm. She was trembling, and her eyes looked old and sunken. "Jennie, Jennie," she said in a low imploring voice, "don't be at odds with me. I must speak to you quickly. Madame is in her chamber, resting.

Come." And she almost pulled Jennie up the interminable stairs to the cold dim little attic room.

Jennie stood, looking dispassionately as her friend sank down upon the narrow bed. She would let the zany speak first, she thought. It could be nothing more pressing than another appeal for money. She wondered, in a speculative way, how much she actually owed this peaked Frenchie. And Mr. Spackle, the old fool, how many florins had he poured into her trunkful of airy beauties?

Melanie stiffened herself and held her hands tightly in her green silk lap. "Jennie," she said finally, "you know the fan you bought, the last one with the black lace and the brilliants?"

Jennie nodded.

Melanie was almost choking. "Jennie, you must let me have it back! Madame Collinswood . . ."

Jennie looked through the little window at the bleak sky. Now that the moment was come for which she had so long waited, she felt near boredom. She felt near something like exasperation that Melanie did not recognize it too.

"Well? Did you steal it, Mademoiselle Groscoeur?"

Melanie moaned and put her thin yellow hands to her cheeks. Her eyes were like puffed black raisins in her face, raisins puffed with woe.

"Jennie," she said hopelessly, "I thought you loved me. I needed the money desperately. I did not think Madame would notice one fan gone from all her Christmas gifts laid out to be wrapped. But this afternoon before she went out she embraced me, like a mother . . ."

Rubbish, Jennie thought impatiently, maudlin rubbish!

"I must put it back, Jennie. Ah, if you'd only paid me a little more of what you owe!"

"Are you implying then, Groscoeur, that it is I who have driven you to crime?" Jennie's voice was slow and voluptuously cold, so that the woman on the bed looked up dully at its sound, shivering. "How many others of the so-called refugees' trinkets have you lifted from old Collinswood? Tell me, I beg of you. It interests me."

Melanie shrugged finally. "A few," she said. "I was mad, a cursed fool, to think that you would ever pay me for the first ones. Then there was more and more need for money. My cousins run a secret printing shop for the Movement. I can send them everything, paper even, from London. And I could see"—and her own voice slowed in a faint copy of Jennie's shrewd iciness—"that you were fortunate enough to have found a protector to help you financially."

Jennie almost gasped with shock. She felt utterly affronted that this confessed thief should thus dare to imply that she, Jennie the proud and the inviolate, could be underhanded about such a thing as money. She felt like striking the clammy yellow face she looked down on from the doorway. She felt like knocking the head on its thin neck from off those sparse, silken shoulders. She came slowly into the little room and sat down beside Melanie on the bed.

"You've made a great mistake," she said in a kind way. "We must discuss this while there is time. In the first place, I shall pay you for the black lace fan. I shall pay you in full for it." She smiled patiently at Melanie's bewilderment and patted her arm. "Then, my dear, I shall return it in person to the Madam."

"But Jennie! No!" the other woman cried out.

"But yes," she mocked softly. "I shall return it to her without any explanation of where I got it."

"But she'll know! She'll recognize it! Or she may suspect you!" Melanie laughed shrilly. "That would be funny, if you caught yourself in my noose!"

"Don't be a fool. And then you will be called back to Paris, won't you, my dear friend, and you will beg the old lady to let me take your place, won't you?"

"No!"

"Then I shall have to show some other things, perhaps the gauze night-robe—I am sure now where that came from—and what of the buff silk shoes with leather tips? I thought so. I shall be forced—"

"But my money! Jennie, if you love me, if you ever loved me, you must get me some money, do you hear? You must!"

Jennie said nothing for a moment and then asked scornfully, "What entitles you to make such demands, Groscoeur? I should think your position rather too shaky a one for such highhanded tactics."

Melanie moaned again and shook herself doggedly, as if to strengthen her sick spirits. "I do not believe," she said in a slow, unwilling way, "that Madame would be any less interested in where you got your funds than in where I got the pretty things you bought from me."

"Are you threatening me?" Jennie's voice shook with astonishment.

"Why not? How much have you borrowed, as you probably put it, from poor old fat Spackle? Who is the thief between us, Jennie?"

They sat, almost touching, on the little bed in the cold room. Jennie waited. As she knew would happen, Melanie sobbed suddenly.

"Ah," she said hopelessly, "you were so loving, so fine and dainty! I wanted to please you. I believed always that you would pay me what you promised. It was not until a few weeks ago, when you seemed to have more money, and things looked so dreadful for my friends—"

"That you started to steal from your adored Mrs. Collinswood?"

Jennie's impassive question seemed more than the poor woman could endure. "Shut up," she cried frantically. "Shut up, you devil!" Then she closed her eyes tightly. When she opened them again she leaned toward Jennie, who watched her without a trace of emotion. "Listen, you," she said brutally, "what do you want from me? What's your game? What's the bargain, eh?"

Jennie drew back distastefully. "You've changed, dear friend," she said with reproach.

"Come on," Melanie almost spat at her. "So you don't tell Madame where the fan came from. So you keep all the other little beauties, I suppose?"

"Of course. It would be somewhat difficult to restore them all to their rightful owners, I suspect. It would be impossible to pay their original cost."

Melanie spoke very slowly. "I must have money. Do you hear, you? I must have money!"

Jennie frowned a little, her eyes vacant and still fixed

on the gun-metal sky outside. "If I get you enough to reach Paris, how soon will you leave?"

Melanie made a choking sound.

"Naturally you would not wish to remain near your old and beloved employer if you were a proven thief. You can go this way without any accusations, with money in your pocket. You may even get there in time for your little revolution."

Melanie stared at her over the white knuckles of her hands.

"Here!" Jennie skimmed suddenly across the room and unlocked her trunk. She pecked like a little bird of prey through the deep richness of the things piled in it, and then held up a tiny fan. "Here, Groscoeur! You think I don't remember our friendship? You see? You may take this back yourself, before the old lady comes home tonight, and you may trust me not to tell her about it."

She watched the other woman stand up dully, the besmirched dainty in her hands. Poor fool, she thought with a kind of compassionate mockery, how easy it has been to frighten her away, away from the subject of the butler's money, away from Jennie!

She opened the door, and as Melanie Groscoeur went past her for the last time, she put a light kiss on the chill, sallow cheek. "Don't worry," she whispered gaily, like a child planning a delightful party. "You'll have your money tonight! Jennie promises!"

There was no answer.

Once the door closed between her and the slow sound of footsteps going down and down, she shrugged. Mr. Spackle would, she knew, be difficult. The last time he had started to question her, to quibble, and then had bent heavily over his cashbox, his fine head mottled suddenly with red. Yes, it would be a little unpleasant. But she felt so full of excitement, so drunk really! Soon, perhaps tomorrow, she would be downstairs, breathing warm, musky air, lying at night as a lady should, in a lady's chamber . . .

She smoothed her hair, tightened the corkscrews demurely on her flushed cheeks, and was halfway down the long stairs to the butler's office before she remembered her open trunk. She would lock it later, she said triumphantly. Nothing mattered except to get the money as soon as possible, to get down into the soft alcove as soon as possible.

Eight

ONCE in February, when London was full of wild stories about the Revolution, the bloody Paris gutters, Louis-Philippe scuttling under an umbrella, Mrs. Collinswood said, "I have poor Groscoeur heavily in my thoughts lately. And you, Jennie? You seemed good friends."

Jennie smiled sadly and held a rouge pot out toward her mistress. "I often weep for her," she confessed sadly. "But her whole heart was with the Republicans, Madam. She was driven as by a fever to help them fight. She was— not herself toward the end."

"Certainly she took French leave." The old lady smiled rather grimly at her tiny pun. "I was fond of her."

"And she of you, Madam. That I know."

Mrs. Collinswood sniffed, but her face looked bitter and regretful through the mask of powder.

"And think, Madam, how happy she must be now to find herself fighting side by side with her brothers, from street to street, from barricade to barricade—"

"Here, give me the rouge, girl! Think," old Julia said tauntingly, "how happy she must be to feel a bullet strike her, to fall spewing blood!" She laughed shortly and gave Jennie a little push. "You are as innocent as a kitten," she said. And that was the last time Melanie Groscoeur was mentioned.

Jennie was glad. The old Madam's unladylike and brutal words had affronted her. She hated them, the way they stuck in her mind, the picture they etched there of a thin face all bloodied . . . Madam had no right to speak so to Jennie.

It was like the time the woman Cairns appeared, a vision that Jennie tried to ignore as casually and easily as she could most other impingements on that delicate shell of her mind which protected her from the world's gross folly. It annoyed her to find that she could not thus push away all her sleeping thoughts: the Frenchwoman bled there now and then, and the meeting with Cairns came back often, a nightmare to make her sit up, menaced in the alcove.

It had happened soon after she moved from the attic, one day of blown sleet when she put on a thick shawl, one Betsy's old mum had made for her, and went out the service entrance to stand for a minute in the sharpness, away from the steam of teacups and chambermaids below-stairs, the hothouse smell of birds and roses and old woman in the Madam's chambers. She leaned against the iron railing of the areaway and felt it, burning cold, through her clothes. But with the shawl, a great crude furry thing, pulled tightly over her curls and about her little shoulders, she was snug and gay, alone there in the white windy air. She stamped her feet and hummed.

When she saw the other muffled figure come toward her it seemed for a second as if she were watching herself, something droll and frightening, in a crystal paperweight, a bent tottering Jennie in a tiny snowstorm, for people to shake up and watch. She felt breathless with horror.

Then she was safe again. She laughed a little and stared incuriously at the woman who crept painfully along the railing. It did not bother her that red, sick eyes stared back at her. She felt impervious, the way a queen must, to anything so foreign to her.

The creature's lips were moving. Finally she yelled into the wind, "Are you waiting too, Miss?"

Jennie started to turn away. Then she realized that this beggar thought the two of them, wrapped as they were in shawls against the winter, were sister wretches, sharing the same mews, waiting for the same crust. The idea was funny. Jennie laughed delightedly.

The woman came close to her. "You look well now," she said. "I've changed though, haven't I?"

"What do you want?" Jennie pulled back. In the cold moving air there was no obvious affront, but she knew the poor thing must have a stench of illness and filth all about her, and in her dead eyes there was a ghost of horrible recognition. It was upsetting. "You must go away," Jennie said sharply.

"But I have a paper," the woman went on crazily. "The old Madam wrote her name on it, if ever I should need help. I need help now, I do!" She cackled. "But maybe she's forgotten, like you, Miss. I'm frighted to ask. Oh, I'm frighted and bad off, Miss!"

She clutched the railing, weaving and chattering.

Jennie wanted to run away, back into the warm solidity of the big house. But she must find out. She could not stop herself. "Who are you?" she called out into the wind, and then she knew, before there was any answer. She was lying on the floor of the railway carriage, with women's skirts held in a wall around her, and a strong countrywoman tearing cloth . . .

The shock of memory, held back so long, so well, sickened her. She leaned, almost gagging, toward the beggar. "Go away," she cried. "Go, go!"

Pain and humiliation in a drowning flood raced through her body. There she was, lying on the floor, she, Jennie, helpless under the kind, curious stares, a cow among cattle. There she lay, weak and soiled, while a stranger tended her and knew her intimately. Never, never, must she think of it again, or she would die.

"Go away!" she screamed, pushing the air with her hands so that the shawl fell back. "I know you! You were eating a big meat pasty, chomp chomp chomp!"

She ran laughing and sobbing down the areaway and through the heavy door, and the woman did not move.

That was the nightmare, afterwards, that she did not move. Jennie would dream of her standing there, long dead, with the bones coming through the red, sick flesh, the hands tight on the iron railing, and she would awaken panting, enraged to be thus made victim of herself, thus reminded of her female ignominy.

Nine

THE months went by too swiftly to be remembered. They were soft pleasant ones for Jennie.

Old Julia Collinswood felt suddenly the weight of a long full life and weakened under the burden so jauntily ignored for many years. Paint still masked some of the weariness on her horsy face, and the feathers in her turbans were still as bright as a macaw's, but she often grew querulous and dozed over the pages of the book she had been writing in the half-century of her widowhood.

Once she opened a drawer that Jennie had never been able to force when she was alone, and with only a trace of wry amusement showed her a stiff little pigtail of faded reddish hair. There was something ghoulish about it, like a dried monkey's hand.

"That, my dear," the old lady said, "is the way a lover showed his passion when I was still pretty. He was in the militia. This was his queue, and off it came for me!"

"Was it Mr. Collinswood, Madam?"

"Of course not, Miss Pert-and-Sauce!"

Jennie did more and more small things for old Julia, so that she seldom had time for even a nod for Betsy Vaughn, and not much more for the Spackles. Back and forth she skimmed all day, making tea with her own hands, toasting white bread just so, mixing a light syllabub while the cook glared silently, and then the little silver tray placed at chairside, bedside, the softest shawl tucked gently over the sagging old shoulders . . .

"Where's Mrs. Spackle? Tell her to come sit with me this afternoon, Jennie! . . . Here, give this new book to Spackle, and tell him he is neglecting his old friend! . . . I'm lonely, Jennie! Fetch Mrs. Spackle for a little chat with me!"

Jennie would cry out, "Oh, Madam, of course, of course!" and speed from the morning-room in her little silken slippers, and say nothing of the kind to anyone. And when the loving people came to the door, most often Jennie stopped them before they could knock, with a finger to her lips, and they tiptoed away, sighing.

Now and then Mr. Spackle would try to talk with her, as she leaned easily against his desk waiting for money, watching his monumental white head flush in the lamp-light. There was no pretense of borrowing any more: she had told him brutally at the first sign of rebellion that Mrs. Spackle would hear a fine tale indeed if, if, if . . .

She had developed a passion for laces, expensive laces. Her trunk was stuffed with them; the old fineries from Melanie lay ignored at the bottom of the pile. A few times Mr. Spackle bought her little lengths of the cobwebby stuff, with a kind of shameful unwillingness, as if to divert her from the money she kept asking from him. Jennie smiled mockingly, and took the presents as if they were, after all, the best his doltish ways could do, and then she stood frowning a little, her hand out.

One night he said heavily, "Jennie, you are forgetting your old friends."

"You? Ah, dear Mr. Spackle, you wrong me! You cannot know how much I lean upon you, how grateful I am for your thoughtfulness of me! Alas, I am so alone, but for your charity and goodness!"

"No, no!" He shook his head like a hurt beast, and his dramatic vibrant voice sounded as if it were trying to harden itself. "I do not mean us. We understand your devotion to Madam. We are happy that she has found you to care for her. But some of the girls who were—who helped you when you first came. Mrs. Spackle tells me that there is some bitterness amongst them at your change of manner."

Jennie straightened with scorn against the desk. It seemed an impertinence that she should be reminded of her old equality with the chambermaids. That they should dare criticize her to the housekeeper was intolerable.

Mr. Spackle went on laboriously, "This is not like most great houses, Jennie. This is a place where we are proud to be servants, because of the finest, most humanitarian mistress in all London, all England, a great lady such as has never . . ."

Yes yes yes, Jennie snapped impatiently with her mind while his voice droned on. The old fool! There were tears glittering in his eyes.

"Which of the maids considered herself slighted by me?" she interrupted coldly.

Mr. Spackle pressed one hand against his forehead, like a statue. "Vaughn, I believe."

She laughed. "I can attend to that," she said.

But it was not so easy, to her astonishment. In the next few days she spent more time in the linen room, and she smiled, and she praised Betsy's magically skillful hands as they moved like great chunks of meat among the Madam's ruffles, and except for a surly sniffle and an occasional mutter there was no response from the big woman. This was ridiculous, Jennie said to herself, to be courting a countrymaid as if she were important. But the fact that the countrymaid dared spurn her made her try harder to be loving. Finally one day Betsy burst into wet loud sobs and flounced away. Jennie sighed with a mixture of pique and relief and thought no more about her.

Old Spack was a different matter. She grew dourer with the months, and once almost lost her dignity, to Jennie's amusement. They met on the stairs. "I am going to speak to the Madam," the housekeeper said unsmilingly. "I can relieve you of her tray and take it with me." She held out her long white hands for it.

Jennie hardly paused; the sherry in the little decanter hardly stirred in her steady progress. "Thank you," she said with a polite smirk that left her face as still as the wine. "Madam is resting."

For a few seconds she thought Old Spack was going to snatch the tray from her, scream curses at her even. There was a look of completely helpless rage, then, that settled over the face so usually calm, like a black wing. Jennie smirked up at it, her eyes very gray and blank.

"Thank you, Mrs. Spackle," she said softly, and she skimmed on. She turned back enough to see that the housekeeper had stepped aside, against the corridor wall, as if to make way for a Jennie already far ahead of her.

When the real scene finally came Jennie felt too powerful to be much upset by the unfolding of it, except, of course, that it was offensive to her to see any lack of dignity in the people about her. Later she grew furious, and hurt, to find herself so caught in other human beings' stupidities.

It started simply enough. Old Spack, as if to apologize for her weeks of remote silence, asked Jennie to have tea with her in her sitting-room. It was the first time Jennie had been invited there since the summer evenings so long ago, when she had sat listening to Mr. Spackle's rich voice, dreaming of what could be inside the package on the table, wondering what Melanie would bring her from Paris. She was titillated, in a mild way. Was it a sign that the woman was finally recognizing her complete loss of power?

The room looked very pleasant, very familiar. Old Spack gave Jennie her own chair, but this time Jennie sat primly in it, not lulled as she had once been by the butler's rolling periods. The two women ate bread-and-butter sandwiches and little cakes, as if they were in one of the reception rooms upstairs. They nodded and smiled distantly, and Jennie was smoothly careful to say "Ma'am" always, as if she knew the privilege it was to be there.

Finally Mrs. Spackle put down her plate and folded her hands easily in her black silk lap.

Good, Jennie thought with a kind of glee.

"Jennie, I know about your trunk."

Jennie looked straight at her, her forehead wrinkled into a question.

"I am sorry that I know. It is not fitting to you or to your station, Jennie, to possess such expensive playthings."

Jennie shrugged and said coolly, "If you know about my private property, then you probably know how I paid for it."

Mrs. Spackle's hands were still clasped loosely in her lap, and her voice was easy. Jennie approved of her poise.

"Yes, I know—as much as I wish to. I have gone over the accounts carefully with Mr. Spackle. It is very unfortunate. It is impossible for you to replace a fraction of what you have borrowed. But we do not wish to have you accused. You will, of course, have to leave."

Jennie refused to let herself show how furiously amused she was. She kept her face smooth, her breath even and slow, but inside she was seething with excitement. At last the thing was ready to be played out! It was wonderful. She had never felt so full of power.

"No," she said, smiling.

Old Spack looked sharply at her. "What do you mean, girl, 'No'?"

"I don't leave, Mrs. Spackle. You leave."

Jennie saw dispassionately that the white hands were suddenly clenched and twisted, like those of a corpse dead in great agony. The black silk skirt hissed a little under them.

"If there should happen to be any discussion, Ma'am, about what is in my trunk—and, of course, you know as well as I do that I could not possibly have bought it all with what I borrowed, and you know where I got the other money, who gave it and lace and suchlike to me—if there should be any discussion of it, I would feel forced to tell your adored old Collinswood about you."

There was a kind of silence in the pleasant little room. Jennie's breath still came slow and soft. Finally Mrs. Spackle gasped, with a grating, inhuman voice, like a woman in travail, "Me?"

"You and Mr. Spackle."

"Tell the Madam?" Her mouth moved stiffly. Her arms were stretched straight as rods down into her lap, where her hands writhed, apart from her. She began to shake, the way a stone statue might shake on Judgment Day.

"Yes. It would be hard on her. She is old." Jennie sighed and then leaned forward confidingly. "But you really aren't married, are you?"

Mrs. Spackle shook more and more, until her head jerked like a doll's. Then she slid slowly down onto the red carpet.

Jennie ran to the door. "Quick," she cried, and to her surprise there was real terror in her voice. "Help me!"

Ten

IN THE warm quiet little alcove, in her soft chair, she felt safe again. How could she have known that anything, especially a chance bit of gossip, would so affect as coolheaded a woman as Mrs. Spackle? Jennie shuddered with distaste at the memory of the stonelike body, the rasping breath, the little line of spittle running from an open, pallid mouth. That was not Old Spack, she told herself: Old Spack would be back, none the worse for a wee shock, tomorrow.

But in the morning all the maids were hushed, and although they stopped their thrilled murmurs when Jennie came into the dining-room, she knew that things were serious for the housekeeper. Mr. Spackle was invisible, in his office with his worry, probably. Betsy Vaughn and a hired nurse reigned in the butler's little apartment.

Jennie sat alone at one end of the long table, pretending to drink her tea without concern, but she felt strangely upset. Should she tell the old Madam anything, she wondered? What? How?

The girls went in and out, without speaking to her. Jennie smiled a little at their histrionics, their abrupt elevation of the strict housekeeper to the pedestal of martyrdom or at least of pain.

The dining-room door opened and closed again. It was Betsy, breathing hard, her face red and determined. "They told me you was here, Jennie," she said. "And what do you think of yourself now, eh?"

Jennie sipped twice at her tea before she answered. She felt cool, and scornful of all this pother. "What I always think of myself," she said casually. "Why should I have changed, my dear Betsy?"

"And don't 'dear Betsy' me," the older woman said furiously, her voice low enough still, but her face redder, her blue eyes snapping. "You know what I'm saying, Jennie. We've seen you and the way you've been treating poor Mrs. Spackle."

"Mrs. Spackle? I thought you usually referred to her as Old Spack!"

"Old Spack then, and you wouldn't know what I'm saying, but we love her, we do. She's hard, but she's fair with us, and maids were never better treated anywhere. And we've been watching all your airs with her, Miss Jennie!"

Jennie sat patiently, waiting for the loutish girl to begin

to weep, as surely she would soon. But Betsy kept on, her big breasts surging, her cheeks mottled.

"And the old Madam, how about her? You guard her and keep us all away from her like she was dangerous, you do! If she was dying in the madhouse, Miss Jennie, she'd still have more sense than you! And now I'm going to see her!"

"You? What would you have to discuss with Mrs. Collinswood, my dear Betsy?"

"I bade you not call me that!" For a second Betsy's voice wavered. Then she went on hardily, "You'll see perhaps, Miss. We girls know more on you than you'd think, perhaps, Miss. And you're not the only lass that can be friends with a real lady like the Madam. I can talk to her as loud as you, and I shall, and now. You sit here, you hear me? And don't come trying to stop me!"

"Why in heaven's name should I try to stop you, Betsy? Nothing in your conversation with your mistress could possibly interest me. Do go. You act so absurdly upset, and I haven't finished my breakfast." She called after the big flouncing woman, "Madam is at her desk. Please remember to knock softly."

The door slammed. Jennie sighed. She felt less disturbed than hideously bored by all these below-stairs melodramatics. It seemed to her that everyone in the world was selfish, living in a tight cocoon, giving nothing, and always sucking at her, draining her of her daintiness, her fresh fineness, asking, taking, giving nothing to her but a stream of words. It was almost more than she could stand, this drowning flood of words everywhere about and above and around . . .

She heard bells sounding, out in the hall. The stupid maids were probably cackling too loudly to notice. She sighed again, resignedly, and went with a cynical patience to see what was wanted.

In the glassed box by the butler's office two signals showed, and the bells still jangled. Why did not Mr. Spackle answer himself? His own flag was up, and hers too. She pushed the little buttons that stopped the suddenly unbearable clatter. Was Betsy out of her mind, to ring thus from the Madam's chambers?

The office door was still shut. Almost in spite of herself Jennie knocked firmly on it: she must see what made such silence there.

Mr. Spackle peered up, squinting, as she pushed her way in, unbidden. He looked, and was, astonishingly drunk. It was as if one of the statues of the Prince Consort, larger and much handsomer than life, had with no warning hiccuped and waved a gin bottle, to see him sitting there behind the brown jug of Geneva, with his fine eyes bleared and his face all out of focus. Jennie felt very sorry. It is pitiable to see a good man lose his innate dignity, she thought austerely.

"Your bell is ringing, Mr. Spackle," she said. "Mrs. Collinswood wants you. The bell rang a long time."

"No, she doesn't want me," he said slowly. "She is a fine person, little Jennie, but she doesn't want me."

Jennie stepped sharply into the thick air of the office, which smelled as if it had been closed in upon this befuddled creature for much longer than one night. He leaned backward at his desk, as if she were going to strike him.

"Stand up," she said, and he shivered at her voice.

"You don't know how I feel," he whimpered weakly. His head drooped, and Jennie sighed with exasperation. "My dear wife . . ."

"Your dear wife," she cried out tauntingly. "Don't be a fool, old Spackle! We all know just how much she is your wife! Yes, all of us! Now, stand up and walk upstairs to the old lady's room, if you're a man at all!"

He shivered again, and his eyes fixed themselves on her with a kind of desperation, as if her little straight figure and her scornful face were the only things that could keep him upright. Slowly they mounted the flights of stairs, into the warmth and muskiness of the corridor to Mrs. Collinswood's chambers, and as they walked Mr. Spackle tried shakily to smooth his rumpled white curls and wipe some of the unshaven cobwebby look from his sagged but still monumental face. Jennie thought disgustedly of the dancing statue, smooth as Jehovah, who had first escorted her along this path, and of how she had leaned upon his great warm arm.

She tapped lightly at the door. Betsy, her face smeared with tear stains, opened it with never a glance at the two who entered. They walked across the woven roses of the carpet, threading their way among the little tables and the golden cages full of silent watching birds.

"You rang for both Mr. Spackle and myself at the same time, Madam," Jennie said clearly to the old lady, who sat in a ruffled crimson spencer, half turned from her desk, the pen quill standing up straight and steady as a ship's mast in her hand.

Mrs. Collinswood cleared her throat, and her voice was flat and white, like the paper she had been writing on.

"Jennie, it is just as well. I have questions to ask you both, and they seem intertwined. This poor girl Betsy"—and at this Betsy threw her apron over her head and started a series of low hypnotic sobs which seemed never to cease again—"this poor good Betsy has felt pressed to bear tales about you. I have felt pressed, in my turn, to look at the contents of your trunk."

The old lady motioned dispassionately with her pen toward the little open trunk beside her desk. Jennie almost gasped with astonishment: it seemed utterly strange to see it there, and open, and spilling out its laces and fans and pretty silken slippers. She looked wide-eyed at Betsy's incoherent figure, like a carved fountain with a duster over it, but still dripping.

"Betsy once peeked into it, finding it unlocked and perhaps feeling hurt at some coldness of yours. The action is not as you or I would prefer it"—and Mrs. Collinswood sketched a tiny bow to Jennie's gentility with her morning cap—"but she was worried about her friendship with you."

Jennie shrugged. She felt herself drowning in all this talk. Friendship! Who there in the room could speak of it to her? Who had been anything but weak and faithless to her?

"There are some articles in the trunk that interest me," the old lady went on flatly. "But first I must ask Mr. Spackle a few questions. Spackle," and her voice softened as she looked straight at the old man from her small tired eyes, "you are very drunk, are you not?"

"Yes, Madam."

"But not drunk enough—is that it, man?"

"Yes, Madam."

"Vaughn here has told me of our good friend's seizure yesterday. We shall attend to that. I should have been told of it at once. But now, Mr. Spackle!" She jabbed her pen into the little golden jar of shot and then thumped her hand on the desk. Jennie had not seen such vigor in her old body for many weeks. "Now, what of the differences in these accounts, eh? I've not looked at your books for twenty years, man, and that you well know. Have you made a fool of me?"

The butler groaned and put both his fine long hands over his temples with a mad look about the room. Then he straightened himself. "No, Madam," he said, in something like his own ringing, throbbing voice. "Not you, never! It is I, lately."

"Since when, Mr. Spackle?"

Jennie thought, now is when he will blame the whole puny insensate business on me, me Jennie! But instead he answered, without a look at her or the weeping chambermaid, "A few months, Madam. I shall show you. I can only beg you to let me put it back, as I had always planned. I discussed it only yesterday morning with Mrs. Spackle. We can manage it. And if you do not wish me here, I will still send it in installments. I will send it from wherever I am."

Mrs. Collinswood shook her head a little. Jennie saw the blue line around her lips, at the edge of the paint, and the slight tremble in her tightly clenched old jaw. It was like watching an aged hunting horse try one more jump, she thought dispassionately: the body still knew what movements to make, still got signals from the mind . . .

"Jennie"—and her face did indeed look more like a

horse's than ever before—"I shall ring soon for you. Leave Betsy here. She is useless and does not bother me." There was a stiff nod of the morning cap, and Jennie was outside the door.

She stood for a minute in the warm corridor. She felt no alarm, but there was in every part of her intricate pretty little body a sense of outrage. It made her almost breathless. She waited to calm herself, and then went silent as smoke to the little back door that let into her alcove, and into the dim musky nest she loved so much. She stood for a minute looking at herself in the glass, and then tiptoed to the thick curtains that almost cut off her part from the big bedchamber.

Voices came faintly to her from the morning-room. She went to the door and pushed it open a little, not even bothering to watch that none of the three people saw the movement. Then she walked easily back to the alcove and stood listening, unable to stop her ears, to the talk talk talk. Scorn boiled in her. Spackle's voice was a droning whimper. Betsy keened like a tipsy mourner at a publican's wake. The old lady rasped on, scratchy as one of her pens. Jennie moved restlessly inside her clothes: this flood of words exasperated her, hurt her very bones. She heard parts of it and let others flow by shapelessly.

"Yes, Madam, it is true. I bought these things for her. I cannot beg any kind of pardon, that I know. I was lonely."

"She is sweet to look at, Spackle."

He groaned.

"Your good wife—what does she feel about this indiscretion? It came late in your life together, man. But there's no fool like an old fool. That I've proved today."

He groaned again, as if he would be sick. "No, Madam," he said through the sound of his suffering. "Not you, but I! The girl was a witch, so amiable and intelligent. We talked of the Revolution. She felt as I did, or pretended to, about the laboring classes here at home. She seemed compassionate."

"But your wife, Spackle?" The weary voice was relentless, and at the same time had a bitter urgency about it, like a surgeon cutting into his own flesh to find a poisoned thorn, knowing what pain he would give himself, and why he must. "What of that good friend of mine and yours?"

Betsy let out a yelp of utter misery. There was a long pause before Mr. Spackle answered, and then he was almost inaudible to Jennie, so that she went a little into the bedroom to hear him say tonelessly, "I suppose she will tell you."

Betsy made a long wailing stream of denials, nonono, like a pig ready to be butchered.

"Not you, not you, Vaughn," Spackle shouted disgustedly, forgetting where he was and what of politeness all his servitude had taught him. "That bitch, that devil Jennie! She will tell you if I don't. She'll see to it, she will!"

"What use to shout? I know already that she has many of my shawls and gauzes."

Jennie felt white-hot with outrage. She wanted to rush into the flood of noise and dare them to accuse her so wrongly. The things she had bought innocently, the rags she had paid all her money for to the infamous Frenchwoman, to be thought stolen by her, as if she were a common thief: oh, God eternally damn it, she cried out at the unfairness of the world.

"No," the butler said, less violently but with passion, "not those foolish little crimes, Madam. Not that. But I say she'll tell you if I don't, or someone will: I have no wife. I never had a wife. We aren't married, I tell you. We are sinners, cheaters. We've lied all the years to you. It's made Mrs. Spackle almost mad with shame. Now it will kill her. For a time I hated her for it. I wanted . . ."

The old lady spoke with effort. "You wanted Jennie?"

"Yes, Jennie."

In the alcove the word was like a low curse. Jennie shuddered with pain, that a man could sound so base, so crude.

"In that case," Julia Collinswood's voice dragged on, "we shall assume that you had her, and that it was worth this present disillusionment. Whoring, mismanagement of funds, infidelity to Mrs. Spackle and to me. No, there are indeed no fools like old ones. And we are both very old. And you are drunk, man, and I am tired . . ."

There was only the sound of Betsy's voluptuous misery in the rooms. Even the birds were still silent, watching and curious behind their golden wires. Jennie wanted it to stay that way. She felt herself drowning, dying, in the ugly words that hung all about her in the air of her alcove. She felt herself stifling in the odious muskiness. She must flee. She must escape from all this. She was almost engulfed by a kind of anguish at the ingratitude, the selfishness, of other human beings, their accusations of her thievery, so hideously untrue, their loathsome assumptions that she, she Jennie, had ever deigned bed herself with an aging butler. Ah, it was a cruel thing to be here, to have heard such things!

She threw the furry shawl that Vaughn's mother had made for her about her shoulders. In the mirror she looked at herself wryly, thinking of her delicious little *canezou*, so airy green, so sewn about with magic silver roses.

Then her eyes darkened with horror, for it seemed for one sickening instant that it was Cairns she looked at, Cairns huddled and dead and upright in the snow, and she was Cairns, or would be, or had been, with nevermore a meat pasty to break open and tuck into the pale, toothless cavern of her mouth . . .

She turned frantically away.

By the time she reached the little door into the back hall she was Jennie again. She smiled, and shook her shoulders, and thought of the sweet, wordless air outside of the great musk-heavy house. Ah, Jennie my girl, she said gaily, you are free once more, gone from such selfishness, such stupid accidents, old Julia's lies . . . free Jennie, pretty princess . . .

III

One

THE train from the west coast to Chicago in 1927 was as good as any in the country probably. It lumbered smoothly across the deserts and the rolling plains and the rich riverlands, and inside it, blinking out upon the skidding, wheeling world, the various travelers endured.

Sand and black grit fell on old women eating tepid fried meat from their greasy lunchboxes, and on Hollywood producers wolfing fresh trout in the sparkle of the dining-car. Hot air puffed in and out of all the human lungs, farmers', salesmen's, with the same muted reek of toilets, of starch from the Negro porters' jackets, and of eau de Cologne and shaving soap and whisky from the caged, sweaty passengers. There were the same clean gray-white pillow cases in the private sleeping-compartments and in the long chair cars where people sprawled like corpses at night, upright under the dim lights, their faces turned painfully toward the cautiously opened windows and the stingy air. The hours went in the same dignified procession for everyone, and a rich man could not pay extra-fare to get to Chicago before the farmhand who smoked patiently beside him in the restroom: he could only comfort himself with the reassurance that the dirt and stench and the interminable turning of the wheels cost several times as much for him.

By the time the cars from San Francisco had met the train at Ogden, and had been hooked on to make a longer, more ponderous monster in the hell of the late September desert, Jennie felt that she was the oldest person in the world. She had forgotten how nonchalantly Americans moved over the face of their country, from their first staggerings in diapers to the last smooth coffined ride in the baggage car, a thousand miles for Christmas dinner, three thousand for new dancing frocks, as many more to sleep beside Mom in the family burying lot . . . Now it was a few days before schools reopened everywhere, and the hot aisles of the train churned and echoed to countless students, gay and gawky as colts. She heard them bumping their way back and forth to the dining-car, past the partly opened door of her room. Their cracked voices whipped at her. She put cotton plugs in her ears, but above the grind of the wheels and the nervous pounding of her own blood she could still hear them, so young, so foolish, so selfish.

How had she blundered onto this train of all others? Could she not have waited? In another week the migration, the educational trek, would be over, and all these foetal citizens safely tucked into their boarding schools and their universities. In another week . . . but ah, poor Jennie! Could the refugee choose her hour for flight? Could the imprisoned bird say at what moment the shell would break open for her and let her out? Could even Jennie know, until the final moment when she fled all the ugliness to be herself?

She went to the mirrored wash stand and stood braced against the swaying of the train, looking at this woman. She was free, and that was what mattered. That was what made everything else not matter at all. She looked at her smooth hair, cut like a boy's, on her little head, and at her wide gray eyes. She was beautiful, much more beautiful than if she were as young as the college girls who giggled everywhere on the train. The boys with them peeked up furtively over their ukeleles and bridge cards when Jennie went past, so cool and aloof, and she knew with a kind of smug revulsion that it was she who peopled their hot night thoughts, and not the thin pretty girls who sang and played closely pressed against them in the gritty Pullman seats.

She smiled a little as she washed her hands for the tenth or the hundredth time. She felt strong and desirable, and most of all she felt free again, away from the petty people who had tried to hurt her. All their injustice, all their talking and talking! She had fled it. Wise Jennie!

Suddenly she was happy, knowing how far past the youngness in the train she had grown, and how good it was. The untried bodies everywhere, the stretching voices and the smooth cheeks of the students, were like a salve to her, so that she began to feel purified, as if she were making a new skin inside and out, one that covered silkily the scars and smudges of old blows.

She took the little cotton plugs from her ears and let the sound of girls singing to a portable phonograph in the next compartment flow peacefully through her head, healingly. "Aheeee . . . ain't got nobaaaahdee," they sang in a crazy, sweet way. The pain from all the old talk, all the things cruel people had cried blamingly at her, melted, evaporated, vanished in a kind of cool gas up through the top of her skull, so that she felt giddy with relief. How wonderful it was, how exactly like Jennie, she cried to herself, that she had chosen this train full of boys and maidens!

She would hide no longer, full of bitterness, in her little room. She put pearls into her earlobes, fitted a Basque beret carefully down over her shingled hair, ate a few grapes from the top of the big steamer basket that leaned heavy and lavish against her berth. She would stay a long time in the diner, listening and watching, letting the complete youngness of all the other people heal her.

Young people are the kind ones, she thought almost drunkenly. They are the ones who have not yet learned how to be unfair.

Two

BY THE time the train neared Kansas City Jennie knew that although the average age of the other passengers was perhaps half her own, she was as far from mingling with them as if she were perched on a pillar miles above their heads. Even if she slid down on top of them, even if she were naked or clothed in green pinfeathers, she thought wryly, she would not jar them into acknowledging that she was, that she breathed and ate and functioned as did they.

They flooded into the luxurious dining-car like a tide, and ordered at length from the elaborate, expensive menus, and behaved properly enough, like the upper middle-class children they were. And except for the inevitable sidelong glances of the budding boys they ignored Jennie as completely, as stonily, as if she were not there. She watched what they did, and how and what they ate, as if she might find some clue to them and their fine healing youngness in such public patterns. She listened to their well-bred table-talk as she sat unseen among them. Finally she shrugged: if it was true, as she still felt, that they were in some way revivifying her, they were unconscious of it, and would stay so. She, Jennie, must be a grateful ghost among them.

It was a new role for her, one that titillated her, like an unexpected caress, so that she looked forward with what was more than physical hunger to her staggering walks along the cars to the diner. Always there were boys who held open the heavy doors for her and let her pass them with the automatic courtesy of older men. Always Jennie felt that this time, or this time, they would react to her as their fathers did, and be disturbed when she stepped lightly past them with her fine little body and her smooth hair. Then she would hear them behind her, calling out in their cracked voices to the girls they waited for, and she would go on, rebuffed and fascinated by her own invisibility, the magic cloak of her years wrapped about her. To them, she, beautiful Jennie, was an old woman. She was past desire. That more than anything amused her, and in a way shocked her: it was the one thing, probably, that she was positive could never be . . .

In Kansas City she checked carefully with her porter, as she did each time she passed that way, to verify the unchanging fact that the train would be there for so many minutes and on such and such a track, and then she hurried through the station and out into the cooling dark air. It blew in little puffs after the hot day. Over the tops of the taxis in the square she saw the high monument to dead soldiers, with the flame. It moved her, as live fire always did, wherever it burned to prove man's eternity in the face of his obviously finite span. She was at peace, and fully herself, after the strange anonymity of existence on the train filled with youth. The stars were enormous in the deep sky. She was well again, forgiving as only a strong person can be of the weak ones who have tried to infect her and hurt her. She breathed the sweet prairie air and felt magnanimous.

Inside the station people sat on the benches in shirtsleeves, in thin cheap dresses, and their sleeping children lolled with dead-white faces against them or wailed thinly, patiently. Jennie bought new magazines, and a package of strong peppermints, and waited for her change with a familiar feeling of panic: each time she left the train in Kansas City she was sure that she would forget where it was, not be able to get back to it before it rolled on toward Chicago, and left her standing there with no hat, no gloves, no tickets or powder . . .

"Excuse me. I'm terribly sorry," a girl said beside her. Jennie put the change in her purse and looked up, unsmiling, attentive. She did not want to be spoken to, not by anyone in the world, but certainly not by another woman.

"I'm terribly sorry," the girl said again, and her voice was breathless, "but I know you're on my train because I've watched you."

Jennie almost laughed with a sudden sarcastic gaiety at the realization that one human being had actually looked at her in the past days of invisibility. And now what was it to be—a plea for money perhaps?

She let her gray eyes widen arrogantly as she stared up at the girl. How dared anyone accost her simply because she traveled on the same train? The girl was like all the others, slender as grass, no breasts, no hips, fine long legs, a small head set well on her tender, bony shoulders, good clothes, shoes wide and short to make her American feet look French. She had too much lipstick on her small mouth, but her eyebrows were not plucked fashionably thin. That takes courage, to be an individual even about an eyebrow when you are eighteen, Jennie thought appreciatively.

"Yes?" she asked.

"But the train's gone," the girl said tremulously. "It isn't on the track. The porter told me . . ."

Jennie smiled. It was because, she knew in a rush, she was grateful to this silly child for being scared for her. Now she was free to be calm, self-possessed, the ruler. Yes, she smiled warmly, and then touched the girl's arm to reassure the two of them.

"Oh, that always happens. The porter always swears the train won't move. Then it does. But it comes back to the same track. Always. I promise you! Come along and you'll see."

Jennie laughed aloud, gay and grateful, and almost loving the tall girl who had been scared for her. "Come along," she said again, looking up at the young face with eyes as candid as a kitten's, and they ran through the station, through the gate, out onto the long ramps. "You see? Our good old horrible filthy train! It's sliding back into place again. This always happens."

They waited side by side until the cars had jerked to a stop. Then the intimacy broke, and the girl seemed to grow two inches taller, and her voice was not breathless. "I'm terribly sorry," she said politely. "I hope you'll excuse me for bothering you. Good night."

Jennie could not bear to have her go. "Is this your car?" she asked.

The girl looked at the number in the end window and shook her head stiffly. "I'm farther down. Good night, and thank you."

Don't go yet, Jennie wanted to cry out. Stay and talk. Did you not say you had seen me on the train? What did you see? Did I look old to you? How did you happen to remember me, there in the station? Was it because of my little snakeskin shoes, my smooth chic hair? Was it because I am Jennie? Stay and tell me . . .

She watched the girl walk with a faint gawkiness down the platform. The lights shone glintingly on her close-cropped head, on the choker necklace of big gold beads about her throat, and as she swung herself up into her car she seemed hardly to touch the steps, so light was she and young.

Jennie yawned all of a sudden, helplessly.

Three

WHEN she saw the girl come into the dining-car the next morning she knew everything would go the right way. If she had gambled thus on rising early and eating breakfast in public, a thing she never did, and the girl had not come, Jennie would have known that nothing else

would come either. But there the girl stood, swaying behind the steward, and Jennie was sure that he would pull
out the other chair at her table and that the girl would sit
down sleepily, ignorant of her at first.

"Good morning," she said in a voice not cool, not warm.
And when the girl looked up, and then smiled radiantly
and flushed, and tried to straighten her face from its
betrayal of delight, Jennie felt a wrench of excitement: this
beautiful slim child is mine, she thought, mine to teach,
to shape, to mold. She saw herself forever young, forever
adored in complete purity and gratitude, traveling and
talking and swimming in blue seas over green sands with
this companion.

But as she began to woo, she was skillful as only Jennie
could be, and her voice stayed impersonal and discreet, and
there was a fine air of courteous disinterest about her, all
so artful that inside she was trembling with a kind of
admiration of herself. She would let the flow between them
lag until just before the point at which the girl would
convince herself that she had been forward or childish thus
to talk with a strange woman, and then she would lean
forward warmly, candidly, and the girl would flush a little
and unfold again.

Their names they told each other finally, as the gray
outskirts of Chicago rolled past the stability of their white
linen table and the silver pots of coffee. It was the final
concession, an admission that soon the journey would end
for each of them, so that they could separate and never be
afraid of having told too much. And with that admission
Barbara Janes bent toward Jennie eagerly, released from
the code of behavior, and told her about the old small town

in Ohio where she went to college, where her father was a doctor, where she lived alone with him and a Negress who had been born a slave. Janesville, Janesville College, Barbara Janes . . .

Jennie held out her case of thick cigarettes and watched with a kind of affectionate amusement as the girl took one too casually, inhaled too deeply. How young, how young . . . and Jennie felt herself grow stronger and fresher than she had been for many years.

The steward told them the train would soon be in the station, and they paid their checks and stood up, polite suddenly and stiff.

"It's been so nice," Jennie said without too much cordiality.

"Yes, hasn't it?" Barbara answered as if she were already closing her traveling case, smoothing on her gloves.

They smiled a kind of automatic, distant smile at each other and parted.

Jennie had her bags checked, and skimmed as fast as if she were flying, in her little snakeskin shoes, to the information booth and then the travel bureau. There were telephone calls, and slips to sign, and bills to pay, and then she was out in the hot streets with a ticket to Janesville in her handbag, and in her sleek head the knowledge that the best room and bath in Janesville's best hotel, the Lincoln Arms, waited for her.

She had three hours left, pause between an old life and a new one. She took a taxi to Michigan Boulevard and then walked along, looking in windows full of furs and jewelry, and just before she must go back to the station bought a heavy silver vanity case, handmade and set with a mysteriously carved jade seal. The weight of it in her bag delighted her, and she hugged it against her ribs.

She stood beside her porter and the little pile of her handsome luggage at the gate, waiting so cautiously, so completely, that it seemed hardly necessary to breathe in and out. She held a cigarette in one gloved hand and watched the smoke rise torpidly from it into the dead station air, and there was nothing but remoteness on her face, no sign of the fast rushing of her blood, nor of her need for reassurance that she was strong and beautiful and Jennie.

At last she heard, above all the sounds of traveling, what she was waiting for, the gasp and the incredulous delight of Barbara, crying out, "Oh, *Jennie!*"

She let herself turn slowly, her eyes innocent. "Of course," she said, looking up, "of course."

Inside she knew now what should never have been doubted, even when the boys had treated her politely, like an old woman past desiring, that youth needed her, felt her power, acknowledged her beauty. Youth was Barbara. Barbara needed, felt, acknowledged.

Four

A FEW days in the Lincoln Arms brought Jennie almost to the point of scowling and stamping with boredom as she went for another enormous rich dinner into the refined hush of the dining-room. She walked to her little table haughtily, knowing that two unattached faculty members, the town librarian, and a handful of desiccated widows stared at her over their cream soup, past the silver bud-vases of late asters, around the corners and cretonnes of the remodeled family room. Hoping she would not snap with exasperation, she waited frigidly for the muted greeting of the decayed *grande dame* who had once owned this pile of colonial charm and now ran it with shrewd snobbery for whoever was willing to pay three times the price of a properly ventilated room at the downtown hotel for the obvious privilege of living with intellectuals rather than drummers.

"Good evening," Jennie said in as near a contagious coo as she could summon.

Mrs. Tapham nodded, smiled, advised turkey pie rather than the chops, and then tried once more to involve her latest and most intriguing "guest" in a game of bridge with the two professors and the librarian.

Jennie looked wan with fatigue and an incipient migraine, and dived resolutely into the first of several well-cooked courses that managed, at least twice a day, to uphold the Lincoln Arms' boast of local gastronomical precedence. She ended with a two-plate dessert, hot mince pie and vanilla mousse, and rose from her table with the caution of a gravid quail. On the way to the door she nodded with sly coyness at the lonely faculty men, laughing to think how she had lied herself out of an evening in their quirkish, tweedy company.

Such was the genteel oppression of the air that she longed for a dish of toothpicks within reach, that she might stick one between her lips and affront the ninnies staring at her in their thick breeding and timidity. She would have liked to put one hand on a swaying full hip and lope out upon run-down French heels, a strayed Sadie Thompson. Instead she knew that her slender body under its discreet dark crepe de Chine showed hardly any movement as she scudded toward the door, and that the heels of her shining gray lizard pumps could click but impotently upon the flowered, well-brushed carpet. She wanted to spit with boredom. Instead she nodded once more, properly languid, to Mrs. Tapham, who came puffing at that minute through the service door, and ignoring a fluttery signal from the lady, she went sedately up the soft stairs to her room, while her guts cried out in panic, panic that she had made a mistake and that Barbara Janes had forgotten her. Jennie felt that she could not live, not face her own face, if the tall young girl had betrayed her, and so soon.

She tried not to remember the joy in Barbara's voice, so far away and long ago in Chicago. "Oh, *Jennie!*" she had cried out.

Jennie could still feel triumph at that sound, and at the memory of the long, filthy train trip down to this God-forsaken, tree-bound village. Barbara had talked of her father the doctor, of Henry who wanted her to quit college and marry him, of Janice the ancient cook. By the time the train slowed for Janesville, Jennie was part of the whole strange, shy picture, so that when Dr. Janes came up and kissed his daughter and listened courteously to her introduction of him, it would have seemed right for them all to go together to the same house. Instead Barbara had grown younger and more remote, and Jennie had felt the father's gaze cold as a scalpel across her face, and then they had parted with not even a whispered farewell from the girl who had seduced her thus far.

Jennie had got somewhat stiffly into the town hack, and found herself put down like a sack of potatoes in front of the spuriously beautiful, impossibly authentic colonial façade of the inn, alone and hateful of her own softness in ever coming here. And for days she had waited, incredulous of others' disinterest because of her passionate absorption in the affair.

Now, overfull of rich food meant for zombies waiting for their physical, if not cultural, disintegration rather than for such a world-hungry soul as Jennie, she went slowly up the stairs, resolved to flee once more, misunderstood and cheated by the stupidity of other people. The gray lizard belt low on her flat hips felt heavy as chain mail, and the silk and lace band that held her little undaunted breasts pressed them down painfully, so that her whole stylish silhouette dragged at her like lines of bitter lead. She thought of her bath, where she could let herself grow round and upstanding and soft again, Jennie the ripe princess . . .

Barbara stood hesitantly by the door of her room, her hands tightly held before her in their beige suede gloves. Jennie looked at her with cool eyes, to give her pulse time to slow itself, and she enjoyed, as a connoisseur enjoys a fine sherry, the way the girl's spine stood up straight with the shoulders, and the hips swinging narrowly from it, and the long slightly gawky arms and legs hanging, and the head like a ringing crystal goblet perched above all. Ah, Jennie thought with her heart beating fast, youth needs me . . . Jennie is not too old for this beauty to come begging . . .

She was formal and polite, and Barbara sat down, and

they lit cigarettes. Jennie talked lightly, watching the fine flicker of emotions, like a scientist with one eye to his microscope, as the girl tried to match her suavity. Finally, "I am hideously bored," she said. "Barbara my dear, take me out of this prison. Take me anywhere." She lay back like a child against the neat pillow cover on her bed and saw her visitor's face flush with delight.

They walked for more than a mile down the silent street under great elms, too fast to see the first leaves dropping irrevocably to the earth, too fast to feel Barbara's father peer at them from the window of a patient, some woman inadequately numbed to a cancerous gnawing. They talked a little of French poetry and Verlaine and Colette and the Comtesse de Noailles, or Jennie did. Jennie talked, or perhaps it was Barbara who did, of being a doctor, a woman doctor but like her father, but not a small-town doctor like her father. And she did not mind blood or smells, she said. But could she be a good surgeon? Was it true that women's hands and minds trembled when they—when they—that is, at certain times? Ah, said Jennie, or perhaps it was Barbara answering herself, there in the cold drifting dark under the great trees, as they walked along so neatly on the ringing pavement, ah, but to be a doctor of the soul, perhaps? Then I, you, she, we could study why people act as they do, could learn first by living of course, could read and think and act and then become a great psychologist and live in Vienna—Vienna! They walked faster and talked and talked.

Barbara went to the door of the Lincoln Arms. "No, I couldn't think of your coming back alone, Jennie! You are so little! And I know every crack, every shadow, in these walks, I swear I do!" She laughed with happiness. "Oh, Jennie, it's so wonderful you're here! May I come tomorrow? But when? I have classes all day . . ."

Jennie wanted to get her, the little fool, to invite her to come to the Janes' house, there with the doctor and the old slave Janice. Instead she stood smiling up, breathing easily under her soft fur coat, waiting.

"Jennie, could you come down to the Sweet Shop at four, maybe? It's on the Square, across from the bank. We're always there at four, all my crowd. I want them to meet you."

Barbara dashed like a shy colt down the steps.

Jennie, her face serene, watched her lope around the corner and then walked slowly once more up the stairs to a room which was less horridly sterile than it had seemed a few hours before. Her cheeks were cool from the night air of autumn, and her heart felt strong as an eagle's with the surety that now she was needed, and by a creature young as apple blossoms. The next day more of them would look at her, and tremble for her, and nevermore look past her as if she were beyond desire.

Five

THE next day though, as Jennie sat on a hard narrow seat, with another straight piece of boarding against her back, and all of it painted crude bright blue and orange, she knew that she was still invisible.

Barbara had stood up shyly from her booth in the candy

store as Jennie strolled in, and had met her at the glass counter where Jennie stood looking absently at trays and boxes of unappetizing chocolates. The record of "Blue Skies," sung in a high, sexless voice, ground on above the sound of what seemed like a hundred chirping adolescents. Jennie wanted to run. Instead she waited coolly for Barbara to come to her, and then smiled and followed the girl in her tight pony-skin coat down the middle of a double row of crammed blue-and-orange booths to where a boy and girl sat, obviously primed to welcome them.

The introductions were slurred over. Jennie asked for a coke. The boy looked once at her and then went into a little dream apparently connected by his gently waving hand with the sweet strains from the phonograph, like an old lady at teatime in a hotel full of aspidistras. The girl got a sulky pout on her face, sucked at her tall glass of malted milk until it gargled, looked fleetingly at Jennie's smoked-pearl choker, and then called across the room, "Hey, hello!" Nobody seemed to answer her, as far as Jennie could tell above the sound of the music and the chatter, but the girl and boy got up as if they were pulled on the same string, mumbled vaguely toward her, and left.

Then Barbara swung around on the hard narrow seat so that she was almost facing Jennie. "Oh, it's so wonderful to see you again," she said passionately, and put down her half-empty chocolate cup as if her wrist would not hold it. "I thought four o'clock would never come. They're all laughing at me for having a crush, Jennie, and at my age! But people like you simply don't happen in Janesville. You make them all seem so damned dull!"

Jennie asked for another coke, and she and Barbara

talked about Paris and whether gin was bad for the complexion, and all the time she was remembering the way the boy's eyes had not even shone to have her sit across from him, the way the girl had not even flickered with jealousy of her femaleness. She felt rage rise in her at the invisibility thus constantly thrust upon her, so that her own eyes flashed and her cheeks looked like ripe apricots, and Barbara sitting cross-ways caught her breath and murmured, "Oh oh oh, but lovely Jennie!"

When they walked out of the steamy room, heavy with the smell of hot chocolate and cold fur and youth, Jennie could feel eyes on her, but undemanding, disinterested eyes such as she had never felt before. They piled rage on her rage. What is wrong with them, she cried out, that they can be so?

Then she felt Barbara close to her, in the darkening air, and as they walked swiftly away from the shops toward the hotel and people's houses, she forgot her anger, knowing her strength with the beautiful girl. She did not remember how alone the others had made her until she was in bed that night, after a grudgingly gay game of bridge with three of the dry ladies from the dining-room, none willing to say more than a word of Doctor Janes either, and that word bitter with frustration.

Jennie went a few more times to the Sweet Shop, and sat like a princess under the blind chilliness of Barbara's friends, and once she went about nine at night to a wretched little lunchroom and ate soggy waffles and waited with Barbara for Henry to meet them. He did not come. Jennie wondered, and felt for her friend a baffled anger, that she should be so treated by a man, and that she should not care.

Henry was an intern. Henry could never know when he would be free, Barbara said with the fatalistic acceptance of a doctor's daughter.

Of course, Jennie agreed, knowing that if Henry were her lover, admirer, suitor, whatever he was to Barbara, she would see his patients dead in their own blood rather than let him keep her at bay in a stinking hash-house. Of course, she agreed, smiling, and she looked into the girl's eyes with such compassion that Barbara caught her breath and stared down suddenly at the smeared tabletop, her face soft with bewilderment.

It was that night on the walk homeward that Jennie asked her straight out why she had not ever been invited to the Janes' house, and it was then that Barbara told her that the doctor had seen the two of them walking down the dark street when Jennie first came.

"Well?" Jennie's voice was so cold and small that Barbara shook with pain.

"Jennie," she said, breathless and almost tearful, "my father thinks I'm silly. He doesn't know how lonely and bored I am here, and how wonderful, how kind you are to me."

"But your little intern?"

"Oh, Jennie! Dad's said something to Henry, and he's furious at me and thinks I see too much of you and says it's—it's unnatural—you know!"

"Oh, my God!" Jennie laughed helplessly. "You mean the locum of the village hospital is thumbing his Krafft-Ebing about us?"

She felt Barbara withdraw from her and went on softly, "My dear child, don't worry about that. I can assure you that I am abysmally, boringly normal. As for you, you are a sensitive lovely creature who needs companionship, which she can't find in the little Midwest town. You need to travel, to expand, to be—"

"Oh, Jennie darling, it's you I need! It's people like you! But there isn't anyone in the world like you, anywhere!"

Barbara threw her arms lightly across and around Jennie's little shoulders, so that her trembling shook them both. They stopped breathing. Jennie pushed her almost roughly away, without a word.

Gradually they arranged, as they walked toward their homes, to have black Janice cook a fine dinner, and to invite Henry to it to see how nice Jennie was, and to make the doctor stay home for once and see how nice Jennie was. Barbara would show them that she was happy and grown-up and able to run a house and invite her friends to it.

People, Jennie cried out angrily to herself, how they distort and twist and crucify whatever is decent! But later, as she bathed in her chaste tub at the Lincoln Arms, she yawned suddenly at the swift picture in her mind of Barbara naked in deep water, green sand beyond, a fish, a star-fish, a pearl . . .

The dinner in the Janes' dining-room was awful, with the doctor looking like one of the badly done portraits on the faded walls, and Janice, a hunched tiny woman, a scowl on legs, thrusting platters of rich food at Jennie as if they were piled with ground glass and Paris green. Henry was in the ambulance heading for the slums around the mills when they sat down. By the time they were cracking pecan shells and pulling pink grapes from their stems he came in, scrubbed, politely surly, with a look of permanent fatigue around his eyes. Barbara talked on, her face stiff. Jennie sat like a princess and felt now and then that she must ask for a footstool or perhaps the family dictionary, to put her stinging feet on, under the high old chair. Dr. Janes was courteous in the same way as Henry, but older and even tireder. Everywhere there was suspicion of her, Jennie felt. Why, why, she cried, must common kindness be suspect?

She sipped coffee, and with a gesture she knew would offend the doctor she pulled her new silver vanity case from her pocket and nonchalantly powdered her nose. Barbara looked at her and then away, hurt that Jennie must do it, after they had laughed together one afternoon at Dr. Janes' quoted dictum that ladies no more did such a thing in public than they washed their teeth or cleaned their fingernails. Jennie smiled, clicked shut the heavy top to the box, and laid it on the tablecloth.

"Did I show you this?" she asked the girl softly, as if they shared all such intimate things.

Barbara smiled wanly at her and picked up the case. "Look, Henry," she said. "Did you see this? Look at the carved seal on it."

The young man bent his dark face dutifully toward the trinket.

The doctor coughed. "Very interesting," he said, a kind of apology to Barbara in his voice, and as the old black woman slipped gnomishly about the room, clearing away the crumbs of the sad feast, talk grew a little easier, about jade and jewels and such, and it was not until she was back in the hotel that Jennie thought of how dreadful the whole business had been.

They hate me, she thought disdainfully, not bothering to hate them in return. I'll not go there again, she thought with scorn, not bothering to recognize that they would never ask her.

Instead she and Barbara began to drive together in a little roadster Jennie rented, long rides through the blue autumn afternoons, through drifting leaves, through the slowing countryside. They talked or not, and now and then stopped the car to sit, each in her corner, smoking Jennie's short thick cigarettes into the leaf-smoky air.

Barbara had never touched her since that one close trembling embrace, nor had Jennie stung to the whip of an unsummoned vision of blue water and green sand and a pearl. If she wondered that the young girl would thus choose her and her silences to the close humming air of the Sweet Shop she said nothing. It seemed natural when Barbara told her, one twilight, that if Jennie wanted to take her car they could go that night to a place outside of town and hear some good music. Jennie felt her heart quicken a little, but she said only, "Why not? When? What should I wear?"

Six

IT WAS the first of a tortured string of nights for Jennie. She hated the thick fog in the little rooms they sat in, smoke so thick and foggy that her eyes felt like red bruises when they finally left. She hated the music: its troubling rhythm, and the epileptic stares and twitchings of the people who played it and the ones who listened to it, disturbed her as no Parisian peepshow could ever have done, and she sat in an agony of orgiastic puritanism through hour after hour of it, afraid to open her lips or even touch her fingers to her knees. The people were what she hated most of all, because she did not understand them.

She even hated Barbara Janes, there in the racked, crowded rooms where they all sat listening to the music. She looked through the dimness at the sweet face and found it remote from her, wrapt in a veil of rhythm, swept by a singing that was like stone in poor Jennie's ears. And it was hard for Jennie to admit that this or that or anything at all was stone to her. She knew herself as a fine creation. She found, in the jazz joints, that she was stone inside stone.

The first night she drove Barbara outside of town toward the mills they stopped at a small house and picked up a boy in a fat raccoon coat and flopping galoshes. He got in beside Barbara wordlessly, and as he closed the door of the little roadster his hand came up in one practiced delicate gesture with a long flat silver flask, its top already off. Barbara handed it to Jennie and then pulled it back and tipped it to her lips, as if to show what to do. Jennie took it. She could tell by the smell on the mouth of the bottle that dreadful stuff was in it, and she tipped it to her own lips with an obvious mockery of swallowing what she had never let touch her tongue, and then handed it back across Barbara's thin body to the boy. He took a long gurgling drink and then held it with womanish precision against his chest. They drove on.

It was not until they parked behind a dimly lighted chile joint that Jennie realized that Sam was the boy who had mumbled at her the first day she went to the Sweet Shop and then never looked at her again. She stared coldly at his slick whitish hair and his pink neck as they were solemnly passed through a filthy corridor and into the heart of the place. She hated him. One reason was that he did not know it, nor care that she might. He looked glazed. She saw that it was not because of the raw liquor he had drunk in a subtly ceremonial way in the car, and she determined, standing there in the smelly hall, that some night she would make him feel, under and past his sexlessness, how much she disliked him, how little she cared for him.

He jerked as the scream of a cornet came to them and said in a high voice, "Bobs, for Christ's sake, get your friend here out of her clothes and into the place! He's playing already, for Christ's sake! And he's hot tonight!"

Barbara grimaced at Jennie as if they were two aunts with a difficult little nephew, and when the fur coats were hung perfunctorily and sloppily on a long rack they opened a door and plunged into what was hell for princess Jennie, a long murky room where none saw her and none cared to, a cave with light at the end beating on five Negroes who blasted out sounds that poked like snag-nailed fingers at her eardrums, a tunnel where countless young human beings sat as if their nerves had been pulled out delicately through their pores and they dared not move for the agony there would be in the moving.

Jennie alone knew how wrong it was. She sat primly, as if anyone cared, with her ankles crossed like a schoolgirl's. She felt her exquisite sweet body a little flower in the fast-thickening air and all the sweat and the stink of hair-oil and toilet-water and marcel-lotion and homemade gin. She glowed with disdain.

It was the first of many times that all this happened to her, and thus perhaps the worst, but always she felt herself, in the low dim rooms Barbara took her to, pull into a knot of perfection and a tight spot of aloofness, and always she pushed away from her the knowledge that not one soul in the joint, not even Barbara, cared how aloof and how perfect she was. She sat there night and night and night, trying not to blink her eyes, trying to shut from her outraged ears the screams of the instruments and from her pelvis the thrusting beat of the traps, trying to explain to herself what Barbara Janes did here. She watched the girl in bewilderment, and never did she see any trouble on the fair face, anything other than delight at the rhythm behind the scat and the flame behind the torch. Barbara is an innocent, she cried out protestingly. But when she looked at Sam and saw the impenetrable youngness of his face when Marty stroked his trombone or Smiles beat out a long blood-song, she knew him to be just as innocent, just as far from a recognizable lust.

They all drank, even Barbara, in the foul air of the rooms where the sessions were held, but neither the girl nor any of the cataleptic youths they drove to and fro in Jennie's roadster ever showed that they had put down stuff her own stomach would have vomited in quick denial. They smoked too, of course, all of Jennie's thick heavy cigarettes she could cram into her pockets, and then unnamed fags they bought in the corridors. Some of them smoked dope: Jennie knew it by the way Sam's chin grew slack; but although she looked like a frantic mother into Barbara's eyes sometimes when they said good night, she saw only the black pupils of fatigue and not a stretched depthlessness. And even that failure in suspicion made her unhappy, poor Jennie, and she resolved never more to go and listen to hot jazz.

The next time Barbara said there would be a session the two of them picked up Sam though, and two other boys, and that was the night Jennie in desperation drank what the barman said was Irish whisky and was perfunctorily sick behind the roadster before she drove it, as she always did, from the parking place up to the roadhouse. That was the night Barbara said, surprisingly, "Get in the rumble, Jennie, and let me drive tonight."

"I always drive," Jennie said, not stubbornly, but think-ing that it was a rented car and registered in her name and not in the name, certainly, of any hopped-up minor to smash it against a post.

"Jennie darling," Barbara said, laughing as if at a shy spinster relative, "get into the rumble and give me a chance at these guys!"

And there was Jennie in the narrow straight-backed seat with Sam dumb beside her, and Barbara sailing along fast in the ice-cold air with two sexless mummies. Jennie felt a kind of supercilious impatience with the girl's silly remark, and with all these children. Were they afraid to touch and kiss? They pretended to know passion, and im-plied pursuit of it in shouts instead of whispers, and then they sat side by side, numb to it even when they had drunk and danced together. It seemed wrong, like a plant grown in instead of out.

Jennie saw more clearly than ever before, because of her emptied body, the way Barbara and all the young people crouched night after night in the foul rooms, close as lovers, and let the beat of the hot music make love for them so there was no other need, drums to the females, each man a part of the black hands that held the artful sticks, trumpets screaming up and down to the men, while they all sat stiff or twitching, their faces dream-still, their mouths sometimes a little open in voluptuous exhaustion. For Jennie it was wrong, because it was incomprehensible. She hated it, because it was unfamiliar. If the boys and girls should writhe and bite each other she would, in spite of her disgust, condone, because she understood. As it was, her puzzlement made her censure, and angrily she asked, close to Sam's ear in the wind, "Aren't you even men? Don't any of you ever want more than that damned music? Is that the only way you can have fun?"

He turned his face slowly toward her, and she saw it under the flapping brim of his soft hat, the eyes dead holes, the cheeks flat with fatigue. She felt impotent, because she knew he looked at her and she could not tell in what way. He was like all of them: he made her feel invisible because he did not let her see anything of himself, almost as if he were another woman.

"Well," she cried out furiously, so close to his ear that she could smell cigarette smoke like a skin that had not yet been blown off, "well, don't you ever have fun like a man? Or do you go home and shut the door and pretend, alone? Is that the way you do it? Are you afraid or sorry or what?"

Sam kept his head turned toward her. She drew as far away from him as she could, trying to see what happened behind the deadness. She could feel the car wheels directly under her, in an unfamiliar but exciting slap and purr upon the road. She breathed with caution, like a deep-sea diver newly unhelmeted.

Beside her Sam stirred, and then to her amazement put one hand surely over her shoulders, like a coon-skin boa, and curved his warm young hand under her breast. She was temporarily immobile, with a mixture of shock and mirth, and then when she opened her mouth and drew back her bones from him, he muttered, "Come on, come on!" impatiently.

It was too late. It was impossible now for her to say, "But I am Jennie!" whether she meant "I am Jennie the middle-aged friend of Bobs!" or whether she meant as she really did, "I am Jennie the inviolate, the unsmirched, the proud!" Sam's soft face turned hard and resolute as it bent down upon hers, and his mouth was like a bird's beak pecking and sucking and pulling unmercifully at her, and his irresolute, delicate hands turned into claws as they touched her, so that Jennie, poor Jennie, was torn under him, his fur coat against her fur coat, torn into a quiver, a moan, a throb.

Is this what they get ready for, part of her cried helplessly, is this what prepares in them as they sit there in all the smoke and stink? Is this what the horns do in their blood, and the cymbals in their private parts? What then about Barbara, Barbara the pure and young, she demanded

angrily as she felt Sam bite at her mouth and heard the
car wheels hum beneath them.

They were going fast. They would be home soon. She
felt Sam pull away as a wave pulls away from sand. The
car slowed.

He looked at her in the light that coasted toward them,
on them, away from them, with the corner street lamps.
At first he was like iron, and as blank. Then as he saw
Jennie's small beautiful face twisted from his assault, and
read in her wide eyes the fury and the response to his
brutality, a kind of amusement blossomed in him. As
Barbara slid the roadster still before the inn door, he sighed
gustily, like a boy, innocent of any shame.

Jennie jumped down lightly to the frozen earth.

"Good night," she said. She touched Barbara's cheek
with one furred hand and noticed how thick her fingers
looked on the roundness. Then she leaned closer. "Your
friend Sam was practicing," she said with impersonal clear-
ness. "But tell him, from one who should know, that there
was no man in his manliness. He makes me wonder about
the maidenliness of local maidens."

She turned and walked with light tapping steps upon
the steel-like earth to the inn, not looking back, and hardly
noticing the abrupt sound of her car as it drove off. She
felt almost incandescent with shock. The boy's stupid cruel
embrace, after what the bad whisky had made her do, spun
in her veins, so that she seemed to whirl within her own
flesh, while her mind staggered and fell, and only her finely
balanced skeleton kept her from falling, whirling, spinning
with it. She was Jennie still, but shaken and affronted and,
above all, angered to the marrow.

She walked silent as a cobweb to her room, let herself in with precision, and fell head first across the floor, as if a pecking, clawing bird beat down upon her.

Seven

THERE was no word from Barbara for two days. Jennie waited, sure that the girl was hurt by her parting sarcasm and equally sure that she would not stay hurt very long. She would come back, stiff and shy and lovely, like a fine colt, and Jennie would laugh a little at her solemnity and then they would walk out swiftly together onto the new snow, close as two flames, easy and intimate under the great bare elm trees.

She sat waiting, eating slowly of the creamy custards and thick sauces and rich buttery mounds of whipped potato, smiling at plump, puffing Mrs. Tapham, nodding and listening to the other boarders as they lisped genteel disclosures of their literary and digestive lives. It was easy, when Jennie knew so surely what she waited for.

That is why she was sent into a tremble, almost a sweat of astonishment, when she opened her door to a firm knock and saw Henry standing there. He was bareheaded, and she could see the white of his intern jacket sticking down ridiculously an inch or two from the bottom of his thick tweed coat. He stared at her for a minute, his hands rudely in his pockets, and then, while she could still feel her heart beating too fast, he said in a flat voice, "I have something for you from a friend. I'll come in for a minute, if I may."

Without waiting for her consent he stepped inside and closed the door to the wide hall. He leaned against the wall and stood looking at her, still with his hands in his pockets, and a queer sick twist on his lips.

Jennie looked back at him. He must be well past twenty, too old for such melodramatic behavior, she decided. She would let him play his scene as he wanted to, before she got rid of him. She was used to jealousy, to being misunderstood.

But when he tossed her heavy silver vanity case upon the end of her bed she cried out, "Barbara! What has happened? Barbara!"

"Not Barbara," he said. "She's all right, I guess you could say. It was your little friend Sam who had it."

"But how? Sam? How dare he take my case? That stupid baby!"

Henry looked distastefully at her. "You're playing it very well, Jennie," he said.

"I playing? How dare you? You are the one who is playing, and I am beginning to feel bored with the whole thing, Henry. It is kind of you, my dear, to feel such an interest in returning my case to me, and I thank you, and now will you get out, please? And don't bother to remind me that you are only doing this for the woman you love," she added mockingly.

Henry walked to the wide windows that looked over the snowy lawn and the street, and with his back turned to her said, "We broke down the door, finally—a regular ambulance call. Sam's mother telephoned us when she got scared enough to forget to be ashamed or proud. He was dead, all right, but the convulsions must have lasted a long time, from the looks of things. He drank almost the whole quart. It was called rye, and if I ever find the bootlegger who sold it I'll kill him. Yes," he said quietly, "I believe I will have to kill him. But how Sam got the clothes is another thing again. They must have been very good-looking, Jennie, before he began to die—the kind you wear. There was a gray silk dress, with a cloche hat and gloves, and underneath he had all the proper pale pink things on, a teddy and all that, but ladylike, not floozy. Little Sammie knew just how to do it. And your case was there on the bed. That's why I was pretty sure you'd be especially interested, Jennie, in a few details that we'll keep out of the newspapers because of public morals, you know. Yes, we'll keep it clean. But you'd better get out."

Jennie asked like a child, "Get out? Why get out, Henry?"

He looked at her finally, and his face was twisted with bitterness, so that he seemed like an old tired sorcerer standing black against the window. "Why get out?" He thought for a minute and then answered softly, with infinite hate, "Because, Jennie, you have a rather unfortunate influence on the youth of Janesville. Because, Jennie—"

She interrupted him coldly, "I can claim no such distinction, simply because one dull and apparently perverted boy steals my vanity case and then proceeds to dress up according to something he read in a textbook on abnormal psychology and poison himself with bad liquor. How could I possibly have anything to do with that? It is horrible, of course, but he is not the only college man in America who has made a mistake in his bootlegger. You're being ridiculous, Henry."

"No, Jennie. You didn't poison the rye yourself. All right. But little Sammie had never in all his mixed-up life drunk more than a courtesy nip, a shot now and then because everyone else had a shot now and then. Little Sammie probably often drank a shot of stuff as bad as this. But after he left you, Jennie, because of whatever it was you said or did to him, he put down almost a quart of it, a gesture, a salute, a proof to himself of something, Jennie. What were *you* trying to prove, maybe?"

He looked at her dispassionately now, as if he were probing at her with long delicate pincers so as not to contaminate himself while he turned her this way and that, poked at this forgotten gesture, that long-gone phrase.

"No, Jennie. Little Sammie is dead, and he was a messy character, it seems, one for the books. But you, Jennie, are one for the books too, and before you manage to help mix up anyone else, anyone like Barbara Janes, for instance, you get out. Yes, Jennie," the tired old sorcerer went on in his flat voice, his hands deep in his pockets and the edge of his white intern jacket showing foolishly beneath his coat, "because I might have to kill you the same way I might have to kill the guy who sold Sam poison and called it rye whisky."

Jennie suddenly felt breathless, drowning in the dark pool of his voice. Words words words, she called out frantically. Talk poured down over her, meaningless unfair lying talk, and she was powerless to stop it, powerless to push it back and away, so that she could be pure Jennie, proud Jennie . . .

She felt Sam's rapacious arms and his claw hands, and knew now how he took her vanity case in his own strange way of paying her back for taunting him, and she knew too, clearly, in a flash, what she had always sensed about the flaw in his manhood, the lack there in him, and his fear and shame. She saw once more the delicate way his fingers had held the silver flask, and how he winced to the first cry of the horns. But how could she say it? What was there she could do to stop the engulfing flow of words?

"Barbara is downstairs. She came here to protect you, I suppose. She's very motherly, really. Dr. Janes and I beat her here, and he's downstairs with her. She knew Sam pretty well. Grew up with him. It might be a good idea for you to take one good look at her and see what kind of poison you're selling, Jennie."

Henry walked stiffly across the room and down the hall, and Jennie could hear the soft thump of his steps on the stair carpet.

She looked at the vanity case, dully shining, with the jade seal like a clot of dragon's blood on the cover. It seemed strange to her that she had not even missed it in the two days spent waiting for Barbara to come back. She shrugged. Then the implications of all that Henry had said to her began to wake and twinge in her mind, like a face that has been anesthetized for a tooth extraction, tingling and tweeking and finally thudding awake. Suddenly she was walking through the door and down toward the parlor, outrage hot in her. The unfairness of the words that had overwhelmed her burned them back, and she seemed almost to feel herself float to the top of the pool, free and strong.

Henry she would dispose of, the dour father she would quell, foolish, weak, loving Barbara she would freeze, all with one glance from her wide gray eyes and one cool smile from her inviolate face. Jennie would show them, simply by being Jennie, how cruelly they had misjudged her. And once having shown, she would forgive them.

She stopped outside the open door to the parlor, magnanimous princess, and straightened the belt around her little flat hips and smoothed back the waves of short sleek hair above her pearl-hung ears. They should never know how their crudity had disturbed her.

"But I do," she heard Barbara insist hoarsely. "I do love her, Father!"

Dr. Janes made a furious sound, as if he were about to vomit, and Henry said sharply, "You don't know what you're talking about!"

"Oh, you both make me sick, sick!" Barbara said loudly and began to sob. "You seem to think I'm still a child, that's all. And you seem to think I don't know anything about lesbianism and—and all that. But I do. And this isn't that way at all. Why, Jennie's too old! She's past thirty! If I went in for that sort of thing she simply wouldn't be attractive to me! And she's a little silly, wearing clothes too young for her and hanging around the Sweet Shop and all that—"

Henry gave a snort of grudging laughter. "Don't let her hear you," he said. "It would kill her, Bobs."

"But it wouldn't," the girl said angrily. "Jennie's the sweetest, most broad-minded, most unprejudiced woman in the world."

Doctor Janes groaned and said roughly, "See? Henry, you handle this. I give up. Of all the God-damned confused young ladies—"

"But Father, she is! I love her more than anything in the world. Father," Barbara said with sudden eagerness, as if she had that instant known inspiration, "I want you to marry Jennie! Then you'll see what I mean, and she'll have someone to take care of her when she's old! That's what I've wanted all along. It is, Father. It honestly is!"

Jennie leaned against the wall. She felt tiny and thin, like a whipped child. She thought of the hours she had spent pouring the richness and beauty of herself into this doltish child's heart, and she realized with a shudder that Barbara was like all other young people, and did not even see her, the real Jennie, the regal donor. Barbara had tricked her, just because she wanted to find a companion for her boorish father.

Then she knew, with a new surge of shock, that the girl was lying, and why? why but to escape whole, leaving Jennie dead upon the field, protecting herself and making a fool of her devoted friend. Bored, stupid Barbara had made her feel young and lovely and necessary, and all the time Jennie was invisible to her.

She was sick with a hurt wonder at the ingratitude of people she had been kind to. She turned slowly toward the stairs. The realization of other people's stupidity almost overwhelmed her, past surprise at their treachery, past anger at their lack of understanding. It was stupid, no more and no less than stupid, for this starved, lonely girl to let her dependence on Jennie's beauty turn into a sexual thing. How could she be such a dolt? How could the grim father and the haggard lover let such a thing come about, and then blame the first passing stranger for it? Why must poor Jennie, just because of her generosity, be made a

criminal, accused of arousing unhealthy yearnings in a
naïve girl too ignorant to control herself? Ah, poor Jennie,
betrayed by her own kindness!

"This is a farce," Henry said with loud disgust. "You
forget, I think, that Sam's dead, with your sweet little
friend's vanity box beside him! You forget that, Bobs!"

Without really listening, Jennie heard Barbara begin to
cry again. There was not even protest, she thought wearily,
from the girl who must surely know how slanderous the
words were.

"Sam was on the wrong track all right," Henry went on
brutally above the sound of weeping. "No, let her listen,
Doc. Sam got help, Bobs, whatever he was headed for.
Somebody gave him a good push, just as much as any bootlegger. And it stands to reason—"

"Stop!" Barbara yelled at him. "Shut up! Go away! And
stay away! If that's the way you love me, talking that way,
I'd rather have Jennie than you!"

Her hoarse agonized young voice filled every corner of
the big house. Jennie heard the kitchen door open, and
the heavy feet of Mrs. Tapham run anxiously toward the
parlor.

"I do love Jennie," Barbara shrieked. "Jennie, Jennie!"

There was the sound of a sharp slap, and then nothing,
no more sobs. The doctor said wearily, "That's still the best
treatment, I guess."

And Jennie almost laughed as she sped lightly up the
stairs. How boring it seemed suddenly, and already how
far behind her, all the messy, clumsy noise, all the small-
town histrionics! How wonderful it was to know that never
again would she have to sit breathing the fumes of youth

and hot chocolate in the Sweet Shop, simply because she wanted to give some happiness to a girl incapable of savoring it! How good it was to be gone forever from the cloying adolescence of long talks under the elm trees, ridiculous, pretentious talks about art and poetry!

She shook the last drops of their drowning words from her as she slipped her arms into her fur coat and pulled her beret down jauntily over one eyebrow. She smiled at herself, proud Jennie. At the door she turned back, picked up the heavy silver vanity case from the bed, and put it in her pocket. It felt good there, weighty and solid and beautiful.

Good-by, all the lonely, uncomprehending Janeses of all the Janesvilles in the world, she said. Good-by, all the jealous Henrys, so obvious, so small. She was in flight, free once more. Jennie was free . . .

IV

One

IT SEEMED impossible to Jennie that the train down from Sacramento to San Francisco could have deteriorated so much by 1882. It was a revolting parody of the plush-hung "silver palaces on wheels" that had begun their run so few years before. The minute it pulled out of town she began to regret angrily that she had not, like most of the other passengers, left its filthy, shabby coaches and taken the boat on down the river.

She thought with fatalistic resignation of the sparkling white private cabin she might have had for this last lap of the journey, and the odorous dining saloon, and the swift sliding of the beautiful riverbanks past decks that would seem almost too stable after four days of the increasingly uneven railroad bed from Council Bluffs.

Most of all she thought about water. There was still in her hamper one little bottle of it, boiled mountain water she had bought somewhere up near Truckee from a clean-looking white woman. And there would be almost enough in the restroom, now that more than half the passengers had shifted to the riverboat. But what was almost enough water? She shut a door in her mind against the distaste she felt for her delicate body, so gritty now and begrimed in spite of the gloves she wore constantly, the scarves she kept tied over her soft fine hair, the veils she put on with her bonnets whenever she got down grudgingly with the other people to rush into a station restaurant while the engine was stoked and the train aired. Was there enough water any place in the world to make her feel clean again?

She stared through the dust-filmed window with a depression that she tried to keep shallow. The hills were low and rolling now. It was time to have the conductor take her to the baggage car, for one last change of costume from her row of trunks. She looked about her, to ask some woman to accompany her, and then remembered with a sense of shock that she was the only one left in the coach that for so long had been fat with them and their traveling capes and their quickly melting reserve.

At first it had been almost as good as fresh air, to be free of their genteel squeals when the conductor pointed out bones on the prairies or avalanches in the overhanging mountains, free of their giddiness in the high places and their discreet pattings of Crab Apple Blossom Perfume in the ladies' room. But now, as Jennie looked about and met the bold eyes of men who before had peeked sideways at her over their mustaches, she wished that she had once more the velveteen bulwark of a respectable female on the seat next her.

It was impossible, yes, impossible even for Jennie the inviolate, to go alone to the baggage car, with the kind, impersonal conductor locked ostentatiously outside while she burrowed into her trunks and braced herself against the deadly rocking and rattling of the Silver Palace. Riffraff from Virginia City would wait leeringly for her return, and no high gray velvet collar, no French veil sewn with discreet beads of jet, could hide her womanly discomfiture as she fought to hold herself upright along the lurching aisle.

She looked coldly at the sooty slopes of her brown plaid traveling costume and ran her gloved finger with cruel pleasure over the grit on her cheekbones. Old Harry will have to take me as I am, she thought, and such was her boredom with her physical state that she dwelt teasingly on the possibility that he might well glance once at her and send her packing. Then she shrugged. Not Harry, not after all the money and thought he had spent on her arrival. And Jennie be sent packing, Jennie the princess? She smiled, confident again in her train-weary mind at least, and opened her hamper for the bottle of mountain water and the little silver cup. She would go with them to the horrid closet at the end of the coach, take a final sip, and then pour the rest over her hands, with obvious futility but a sense of pleasant extravagance after the warm stale water she had tried to wash in for so many days.

When she came back she finished eating the English wafers she had bought in Chicago, and then pushed the hamper and its remnants of chocolate and its little linen napkins and the unemptied pots of meat paste and preserved plums far under her seat. Perhaps, she thought voluptuously, some kind old Negro will find it as he scrubs the corner, and will take it home to his starving pickaninnies, or a kind old Irishman.

She grinned faintly at her rush of sentimentality. Kind old Harry, she thought. He is kind truly, and old truly! He is Harry the English swell, the poor fool, to fall in love so late, too late, with Jennie so deathlessly young . . .

As the train slowed in Oakland she leaned back primly against the plush, her face like a smooth stone and her eyes wide and gray behind her veil. She showed no surprise, nor really felt any, when the conductor brought a tall Chinese to stand beside her.

"Got on at the junction, Ma'am," he mumbled with added respect, and went on down the aisle heavy and anxious with duties.

Jennie looked up. "Li?" she asked clearly. "Sir Harry told me of you."

The servant bowed, his hands folded under his wide black sleeves and his coiled queue like a burned muffin on the back of his copper-colored skull.

"Li help Missie," he answered, and Jennie felt as sure as she was Jennie that he could speak English better than her own. Some day I shall find out, she decided. Meanwhile she must look no farther into him than he did into her. She handed him all her checks and tickets and baggage papers, and as she watched him walk lightly down the coach, narrow and tall and like a dry old woman with his bun of hair, she realized that she was almost in San Francisco again.

Her skin crept with an old excitement, and it was as if she held her spiritual breath, waiting to feel once more the Bay beneath her feet, and to smell the hill-torn fog blown eastward from the Gate. When finally she stood forward on the ferry, watching the city come toward her, so big and tumbled now and strong-looking, with the Palace standing up like a square, luxurious giant, she forgot the filthy past days, all of them, the ones on the train and more and more behind those, even filthier. Soot seemed to melt from her into the winy October air, and the little uncouth boat she stood on danced like a filly on the sharp wavelets of the Bay, so that she felt the fine bones of her skeleton move, free and balanced, as she had never felt them anywhere but here.

She saw Li once or twice and smiled to his bow. At the dock she followed him as if she had always done it, through the wild yells of the hotel runners in the ferry shed, out into the ugly cluttered street.

It was typical of old Harry, she thought, that he should wait there for her, massively tweed-hung, beside the little carriage, instead of crossing indiscreetly on the ferry with her. She had forgotten how British he was. It was hard not to smile at his monocle, and at the bareness of his clean-shaved pink skin and his pale slaty eyes. As she walked lightly toward him through the path the Chinese made for her, she looked with a complete impersonality at the well-rubbed wrinkles, the firmly controlled tremblings, of the old man who wanted her so insanely. What a clown, deaf and senile, she thought, full of scorn and pride. Look at him, dressed like a young dandy in his London clothes, with his Chinese slave and his pretty little carriage for his fancy-woman!

"My dear," he said, and bent over her hand. "My dear Jennie!"

She wondered if he would embrace her in front of all the dockside oafs who goggled at the fashionable tableau they played, but then she was in the carriage, alone.

"I shall hope to see you later today, my dear, with your permission," he said politely through the little window, and its heavy curtains hid him before she could nod yes, or say one word to him in the high clear voice she had coached herself to use against his deafness.

She rode dizzily through the rough streets, blind and exhausted, Jennie always, but now ignorant and almost uncaring of where next she would find herself. Where was Li? Where, in plain fact, was she? Was it tact or disinterest that made old Harry thus desert her? What if he had indeed lost his passion, waiting for her to come across such deserts and over such mountains to be his lady-love?

Jennie smiled again at her foolishness. Was she not Jennie? Who would betray her so? Once it might happen, but not twice, not this time. Once she might have had to flee, betrayed for fair, but never again. Now she was armed against the selfishness of the world . . .

The house was small and exquisite and perfumed. Harry was not there. But Li stood waiting, and led her past the rich canopied doorways and up the soft stairs to her apartment, glimmering with rose-embroidered satin and a hundred beveled mirrors. Jennie shed her hateful clothes and walked naked across the pelts of wild leopards into a room where a tub shaped like a gondola swam in the center of the velvet floor, a tub filled with more water than she had ever hoped to see again.

Beside it lay a pair of little slippers, like a ballet dancer's, made of polished snakeskin, with dull horny rattlers instead of buckles on the toes. They were incongruous in all the delicacy and perfume of the room. Jennie pushed at them fondly with her foot as she stepped up into the tub: Harry had remembered everything about her. Harry worshiped her in spite of the fact that he sometimes seemed deliberately to make her hate him for the mockery behind his impenetrable breeding, to laugh as if he recognized a joke about her, her, Jennie, that she would never catch.

Two

JENNIE went down to dinner in her own house, calm as any matron, her shoulders and fine little breasts gleaming above peach taffeta, and about her throat a necklace and pendant of yellow diamonds. She felt them like fire on her skin, and like a triumphant fire inside her, so that in spite of herself she warmed, through them, to the passionate note that had been in their box when Li brought it to her. Sir Harry, of many lives and many wives, begged to be allowed to dine with her, begged that she wear this welcoming trinket, begged . . .

He stood by the English grate, almost slim in black clothes, his face smooth and ruddy. He had an innate gaiety about him, an insouciance in the face of near senility. Jennie felt excited and amused and grateful all at once, and consummately sure of his need for just such daring as her own.

"Sir Harry," she said, curtseying before him after he had looked silently at her as she came toward him, "you are the most charming man I have ever met." She peeked up at him, a picture of gracious femininity, demure worldliness.

He pulled slowly at his long cigarette and then held out one hand to lift her to her feet again. He was strong and sure and did not let her go. His mouth moved lightly against her cheek and down her powdered throat, and she felt him bite once with a soft nibble at the pendant stone of her necklace.

"And you, my dear Jennie, are by far the most amazing whore that I have ever met." He laughed a little. "You are beautiful too, my dear. I am proud of you. I think this arrangement will be a delightful one. And now, will you permit me, this first night, to escort you to your own dinner table?"

Jennie felt a familiar mixture of fury and baffled amusement at the old nobleman's manner with her. She put one hand through his arm, and with the other she pulled reassuringly at the diamonds about her throat. He was impossible thus to tease her. No man had ever acted so before. Jennie, like a princess, was accustomed to the bent knee, the veiled breathless gratitude of any male who knew her. And now this arrogant, mocking dotard laughed as he looked at her and called her whore as if he paid homage with the word. Yes, he was impossible: and he was a gentleman who could teach much to her, a libertine to whom even she could teach very little, a cynic who appreciated her ambitions, above all, a man fantastically rich in a city filled with plutocrats.

"Yes, I fancy I'm safe in saying that I enjoy you more than any woman I've ever known," Sir Harry continued pleasantly as he seated her, and Jennie realized that she felt a little that way about him. We are much alike, she thought. We are gamblers. She leaned toward him across the small beautiful table, conscious that anger and excitement had made her cheeks flush and her eyes brighten. I shall tell him, she thought recklessly. I shall let him know that I feel close to him, not quite cold-blooded as I've always thought . . .

"Of course," he went on, holding a decanter up carefully against the candlelight and frowning a little at the deposit from the amber-red wine, "of course I enjoy a pretty filly more. I have never met a woman yet who could compare with one. Except, perhaps, you, my Jennie. You have the same light-stepping feet—in a clumsier human way, of course."

Jennie laughed helplessly. Li came from behind one of the teakwood screens that made the large dining-room more intimate. Dinner was delightful. There were long white fillets of a local sole. There were grilled truffles from Sir Harry's farm in southern France, sent in olivewood sawdust, he said. There was a haunch of antelope, aromatic as rotting wildflower stalks. Always there was wine in the tall ringing glasses between the candles, and when at last Jennie leaned with schooled caution over a flaming silver bowl of hothouse strawberries, and felt her yellow diamonds swing away warmly from her throat, and touched with respect the crystal stem of another glass, she knew that she was a little drunk. Harry would never guess it: of that she was sure. She had skirted the edges of inebriation too often and too expertly to let anything trip her now, this night when she must lay all her plans. She held out her glass through the light and let her face glow upward toward the old man's.

"Tokay," he said abruptly and took the bottle from Li's hands. "Thank you, Li. Good night." The shadowy Chinese bowed and faded behind a screen. "Tokay is your wine, Jennie. We shall serve it always here, in your house. I should like to kiss you."

She smiled at him, knowing that in the clear light from the candles and the fire her skin shimmered, her hair gleamed, her whole body sent out a fog of desirability.

"But I think not," Sir Harry went on, pouring the golden wine slowly into their glasses. "This is Tokaj Aszu, more than thirty years old—fit for you, my dear. I have laid down a good cellar here, most of it this sweet fiery stuff. We must always serve it in your house. It is like you. You are heady as hell. And now—" he rose as slowly as he had poured and stood stonily beside her while his glass touched hers with a small fine ringing note— "now I want to drink to Tokay Jennie."

She watched him with her wide eyes sleepy and laughing. That this old tipsy body could move her was a constant surprise, and was, she admitted, one good reason for her being here at all. But the way he stood so breezily in his swell clothes, and the way he taunted her and yet spoke to her prince-like, it all made her wish that she could stop being Jennie for a few days, a few hours, to drink with him and love what was left of his nobility.

"Tokay Jennie?" she asked coldly.

He nudged his glass against hers again, and she sipped in spite of herself. "Yes, my dear. What could be more flattering than for me to call a racehorse after you? It is the nearest thing I have ever come to a proclamation of love. But I need not tell you that the name is a private one. My filly will wear it, and proudly, but in this God-forsaken outpost you are to be known only as Jennie. The fact that you serve superlative Tokay will be taken as nothing more than a proof of my good taste—as will you yourself. The joke is one between the two of us."

She stood up carefully and walked to the fireplace where Li had left two little plush-covered armchairs knee-high with knotted fringe.

"It is apparently time to talk," she said, and as she sat down she wanted to throw her wine into the flames, in outrage and anger at the insolence of Sir Harry's knowledge of her. Instead she sipped and smiled up tenderly at him.

He leaned against the draped mantel for a minute, looking at her fine hair, her skin, her little body, with a dispassionate regret loud in his eyes. He sighed and sat down in sections, older than at any time that day, in the chair across from her.

"Yes, Jennie, Tokay Jennie. Hold out your glass. This wine becomes you. Did I say that?"

She saw his big wattled hands tighten on the bottle, as if he called all his nerves nippingly into line against the warmth and the wine and the years, and then his voice sounded firm again and young across the firelight.

"Jennie, you are everything I knew when I first met you. You have carried out all my wishes. Your clothes are perfect. And now what I want you to do is wear them, and more of them made here or ordered from Paris, and act as my hostess. This house is yours. Li will run it for you and will take care of all the marketing and such. He will bring the bills to me. I have purposely not hired a maid for you —they are all gossips in this sprawling village—and one of Li's relatives will care for your clothes. I want you to entertain here for me, in this room and in the cardroom, which you have not yet seen. I refuse to call you my niece, my sister-in-law, as so many of our lonely citizens find it necessary to do with their mistresses."

"That's plain talk," Jennie said in the high clear voice that was for his ears.

"As always, my dear. Don't bother to act ladylike with me. In public you are an exquisite well-mannered creature who will never be received socially by the millionaire barmaids and ex-midwives of San Francisco. In private you are the God-honest female who can say what she likes to me and know herself worth ten thousand of the matrons who will spit on her. You are, Jennie. And they will. Your life here will be lonely. The best you can do is strike up an occasional low-bitch friendship with the painted lightie of one of my poker-companions."

She shrugged. "I'm not afraid of being alone," she said casually.

"That's one reason you're here. Drink more, my dear. This wine is made for you, of small rich, ripe, frost-bitten grapes. It has fire in it." They touched glasses again, and the coals slipped down in the grate. "Lovely, lonely Jennie! But I shall deposit fifteen hundred dollars a month to your own account at the Wells Fargo bank. Here is your check book on the table," and he slapped it down, smiling, among the fruits and the jewel-studded coffee cups. "The house bills will be paid, as I said, by Li. Li has always done that for me. What you yourself must do is be ready to entertain my friends at dinner, to go with me to the theater."

"What of my costumes?"

"Can you not manage them on that sum?"

"No."

"Then I shall open charge accounts for you tomorrow." Jennie laughed. "Thank you," she said demurely.

Harry lifted his glass to her, his ruddy, smooth face empty of the mockery in his voice. "And do you think you can take care of your bonnets with fifteen hundred a month, my dear? Or your fans perhaps?"

"I am doubtful of it," Jennie said. "The theater calls for so many changes. . ."

"We'll purchase them together then, after you have been seen a few times with me. And now are you puzzled about anything?"

Jennie touched one hand gently to her forehead among the little curls and let her eyes stray immeasurably beyond the gilt and leather panels of the dining-room. She knew with some faint embarrassment that her pose looked much like a widely distributed postcard picture of a leading actress, but the wine had taken the fine edge off her caution, and at least it was certain that behind her coy histrionic mask her mind breathed with as cold a breath as ever.

"I? Puzzled? Oh, my dear Harry, you have been so thoughtful! But your friends—who are they? Will I be able to entertain them fittingly?"

Sir Harry stared delightedly at her for a full minute and then tossed down the wine in his glass with a snort of amusement. "Fittingly? You? My dear Jennie, they have seen nothing like you since they left their—in San Francisco we are careful not to inquire where people came from, which is one more reason for your own inevitable success here, but I can assure you that my companions in racing and poker, at least, will appreciate every move you make— as my hostess of course."

They looked thoughtfully at each other. "Li is my confidant as well as my steward," he said at last, and there was soft silence in the room.

Jennie slid forward on the stiff whispering silk of her train and lay against his knees in the firelight. "Your friends shall be my greatest concern," she promised in a murmur that made him bend close to her. "I shall do whatever I can to please them, Harry."

She laid her head like a child against his hand, so that even when he kissed her he could not see the triumph and the ferocious excitement in her wide gray eyes. Jennie was busy, once having caught the scent.

"Yes, I shall try to make them happy," she swore gently.

Three

THE intricacies of Sir Harry's presentation of Jennie to San Francisco were a constantly amusing game to her. Each night he would give her directions for the next day's moves, like a chess master instructing his pupil: she might shop from eleven until one, wearing her gray taffeta costume with the sealskin sacque, no jewels, and no veil; at three he had arranged for Madame Jamison to come to give her a fitting for her new riding-habits; there would be five gentlemen for dinner at eight-thirty, with poker later.

Or he would call for her at four o'clock and take her to look at the new imported laces at Newman and Levinson's, and bow ironically to the fat curious ladies who smiled at him and stared angrily at her over their high trussed bosoms.

Or on Sundays they would go dashingly through the sandy wind-swept Park in his shiny flyer, to the Figure-Eight Drive, where Jennie knew by the glances of other beautiful women sitting beside their "gay blades" that her ankle-length skirts and her little Homburg were the most stylish within five thousand miles of the Golden Gate.

Gradually the blades began to bow to her, their hostess of the week before. Jennie smiled, and let her hand rest with discreet implication on the crook of Sir Harry's formidable length of arm, and looked through the blades' companions as if they were fog, knowing herself to be the same.

Familiarity with loneliness had bred a fine contempt for it in her, and she found her days too short. She grew to enjoy Li's midmorning consultations, along with all the other diversions: he told her in his thin high voice what each night's menu would be, and gourmande Jennie learned dishes she had never dreamed of.

"Do you Chinamen eat ground squirrels, Li?" she once asked teasingly, and he said, "Railroad coolies, perhaps, Miss. But Li eat abalones."

"Li, get abalones for me," she begged.

That night they were served, and the rich white gentlemen who ate them in Jennie's warm dining-room were as excited as children with forbidden sweets. Sir Harry praised her for her daring, and Jennie looked at Li, and smiled, and led him on to find other Chinese delicacies among the local inedibles for her, so that her exotic little banquets grew to be talked of in the Union Club and the Bohemian, and the Russ House bar.

"Li, let the peddlers come up here," she asked once, sure

that he would not, but the next day into her rose-silk room two short Chinese stepped with little bows and cluckings, and spread squares of yellow cotton on the carpet, and Jennie bought porcelain cups and a box of silver-lacquered wood with twenty tiny drawers inside it, and some powdered sandalwood. When they stood up and tied their yellow bundles neatly again, they left little presents for her: incense, a tight grass basket packed with rose tea, carved black chopsticks.

Once a silk merchant came, and she bought lengths of cloth as delicate as moonlight, with poems woven into the edges. And once she sniffed at a wee box of white powder held out to her, and Li caught the peddler a cruel blow across the head and kicked him moaning from the room, with never a word to Jennie afterward about it.

For a while there were no more such scented visits, but still Li told her when the men with flowers and fish and vegetables came, and she stood in the pantry watching through the door and laughed like a child at the singsong haggling. He paid for the fresh clean food, as he did for her silks and teacups, from some bottomless pocket under his black robe, and bowed a little more deeply to her, his eyes invisible, when he gave her the flowers or the beautiful grapes or the polished sea shells that the men left as their thank-offerings.

Jennie went back to her soft carpets regretfully after those noisy meetings, and found herself pretending new reasons for Li to consult with her, drawn as she was by his silent intelligence. It was, perhaps, her one admission that she needed anyone other than herself and Sir Harry in the town of shut doors and shut faces. Certainly she preferred Li's almost affected pidgin English to the artificialities of one or two women she went shopping with, girls Harry always referred to as lighties.

She called for them in her little carriage, very properly, and they exchanged ladylike chitchat about nothing, and walked primly up and down the board sidewalks of fashionable Kearney Street, looking in the shop windows, and went to the Viennese bakery for coffee and little frosted cakes, just as if they lived on Nob Hill and were not well-paid refugees from the red-light district. Then Jennie took them to their charming little houses, so much like her own, and when they met a few nights later in her drawing-room they laughed with gay shrugs and grimaces at the provincial amusements of San Francisco, and Jennie looked at them over her glass of Tokay and loathed them, and Harry for forcing her to entertain them. She never loathed herself, being Jennie.

Once she went with Harry to Dupont Street, and there was Li standing in a doorway waiting for them, and they drank tea and listened to girls sing and bought spinach jade.

And, of course, there was the theater often, with Jennie blazing in a new costume every night, sure of Harry's pride in her. One time she wore stuffed humming-birds from the Amazon wired into her hair and the shoulders of her gown, so that they trembled and fluttered as if they were alive. Every opera glass in the dress circle of the Baldwin fixed on her, and she lifted her head high, tiny princess Jennie.

Life grew gayer. There were parties, late ones, when Harry would call for her after a ball on the Hill and take her with some of the giddier guests from it to the Poodle Dog or Marchand's, and Jennie would listen to talk of the evening's splendors and despise the fat snobs who had not dared ask her to share them. She drank a great deal of champagne, glad to escape from the rich nightly rounds of her own Tokay, and Li without consulting her had the old Negress Liza Bellamy come and bathe and rub her with her famous restorative unguents after such parties, so that by noon Jennie felt calm and smooth again.

Liza knew every courtesan in San Francisco, and most of the snobs too, and it was fun to talk with her. She told Jennie things about the gentlemen Sir Harry brought there. She gave Jennie powders and salves now and then, all magical, and Li paid for them. Jennie felt that she had two allies, both tacit, a Chinese steward with a pigtail rolled on his skull, and an old colored woman in a notorious white starched sunbonnet. She lay purring under the bony hands that smoothed at her so sensitively, and was certain that when she asked Li to put this or that powder of Liza Bellamy's into the coffee or the wine, he would understand her.

The first time she used one, except on herself, was the night she knew Marc Raphael would ask her to leave Sir Harry for his own equally unlimited fortunes and fornications. He had looked seriously at her with his long dark eyes over several dinner tables, and she knew increasingly as she passed near him with the carved box of fine cigars, before she left the gentlemen to their cards and whisky after one of her little banquets, that he planned a move to get her. She wondered how he would do it, there so close to old Harry's lordly nose.

His final attack was audacious. "Harry," he said abruptly, as Jennie turned to leave the room to her guests and sink happily into the gondola of warm perfumed water she knew awaited her upstairs, "I've seldom pretended to be a gentleman, but, by God, I shall have to stop coming here as long as you disturb me with your lovely lady."

Harry looked up from the cards he was arranging. His face was smooth and ruddy as ever, and his voice showed only a trace of the intolerable tolerance Jennie knew was there.

"Marc, old boy, you're gentleman enough for these parts," he observed.

The young man bit at his lip, and then, miserably unmanned by a granddad, stared full at Jennie.

She looked away.

The other men humphed and harrumphed uneasily, while Sir Harry tapped at his cards and rubbed one speckled old hand gently against his beak.

Jennie turned with a little rush of lace and silk petticoats and clicking satin heels and ran to her apartment. Now was the time, she knew, to try what Liza Bellamy had whispered to her. From the silver box with twenty tiny drawers she took a brown cigarette paper folded small as a pea, and then she ran down again into the pantry.

Li stood there, ready to leave as always at ten each night for his own pleasures. He looked at her and past her, and when she said, "Another bottle of wine before you go," he brought out one of the oldest Aszus as if he were waiting for her request, and she was not surprised to find it uncorked. He put glasses on a tray and then stood back against the door to the outside, his hands in their sleeves and his eyes covered with his bird-eyelids.

"Good night, Li," Jennie said slowly. She turned from him, so sure that she would hear the door close that she did not consciously listen, and equally sure that if she did listen she would never hear him walk down the boarded path to the street.

In a minute, thoughtfully, she unfolded the little brown curd of paper in her hand and tipped its powder into her palm. Then she picked up the silver tray with the bottle and all the glasses on it and carried it as if it were a sea shell down the long warm hall and to the cardroom.

The men sat almost as she had left them, and looked up with jovial relief when she stood in the doorway. Harry still tapped at the clean cards. Marc Raphael still stared miserably at her, as if his eyes had never left the spot where he had last fixed them upon her.

"My dear Sir Harry," she said softly and let the tray tip a little, as if unbearably burdened. At that they all sprang toward her, except the old Englishman who still sat on, smoothly. Raphael caught the tray an instant before it seemed ready to crash, and Jennie swayed exhaustedly into the room and leaned against the thick brocade and gold fringe of the mantelpiece lambrequin. Harry looked impersonally at her, and she felt angry enough to hit at him, and yet cool because of the powder in her hand and what dark Bellamy had said it would do. Harry is a fool, she said to herself. She smiled at him, and he smiled back, prompt lover.

"Tonight I felt—I felt with all of you here," she said, making a circle with her little hand to draw each fat, overstuffed adventurer nearer to her, "that I was back in Buda-Pesth—Sir Harry, you remember?—I felt that we were gay again, and young . . ." She looked like a homesick troubled child.

Harry rose at last. "I too, Jennie," he said. "Jennie, my dear friends here in this magnificent outpost, shall we drink to an older civilization?"

Jennie trembled with rage. He was overplaying it in such obvious mockery of her that even these fools would see.

But they bowed humbly over their glasses as Harry reverently poured the gold liquor, and then she gave one to each man, and Harry and his whole crew lifted them to her, tiny, exquisite, and she smiled a tiny exquisite smile to reward them. Marc Raphael, young and dark and troubled, drank down the Negress's powder with the wine and stood back politely, feeling somewhat assuaged. Jennie bade the room a gentle good night and retired contentedly to her gondola of tepid but still perfumed water.

It would take about twenty-four hours, Liza had told her.

Four

JENNIE always slept like an untroubled child, but it seemed to her that she had never felt fresher nor more rested than she did the next morning, as she talked happily from her nest of pink ruffled pillows to Li.

He stood like a thin white cotton post with a carved nob on top, his hands hidden, while he told Jennie of the night's menu. There would be eight gentlemen, Sir Harry had told him.

Jennie smiled. There would be one, she said surely to herself.

Sir Harry wished a full dinner, Li went on, with a buffet Russe beforehand and both game and roast.

There would be a light supper, Jennie said silently, of oysters, grilled quail perhaps, and a soufflé.

Sir Harry wished both white and red Bordeaux and a red Burgundy to be served, with Tokay and liqueurs and later his own Scotch.

There will be champagne, Jennie went on to herself while she smiled at Li and nodded, and later there will be more champagne.

She discussed the way Li had last served venison and agreed with him that it might be better to substitute a roast of beef in the English style tonight, and a clear soup after the buffet instead of the rich creamy one Sir Harry always wanted. And instead of a Roman punch after the roast, why not serve a well-chilled salad of chicken with mayonnaise, to lighten the pattern of the meal? Li bowed approvingly. The fish would be sole, of course, and could he not make an aspic of the little Bay shrimps to follow the salad and precede the game? Li bowed again.

Jennie went on, almost breathless with amusement at the game she played, and decided that a pudding of apricots served with an egg cream could easily be followed by one of Sir Harry's required savories, tonight made with anchovies baked in little puff-paste cases. She checked the plan once more, agreed with Li that the tiny local shrimps would be a sensation among a group of gentlemen who thought that all shell fish must come in tins from the East to be socially acceptable or even edible, and then she lay back, waiting in her pillows for word to come that the dinner must be postponed, as she knew surely that it would be, because Liza Bellamy herself had made the little powder . . .

At noon a messenger arrived with a sealed packet from Colonel Andrew's Diamond Palace. "Wear these tonight!" begged the perfumed card that lay upon the parure of topazes, and so sure of her plans was Jennie that she was surprised for a second that it was Harry who had sent them. He still believed he would see her at dinner then! She smiled and waited.

Li's cousin came and carried away a great wicker box of clothes to be freshened. Mademoiselle Alice called in person to say that a new shipment of bonnets from Paris was at that very moment being unwrapped and would be ready to view the next day. Jennie experimented with a pomade that promised to improve her bust magically and then washed it off what could obviously not be bettered, even by coconut milk and whatever unnamed ingredients the nostrum contained.

By then it was three o'clock, but she was unruffled.

Fifteen minutes later, as she read the advertisements in a month-old copy of the *New York Times*, Li knocked at her door, and she knew before he spoke that the dinner party was postponed. Sir Harry sent all his apologies: unexpected business in Los Angeles . . . return in six days . . . reach him in care of Mr. Baldwin at Santa Anita if necessary . . .

"But the gentlemen who are invited for tonight?" Jennie

asked, putting one hand to her forehead like a proper little housewife and staring up anxiously from under her curls, while inside she smiled with delight.

"Sir Harry tell, all gentlemen say all right, come next week."

"But the dinner, Li! All your beautiful food!"

"Li fix. Missie have little supper, maybe. Li rest, maybe go Dupont Street. Missie all right." He bowed and left her.

Jennie could finally laugh aloud. She felt gay and excited, like an actress who knows that she is playing her best part better than anyone else could ever do it. She called Li back into the room and asked him to go for Liza Bellamy: since she would be alone tonight, it seemed wise to rest completely and have a massage, an oil bath, a "treatment."

Li nodded wordlessly, and within a few minutes brought the old woman to the door. Jennie grinned into her dour face, framed in the starched white sunbonnet that none had ever seen her untie and take off.

"Did you do what I told you to, Jennie?" she asked severely, like a teacher.

Jennie nodded.

"Sir Harry is gone away then, as I told you he would?"

Again Jennie nodded, her wide gray eyes dancing.

Liza tossed her head. "You see? I tell you a thing and all you have to do is believe me, Jennie, because what I tell you will always happen. I have powers unnatural to white people, unnatural to most people in the wide world, I tell you."

She sounded as if she were scolding. Jennie nodded like

a child to her phrases and, reaching out, she pulled the old woman's hand to her and rubbed her cheek softly against it.

"Now I tell you to make yourself ready, Jennie," Liza went on as if she were lecturing instead of pouring a full pitcher of happiness into the other woman's heart. "I tell you to trust me and make yourself ready, whilst I go down and confer and consult and decide with old Sir Harry's Chinaman, and then whilst I go out to deliver a certain message to a certain white man."

She pulled her hand austerely from Jennie's soft loving grasp and tightened the starched bow of her sunbonnet. "There is still much to be done. But trust Liza Bellamy, Jennie, and you are as a plain fact trusting God Himself. So get up off that sofa and set yourself to rights. I shall return before you know it."

By the time Li came in to light the lamps Jennie was bathed and sweet smelling, in a peignoir edged with ermine. He wore his street clothes. At the door he turned and said in his thin high voice, "Li go tonight to family funeral. Bellamy stay here. Li fix little supper, two people, Missie and Bellamy maybe. Fine oysters all ready, quail, Bellamy make soufflé."

He turned to go. Jennie held her breath, waiting for one more thing to happen as it should, and he said as the door closed, "Missie sad alone maybe, so champagne in ice-chest."

Jennie kicked her feet recklessly high over her head as she fell back on the sofa and laughed like a boy, looking up at her gleaming little toenails and thinking of the pinch of powder, ram-horn ground in the moon's full perhaps, and of the way it came when and as and how she needed it.

At eight o'clock Marc Raphael was shown into the rich dining-room, where light from the little English grate shone on the leather and the carved wood and on the glasses set just so upon the damask cloth. Liza Bellamy summoned Jennie, who came down like a golden cloud, with topazes from Harry in her ears, her hair, her half-bared bosom, topazes in a heavy circlet about her golden throat.

"Mr. Raphael," she said softly, as if the sight of him were almost too much for her credulity. She made a low curtsey, and he dropped his elbow sharply from the draped marble mantelpiece and brought his slim heels together in a bow that betrayed God knows what hidden background of student-corps and duelling-school precision.

"Mr. Raphael," she sighed again, lifting her wide eyes to his face, and he flushed.

"Jennie—the nigger-woman sent word to me—I am your guest tonight." He bent slowly to her, and she let herself be lifted, light as a golden feather, into the avid circle of his arms.

The next afternoon Liza Bellamy informed her of what had been deposited that day to her account at Wells Fargo, and Jennie in turn handed another check to her ally and then put pomade delicately upon her lips for her rendezvous with Marc Raphael at Mademoiselle Alice's bonnet shop. Once there, she made it plain that a wager was to be paid off, a strictly decorous gaming debt, and with laughs straight from the last production at the Baldwin Theater she let the hollow-eyed blood pay for three mounds of maline and gauze and feathers, which she watched the apprentices pack into round paper boxes for her. Then she and Raphael walked out into the foggy dusk, two separate human beings.

Once on the sidewalk she put her tightly gloved hand for a second on his arm, time enough to feel him start away from it.

"May I come?" he asked with the voice of a hoarse boy.

But Jennie knew better than to nod yes, for had not Liza told her? "You? Tonight? To my house?" Her voice was incredulous, and she made a birdlike mocking sound. "My dear Mr. Raphael! I hope to see you sometime next week, for dinner—Sir Harry will tell you the night. This has been delightful. And if you will please see me into my carriage . . ."

The young man, his eyes veiled and his face anciently polite, bowed her away, and then stood for several minutes in the filthy gutter mud thinking of her sweet cries in the night, before he walked stolidly to his club.

Jennie, on the other hand, unwrapped the bonnets happily in her rose-silk apartment, and then looked once, very quickly, at her check book before she climbed into the gondola full of water. That night she pulled her hair back from her forehead and oiled herself with honey-and-almond balm.

In the morning Li appeared, as if he had never been gone two nights to a family funeral. "Sir Harry telegram, only to Santa Maria. So eight gentlemen for dinner tonight, late, for dinner party," he said, bowing. "Missy think shrimp good after the chicken mayonnaise, like other day?"

Jennie sighed. Already she could taste the Tokaj Aszu

under her tongue, and feel Harry's mocking eyes slatily upon her. "Liza has gone then?" she asked.

"Liza?" The Chinese shrugged a little. "Missie think maybe a mousse of vanilla, no apricots?"

Five

JENNIE wore her topaz parure to the dinner that night, and there was no more explanation of a little red kiss-bite on her throat than there was of Sir Harry's sudden return from Santa Maria, less than half his announced journey away from her. He was smooth-faced and suavely laughing, and she was, if possible, more charming than she had ever been.

The eight gentlemen turned their heads toward her as if she were their sun, while Harry smiled, and Jennie guided talk to the hunting in the antelope valleys to the south, and got a promise of game for her table such as no African queen had ever seen. Two weeks from tonight, she promised, her head high behind her glass of Tokay, two weeks from tonight a soft omelet with antelope tongues wrapped in the eggs, and Sir Harry's truffles from Provence minced finely among them! The gentlemen's eyes glistened and searched out her stone-crowned breasts. Jennie laughed and tilted her wrist high under its bracelet when Harry nodded heavily to her and gave a toast in French, his slate eyes dancing.

But later, alone, he was, as much as he ever could be or had been, her slave. She hated him, and made him dance before her, and then suddenly forgave him and fell sobbing prettily into his still powerful arms, while her mind crept with the memory of Horace James the shipper, who had stared at her since he first came into her house that night. He was a new one. She must ask Liza Bellamy tomorrow. Meanwhile she drank more Tokay and laughed when Sir Harry solemnly poured a little from his glass into her navel.

Horace James, said Liza, was from Philadelphia, at least lately. The girls told her he was mean. They said he knew a lot of things.

Jennie lay quietly under the black hands, listening, and in two weeks when the gentlemen smacked their way through the great soft fine omelet studded with tender tongues she let James stare at her until she saw Sir Harry watching the two of them. She smiled and then looked back into the small hard eyes of the merchant-shipper.

The next time he came she put one of the powders, spilling out tight as a brown pea from its paper, into his Tokay. Within a few hours Harry started suddenly for Sacramento, and Bellamy came and Li disappeared, and Jennie and the ship owner spent three days together, mostly in her apartment, but also in one indiscreet, beautiful ride through the Park toward the fog-bound sea, with the horses' hooves invisible and even the granite face next to Jennie's own soft one acceptable for once. Home again, Jennie made toast in the grate and warmed a ragout Bellamy had left for the two of them. The next morning the colored woman stood beside her bed, and Jennie looked contentedly at her deposit book and signed a check for Liza, and turned over and slept like a child until Sir Harry stood in Liza's place, his face travel-thin and his gray-white eyes mocking and hungry.

There was a pause then: Jennie felt a profound satisfaction at the state of her bank account, with no need to work for once. She kept on buying finer and finer jades from the Chinese who came up especially from Dupont Street, and now and then she let herself fall into the pleasurable trap of an ordinary peddler, who might show to her a wee enameled singing bird in a cage lacquered with kingfisher feathers, or a five-paneled screen no bigger than a tooth-pick case. Li paid for all such toys, and Liza Bellamy rubbed and soothed her daily with never a word of pay. Jennie let herself grow whiter, softer. Even the Tokaj Aszu tasted good again, and when Harry told his interminable stories of leopard hunts and jungle-beaters she smiled gently at him. It was a kind of Indian summer, full and fallow.

Everything changed, as it must, when Jennie almost fell in love. That was with Coll Hemingway, who was younger than she and owned more pretty horses than Sir Harry. He wore black uptilted mustaches, like a Prussian, but even so the French colony in San Francisco loved him for his good Parisian accent and his taste in claret and jewels and the women who wore them. Jennie knew poignantly that on his arm she could enter drawing-rooms where not even a titled Englishman would be able to take her, and for the first time in her life social implications became entangled with her purely sexual plans. She dreamed of leading a cotillion, of standing in a receiving line when a young girl made her debut, of bowing on Sunday afternoons to other ladies, *other ladies*, in Golden Gate Park.

"Coll darling," she dreamed she would say, looking up at him from the Dresden teacup in a Nob Hill music room, "Coll darling, tell Millicent our plans for next summer in Bad Nauheim. . . . Yes," she would drawl among the white marble and mirrors of Colonel Andrews' showroom, "have the tiara sent to Mrs. Hemingway, at the country house in Burlingame. . . . Oh, Coll," she would say from his lean black-haired arms, for she was still Jennie even in her dreams, and all of them ended properly in bed or at least upon a silken sofa, "Coll . . ."

Liza Bellamy looked dourly down upon her as she lay feverish and tearful in the rumpled pillows. "I tell you, Jennie, and you listen well to me, that you are acting very foolish. You can't play with what I tell you to do and give you to do with, that's all. You use my medicine properly, and what happens will happen. But you can't change in the middle of the happenings, Jennie. Have I ever failed you? You tell me that, now."

Jennie shook her head and tried to look away from the proud old woman.

"No, I have not. Haven't I always made Sir Harry leave you, and then told you when he would be coming back?"

Jennie nodded, pouting.

Liza drew herself up taller and spoke even more sternly. "Well, you remember all that and behave yourself with gratitude then. I tell you Sir Harry is in Sacramento for at least two more days. You have two more days with Hemingway. Enjoy them, I tell you."

"But that's it, Liza—two more days! I want him every day, always!"

The Negress snorted. "Isn't any charm in the world, Jennie, can get you that! You shake these notions out of your head now and have some more pleasure! Anyway, my medicine makes the gentlemen want more, doesn't it? Mr. Raphael still comes back, doesn't he, begging at your very bedside? Mr. James still begs at your very bedside, doesn't he? Well, you see if Coll Hemingway doesn't arrive to join them!" She laughed fiercely. "Three fine gentlemen, three dogs in heat! They are your slaves, I tell you right here and now, Jennie."

"But that's it, that's it," Jennie moaned. "I don't want a slave. I want Coll Hemingway, the man Coll, all of him."

"Scat! You are acting very foolish, Jennie, I tell you. A girl like you will always have slaves, and there's no way to change it, no charm even I could make for you. Mr. Hemingway will come back, and he will make your bank book look finer than you ever dreamed of, Jennie, but you get any silly notions out of your head, is all I can tell you. Here"—she turned her back on Jennie and felt deftly up under the brim of her sunbonnet—"here's a little sweet powder. You take it and rest, and you will be so pretty to-night you will forget all about these silly notions."

She put the medicine in water, watched sharply while Jennie drank it, and then rinsed out the glass and went to the door. "You can have almost anything in the world if you do what I tell you and use what I make for you to use—almost, I say!" She tossed back her head with a proud angry laugh, a puff of laughter, and she left.

True enough, Jennie rested pleasantly that afternoon,

and by nightfall was so happy to see her lover that she went without any thought that only a whore would do it to an apartment on the disreputable floor of a highly reputable hotel, where they dined well and then watched other delights through little windows of stylish many-paned glass. The next day was the same: fevered regretful dreams in the morning, and then one of Liza's powders and a night full of excitements and satisfactions. And on the third morning when Jennie wrote a check for her witch and saw from what newly fattened sum she drew it, she lay back smiling, sure that Coll Hemingway would not forget her, even though he might never lead her across the Palace ballroom on his arm.

Li and Sir Harry returned within a few minutes of each other, as usual, laden with gifts. Jennie fingered the necklace of carved coral hung with pearls and listened to the draymen bring in cases of new Keller wines from Los Angeles, and smelled the delicate perfume of the fine tea the Chinese servant brought to her in a milk-green cup sent by his mother from Canton.

She was seen more with Sir Harry for a time and went often to the races with him, to watch her colors of rose and gold come home first. He brought a jockey from Chicago to ride Tokay Jennie and no other horse, and when they stood up at the finish more glasses were turned on the famous pretty woman than on the filly named for her. Jennie smiled through the cold stares of the ladies and held out her little gloved hand like a princess, a queen, to the bloods and the fat bankers who bent over it. Her costumes grew more exquisite as Sir Harry's pride in her demanded new proofs of his skill in picking horses and mistresses, and Jennie began to wear some of the jewels other men had given her, sure of the old Englishman's blind pleasure at the sight of her.

As for her generous lovers, she called back James and especially Marc Raphael whenever Harry left for Santa Anita or the horse-trading in Sacramento, to help her forget the nagging fever Coll Hemingway always left her in. And Liza Bellamy helped her add two more to her list, the rich young Spaniard Sanchez from San Diego County and a banker, Hemingway's partner in the city. Jennie felt full of power and confidence. She gave Liza a bonus once, and kissed the thin skillful black hands, and wished there were some largesse in the world that she could pour out upon her other ally, the pig-tailed steward of her house and destiny, Li the Chinese.

Six

ONE day Sir Harry came earlier than usual to her apartment. Li knocked at the door of the smaller room, where Jennie dried herself after her bath. "Master here," he said in his clear voice. "Master wait."

There was nothing to do but hasten, a thing Jennie despised. She patted a touch of a new embellishing-wax upon her throat, just for the fun of it and to see what liars the newspapers could be, and then with a grin at herself snapped on a high collar of garnets and gold. Marc Raphael had given it to her, the night before he was married and tried to drive his rockaway over the cliffs near the

< 234 >

beach. She thought of his bandaged head as she had last seen it at the races, and his bitter pale face beside his bride's. The necklace felt good, heavy and solid and full of worth.

Jennie put on her lightest corsets, the ones with the rose-colored silk lacings that Harry loved to tighten for her, and a thin peignoir. She rubbed some attar of roses, a gray gritty salve sent from gardens near Nice in France, under her arms and upon her nipples and earlobes, and then walked with a completely natural regality into the other room.

Harry stood, a Gibraltar-like bulwark of unconventional tweed, upon the hearth. Behind him the little fire crackled, and Jennie could smell the dried flower petals Li always put upon it at this hour. There was a tray on an inlaid table before her sofa, with two glasses on it and the dread familiar shape of a bottle of Tokay.

"Dear Sir Harry," she murmured, close to his massive old ear.

"My dear little Jennie," he said in a matter-of-fact voice and with a fleetingly passionate palping of her left breast. "My dear Jennie—I say, shall we have a talk? It's about time, you know. I mean—well, you've been here several months now and all that."

"Oh, for God's sake, Harry, stop chuffing and huffing!"

He stared at her like a wounded lion through his monocle and then put back his handsome head and roared with delight. "By God, Jennie, but I adore you," he said finally, as if with that statement he conferred on her a celestial order of merit complete with wings made of dia-mond-dust. "Chuffing and huffing!" He gazed jauntily down at her. "That's what it must be, my dear. I'm broke."

Jennie listened to the flower petals crinkle into ash on the coals and felt the attar of roses burn under her arms. Her corsets were unfamiliarly loose. "Harry," she cried out sweetly in the high voice made for his deafness, and she lifted her peignoir, and the old man bent over her, pulling and tugging discreetly, his eyes everywhere but on the fine embroidered places for the strings to go.

"What did you say, you beast?" she asked softly a few minutes later.

He shook his head helplessly.

"The huffing and all that sort of thing, old dear," she mimicked.

There was a little silence, and then Sir Harry pushed her from him and sat down with a thump upon her rose-satin slipper-chair.

"Yes. Yes, that," he said at last. "Jennie my dear, I need some money from you. I hate like the devil to ask it, but my checks from London are slow in the coming, slower than usual this month unfortunately, and I can only tell you that I'll put back twice what I—what I must borrow from you."

She touched one finger delicately upon her brow and let her mouth droop like a tired angel's. Then she sighed.

"Well," he asked at last brusquely, "what about it, my dear?"

"But my dear Sir Harry, much as I adore you . . ."

"Look here, old girl . . ." He sounded furious for a second and then changed his voice back to at least a shadow of its old jovial monotony. "Look, my dear Jennie, I have put fifteen hundred dollars every month into your account.

I have paid all the bills for this little place of yours. Li has made a full accounting to me. I have paid Li. Through him I have paid your somewhat unusual confidante Bellamy. Furthermore I have paid several times the amount I planned to your milliner and dressmakers and habitmakers, and God knows what I still owe to the Dublin saddler who cut such a wide path through San Francisco two months ago. Furthermore, my dear," he added as he watched Jennie pull herself stiff in her skin, every bone as long with hauteur as a human bone could be, and her head perched like a female quail's upon its gleaming neck, "furthermore I have not failed to give you all the respect, admiration, adulation—"

Suddenly his voice choked, and Jennie was astounded to see that he was laughing. She could not believe it for a moment. But there were his slate-blue eyes dancing at her. There was his toothy mouth stretched into a caricature of a stifled roar of mirth. She caught his look and forced him, as if she slashed a little whip across his red face, to *stop*.

"My dear," he said finally, "I do adore you. You are the damnedest little tart in all the West, and you damn well know it. And I believe that you are also the best paid."

Jennie turned away from him. She walked like a cat to the low table with the wine on it and poured two glasses full to the brim. Then she picked them up, and stepping back to where the old nobleman stood, she held one out to him and let her fingers rest with an insulting languor on his as he took it, and then lifted her own to her lips.

"May I drink to you with your wine?" she asked sweetly.

Harry looked at her and then said, "Now, I say, Jennie!

Stop it, old dear! It's your wine, this! You damn well know it is. And you've paid me for it as no other woman could. But the whole thing is, will you let me have some of your money, on tick as it were? I need it now. I need it tonight, or at the latest tomorrow night. In two more days you shall have it back. Give me a check for fifty thousand dollars. In two days you get back double. I'm not begging you for it, Jennie. I'm telling you that you must. Don't be a little God-damned fool now, at this point in your life."

Jennie looked at him leaning toward her, with the firelight kind to his craggy face. She smelled the fog on his clothes. She knew the aristocracy of his bones in their decaying flesh. She remembered the mockery and the live recognition of her as less than a princess in his slaty eyes, and his last burst of laughter, and without hesitation she said, "No."

Finally he asked, almost sadly, "Are you sure, my dear?"

Again without hesitation she said, "Yes, I am sure. I have no money that I can lend you."

Silently she sang a wild song of all the rich fools who would pay for her now, of all that she had done to sew them like sacrificial feathers into her protective queenly cloak, of all their stupidities that would make up to her in small measure for the ills the world had ever borne her, and the slights the world's people had ever heaped upon her . . .

"I have nothing at all for you, Harry."

He sighed as if he had known her answer. She expected him to ask her to say it again, but instead he bowed over her two little hands, with a gentle kiss. Then he kissed her throat, her earlobes, and her nostrils.

"You know, if anyone does, my dear Jennie," he murmured politely, and the door closed, although that night they were supposed to see one of the numberless performances of *Camille*, and Jennie had laid out a costume that would have let few eyes rest upon the train-weary actress behind the footlights.

Seven

ABOUT ten o'clock Jennie, alarmed at last to be so alone in the little night-bound, fog-bound, snob-bound house, had Li go for Liza Bellamy. Five minutes later he would have been gone himself, silently into the salt air, to meet his cousins or his smoke-filled friends. Five minutes before he was sitting with his hands folded over two white beans of jade on a checkered board.

When Jennie spoke to him, hating to do so because of her pride, but sure of her remote hold over him, he said, "Certainly, Miss Jennie. I shall go at once. I think this is the right time to speak with the Negress, as you suggest." He bowed, his eyes and hands invisible, and went toward the back door, like a tall pole, and Jennie realized with a feeling of faint hysteria that at last, this dreadful night, he had indeed spoken to her as she first knew he would, with scholarly preciseness.

Soon Liza in her white unwilted sunbonnet was there, standing with hands folded like Li's. "What is wrong, Jennie?" she asked in her strong voice, but with such an extra measure of sour hate and censure in it that Jennie hesitated. "What did you tell the Chink was wrong?"

"Liza," Jennie said at last, "Sir Harry came tonight and wanted me to give him money."

"And what did you do, Jennie?" Liza's voice was rich and trusting now, as if she recited a familiar litany. "What did you do, Jennie my dear? Did you say yes to the old man?"

"Liza, I said no."

Jennie waited for what seemed a long time and finally heard the Negress's starched bonnet strings crackle against her old dry throat as she asked sternly, "And why did you say no, Jennie?"

The query seemed intolerable and insolent to the little exquisite woman in her silken nest, and suddenly, knowing at last that she was committed to a certain pattern of foolery, and hating the old witch who had helped her into it, she said in a sweet weak way, "But Liza did not tell me! Liza was not here to help poor Jennie!"

Liza stood tall and stiff with scorn. "You have misused my powders," she said coldly. "You have gone against them. I made my powders for you because I thought you were right for them, and now you have done the wrong thing with them and crossed them, I tell you."

"But I did not! You're unfair to me!"

"You did, foolish, foolish fool, or you would never have said no to old Sir Harry! What made you think you needed all that money? Money must come steady to stay steady. With me it would have come steady and it would have stayed steady for us both. Would the old man not have doubled what you loaned him? Would he not, you— you—"

Liza raised her arms in a frightening unfamiliar gesture

high above her bonnet, and then, slowly, as if she cleared her spiritual throat of a kind of puce-gray miasma, she spat at Jennie's feet and left.

Eight

I<small>N THE</small> morning the house was cold, and there was no delicate tea for Jennie upon a lacquered tray. But about eleven Li appeared, looking no more like a real human being than ever, with his bun of braided hair and his invisible eyes.

"Missie pardon," he said. "Li get in accident last night."

There was no sign of bruise or cut or weariness on what showed of him above the dark blue house-coat, and Jennie reassured herself by imagining a night of smoke dreams for her prime minister.

"Sir Harry call," he said suddenly as he flicked one finger like a trout fly into the gondola of warm water he prepared for Jennie, while she waited in a cloud of *mousseline* upon the bath rug.

Finally she replied, like a dutiful convent girl, "Yes? Sir Harry?"

Li put another handful of the Baden crystals into the tub. "He say five gentlemen come tonight for extra-fine dinner, honor of big race tomorrow with Tokay Jennie." There was no query in the thin voice, and as Jennie looked at him the Chinese sketched the shadow of the ghost of a shrug under his fine blank face.

The menu was a good one, as always. Jennie and Li

decided that they would astonish San Francisco gastronomy by serving a croustade of little local oysters coated with béchamel, to be served instead of either her favorite salad or Sir Harry's Roman punch between the roast and the game. And there would be a creamy cheese beaten with sauternes and made into a ring for hill strawberries. She would use several of the Keller wines, and then a high sauterne with the dessert, to please her lord. There would be Tokaj Aszu, of course, and she would gag it down while Harry's guests saluted her and the honey-colored filly named for her.

Jennie dressed lovingly, as always, but with her mind more than usual tonight upon immediate happenings. Why had Liza gone out so ungratefully, she asked herself. It was an ugly thing, to spit at her! What had Jennie done? Ah, poor Jennie, thus to be spat at! And Old Harry, to walk out as if he owed nothing to her! Had he forgotten that Jennie, little Jennie, was in the same rosy perfumed room with him? Was that not more important than some silly debts he owed? Jennie felt magnanimous suddenly, and wished that the two of them, the old stiff-hatted Negress and the great senile Englishman, could be there to admit her generosity. Let them hurt her, she said; let them cut into her and misunderstand her! Liza was an ignorant slave woman, a few years from the whipping block. Harry was a man in refuge, alive on remittances from his home, grateful to anyone who succored him in spite of his name and his bank book. Jennie could still be kind to them in spite of their ingratitude.

She wore pearls upon emeralds and topazes piled on pearls that night, and her gown was a froth of crystal-heavy gauze, the color of champagne, from which her little toes in tea-colored slippers peeped out like sly mice. She wore crystals trembling everywhere in her curls, and upon her upper arms thin gloves of champagne kidskin molded the soft physiognomy of her being, like a drawing of a goddess in the sky. She floated on a decorous fog of scent, and the rouge on her cheekbones was discreet. She was, to all intents at least, a lady.

And Harry was a gentleman, as he stood easy and gaily supercilious before the dining-room grate. Jennie saw with astonishment that he wore, instead of his braided theater-coat, a soft velvet jacket he had never used before except when they planned a long intimate evening beside her boudoir fire. It became him. She looked at it and smiled with a lift in her breast at its promise, until he said, watching her, "The gentlemen tonight are all friends of ours, my dear, and I have permitted myself the luxury of this lounging-habit."

"Friends?" She raised her eyebrows, and in spite of herself asked sharply, "Have we any friends? I thought you always went alone to the balls."

"To the balls, yes, my dear. But these are, as I said, our friends—shall I add, sporting, of the world sporting?"

Jennie stood graciously by the grate, drinking almost nothing from the glass of pink Plymouth gin and Italian wine that Harry had stirred for her. Her mind raced away from Liza and impenetrable Li to the men who might soon gleam gratefully at her table. Who in San Francisco could thus invited come upon Sir Harry in his house-coat? What trick was he playing? She was amazed, and in an ominous way puzzled, when finally they appeared, a refutation of her opinion of her old Saxon lover and his blindness. There they were, gathered neatly into one tight cautious group: Marc Raphael, still bandaged from his wedding death-ride; James the shipper, with his eyes like nuggets of slate, colder than Sir Harry's; Coll Hemingway, gay and pressing even in the small room, with his urgent black-haired wrists and his mockery so like Harry's; and the last two, the limp-eyed Southerner Sanchez and Coll's unsuspecting partner.

Jennie looked at them all and sent out from herself a kind of self-protective mist of desire, to hide her perturbation at the strange turn of things. She felt impotent but innately optimistic, like a beast in a maze.

She sat at the head of the table and had one of Li's cousins hand the dishes first to her, as if to prove their dearth of active poison, before she let the gentlemen scoop into them. She tasted each wine with a small dip of the glass to meet the deep salutation of Sir Harry facing her along the board. She sped ahead of the guests into the warm beautiful little drawing-room, so well lit by the Venetian wall-candles, to crouch in a kind of elegant cramp over the low coffee table and the row of jeweled cups.

"Coffee?" she asked softly. "Coffee, Sir Harry, Mr. James, dear Mr. Raphael? And you, Mr. Sanchez, and you, dear sir? And you, Mr. Hemingway?"

She looked for the first real time at any of them, and saw Coll standing like a fir tree in the light, and felt herself ready to vomit with desire. A small Chinese with a bun of hair like Li's waited at her elbow, and she waved away the webby bottle he held toward Sir Harry, who stood ready, as always, to pour his Jennie's wine.

"Tokay," he cried out hoarsely, so like himself that none

but she noticed his helpless theatrical croak. "Coll, old boy . . . Marc . . . taste this wine, I say!"

Jennie got up as decorously as she could and fled to the cool halls near her apartment. She still heard Harry's harsh voice, and saw against the soft light in the drawing-room the bones beneath the cloth, the marrow in the bones, of Raphael and James and the two others and . . . and . . . and reeling sharp as porcupine quills and soft as bacon grease and loathsome and delightful was the shape of Coll, Coll the one who had really tricked her, Coll the man here at the world's edge who had spoiled everything for her and made her forget even for one millionth of one second that she was Jennie. Indeed she hated him, as she stood there breathing in and out beside her doorway.

She listened. To the back of the house there was no sound: Li had gone already, perhaps, and without more than the one clear word to her, to let her know how much more perfectly than she he could speak any tongue in the world's books. She hated him for that, and for not letting her know him; she hated him for leaving her his debtor. And Liza Bellamy was gone, richer by thousands of dollars, but with the unforgivable stain of spittle upon Jennie's spiritual shoes. Ah, poor Liza! Jennie pitied her the way a scientist pities a yeast germ which will move and die to his piping. Liza could not do that to Jennie . . . or should not think she could.

Jennie shook away the uncertainty of her anger and moved back toward the drawing-room. Inside she could hear the old fool Harry talking, in his mocking way. How could he ever know her hatred of him for that poised voice that was as much a part of him as his chin? How could he know the insult in his easy laughter, and the goad of his teasing certainty of her, her, Jennie? She, if she were not Jennie, could spit on him as surely as old Liza had ever done on her.

She shuddered and pushed open the door. "May I help you, my dear Sir Harry?" she asked gently, lightly.

He lifted his head from the tall glass he frowned upon and looked suddenly like a young man instead of an old tired one trying not to let his hand shake as he poured the wine.

"Ah, Jennie!" His voice was warmer than the Tokay.

It is too bad he is such a beast, Jennie thought. If only he had never laughed at me I could love him.

"May I help you, my dear?" she asked again. She picked up the bottle and held it carefully, while her wide gray eyes slipped over the men watching her. There was an almost visible pause.

Then Harry said, "Go to the vestibule, my dear, will you, and bring us fresh cards? We have decided on a little match."

Jennie sped from the room and down the dark rich hallway, where there still hung a shadow of the brandy that had been poured flaming over hothouse fruit in the dining-room. The cards felt cool in her hands. She stood touching them gently to her cheeks, outside the drawing-room door.

"Of course, man! Of course I hate to get rid of her, especially at this point," she heard Sir Harry agree with one of his guests, his voice nonchalant and very British. "Little Tokay Jennie . . . finest filly I ever owned, and I've spent a lot of time and money on her."

"She shows it," Coll Hemingway said.

"From you, Coll, that's a fine compliment, old boy. I bow to you as an even better man than myself in such matters, in spite of your relatively tender age!"

There was a roar of laughter from the company. Then Harry went on, "It's hard to admit even this temporary set-back. I needn't tell you that. But I've put too much into the stable, shall we say? It's costing me too much to keep my colors up in front, in spite of what all you gentlemen have contributed to Tokay Jennie's upkeep with your generous betting."

Jennie let her hands drop slowly to her sides, so that the cards fell down onto the thick carpet. She was frozen with shock. They were talking about her, about Jennie the princess, laughing and treating her like a horse, a filthy four-legged creature! Her heart pounded so that she could hardly hear the men in her drawing-room, but their gay coarse voices finally rose above the red storm in her ears.

"Where on God's earth did you find her, Harry?"

There was a little pause. Jennie could see the eager eyes watching, the vile mouths ready to shout more laughter, and she heard Harry pour another glass of wine. Then he said, his voice rising on the swallow, "It's hard to believe, old chaps, but I give my word—Virginia City!"

There was another many-throated roar from the men, who as tried Westerners knew the look of the exhausted drabs from the mining town too well ever to see exquisite Jennie there. In the hall she raised her head proudly, grateful for their disbelief in spite of her fury.

"Yes," Harry went on, "I found her up there, working like a good little hustler too, and it cost a fortune to buy her away from Old Bertha, I can tell you. She'd once been right here in the city, incidentally, but not in any place you gentlemen would have visited. I sent her to Chicago, took her in hand myself until I thought she was fit to wear my colors—you know the rest—and thanks to old Bellamy's little rigmarole about magic love potions and my good Li's expert chaperonage, I have been able to let each of you gentlemen try out her paces for yourself."

The old man's voice was round with satisfaction. Jennie could see with her mind's eye the half-amused, half-angry looks of the five men who had with such wiliness been brought to share her. What fools they must feel, she cried out desperately, trying not to recognize their robust merriment, trying to tell herself that she had put horns on every one of them and that they hated one another for it.

"The trouble with Tokay Jennie," Harry went on comfortably in his deaf-sure voice, "is that she is so stupid. She forgot to remember that other people might be even less so. She takes herself too seriously, that is!"

It was then that Jennie killed him, in spite of herself. She murdered him in her mind as she stood there shaking in the dark hallway, as surely as if she had stabbed, poisoned, shot, slashed, bitten with acid, burned with oily fire, and as she saw his taunting body fall, bleed, flame, disintegrate before her, she turned slowly from the closed door toward her apartment.

"Fifty thousand is stiff, I know," he was saying, "but you all agree that she's worth it. At least, thanks to me, the man who wins will never need buy her the etiquette books!"

Coll Hemingway laughed loudest and said, "Tokay Jennie

looks more like a lady than anyone in San Francisco, by God."

"And now let's cut for it, gentlemen, as soon as the cards are here. Low card wins."

Jennie was in her room, peeling her clothes from her like old skins, throwing them everywhere onto the leopard-skin rugs and the rosy little chairs and tuffets. Naked, she looked with cold regret at her cases filled with carved jade. Half-corseted, she turned over the piles of jewels on her dressing table with an icy finger, past caring that she must desert them. Clothed in black, with the little snake-skin slippers rattling invisibly under her skirts, she picked up her check book, looked once at its pleasant round figures, and without another glance left the apartment where she had been so generous to the swine who betrayed her by laughing and making light of her together. She despised them as only an outraged queen could do, and as she swept lightly down the thick stair carpet, the pain and fury she had let herself feel a few minutes before dissolved into a kind of peace. She was fleeing, yes, but she was once more the real Jennie, untainted by men's greed, unsoiled by their trickery. No more need she smile and feel herself drowning in their words, their dark ingratitude. Jennie was free again . . .

. . . and . . .

yes, she was laughing like a gargoyle . . . in the room with the thin champagne-silk curtains, in her waxed and lovely house, with a jewel box in her hand and a little cap upon her head and high-heeled shoes of snakeskin on her feet, while in the patio the old man and the young one and the old woman and the girl sat deep in their dark soft pool of words. She went softly as far as the door. Then she listened again, her mouth still stretched with her own brand of merriment at the trick she would play them for waiting there for her to come back and feed them, soothe them, comfort them.

Paul's young voice said grudgingly, as if the words sounded themselves in spite of him, because of his youth, "Let's tease her, our witch-hostess. She's listening. That I can wager. Let's melt her snow, give her the shock treatment. Let's break our proud little Jennie for once!"

"But why?" Barbara cried out breathlessly. "Why should we? You can't possibly love Jennie, to say that!"

Paul laughed. "I can't? What do you know about love, Missie? You're a girl. You're still nothing but a girl."

"My dear Paul," Julia said in her deep beautiful voice, as if she were a stage dowager, "you apparently don't know as much about women as you seem to, if you think sex, or years, or even the lack of years, have any connection with passion."

"Passion? Did you say passion?" Old Sir Harry sat up a little. "That's not a word to be bandied about. It should be treated with respect, old boy, as should the fair creatures who arouse it. As for Jennie," he went on with the uncanny conversational ease of a deaf person who is seemingly removed from talk which all the time has been seeping into his inner ears, "our charming Jennie knows less, probably, about passion than any one of us, than all of us combined."

"Oh, look here," Paul protested, full of it himself, and in the dark silkiness of her room Jennie started as if she had been stung by a poisoned wasp. Rage flamed in her, so that her blood felt like steam racing under her skin, to hear Harry, of all people in the world, thus calmly strip her of something which he more than anyone should have recognized in her.

"Exactly," the old man went on in a ruminative way that seemed distilled insolence to her. "You protest for her because you know too little of it, although somewhat more than she. Passion, old boy, is a shared thing, and rightly a part of love in one form or another. It's not something you give consciously, so that you can get back equal measure in return. You don't make a rendezvous for it, set a time, and then weigh what you give and get, the way Jennie, for instance, invites us here and then waits for us to give her back the proper matching amount of gratitude and lust and palaver for her damned good food and her damned fine figure."

Paul said, the sweat of embarrassment wet on his voice, "Look here, sir! I was joking when I said Jennie was listening. But she might be! Good lord, let's—"

"Yes, really, Sir Harry," Barbara begged breathlessly, "don't you think—I mean, Jennie is so marvelous, and we're all joking, but even she might not understand—"

Harry snorted. "Of course she'd understand," he said in the amiable overbearing way of an old person. "If she hears us she'll simply think we're mistaken! Jennie's no fool—except about herself! She worships at her own shrine, that filly does. But it can't hurt us any to add a little incense, especially when she spurs us on with such excellent brandy."

Julia laughed, in a grudging way, and in the throbbing stillness of her room Jennie could hear someone, Harry or Julia or perhaps even weak traitorous Paul, sip at the liqueur and then breathe it out voluptuously.

"No," the old Englishman went on, "if Jennie were listening she wouldn't really hear us. That's what will always save her, and always has. She never hears anything the way it is said, but only the way she wants to."

Jennie put one hand gently upon the curtain beside her, and it was with a real surprise that she felt it cool and loose, not crumbling with the acid of her anger, not smoking with the heat of her disgust. They sat there, all four of them, and not even the girl who told Jennie's name as she told her beads had anything to say. The world spun and rocked.

In the soft air Paul laughed harshly, as if he were clearing some cobweb from his soul's throat, and he said, "I can't agree with you, sir, that our goddess is not at her window. But you're right that what we might say could not hurt her. She can't hear anything but the benisons." He raised his voice impudently. "Jennie! Jennie, we love you!"

There was such stillness in the patio that Jennie could hear above the thud of her heart a beetle in the dry cotton-wood leaves under the cactus plants. It was walking cautiously, foot after foot . . .

"Jennie! Come back! We want to worship you! We want to tease you a little, Jennie!"

Barbara laughed unexpectedly, helplessly, like a child being tickled.

Harry said, "I know a good way to get her out, if she's gone to earth. We'll simply tell where we first met her, each of us! What do you say? That will smoke her out, the little vixen!"

Julia laughed in a cracked caricature of the young girl's excited giggle, and then, "That's horrible," she sighed. "We've all drunk too much of Jennie's good wine." Her voice said that of course she would tell, that she would love to tell.

"Right," Paul said. "You know, not now but *now*! And I'll jump first!"

Jennie stood back from the window. She felt like a pin pricking and pointing her way across the floor, or like an infinitesimal dagger, so sharp with rage was she. She felt like a wind, cold from the heart of a subarctic, subexistent iceberg. She felt like the color blue, if for once in the world and time there were a true color blue. Then, as she pointed, cut, blew, bit, toward her freedom, she stopped, and for a second or part of a second she remembered all the people waiting there in the patio to take revenge on her. It was not their names or their faces or the touch of their skins that she remembered either. It was the way she had ever fled from them. Suddenly, for an immeasurable moment, an hour of a second, she recalled flight, so that she faltered in a kind of weariness. Not, she said so fast that it was not her own mind that protested, but the minds of other Jennies in other times, no, not again, yesterday or tomorrow or now.

All this will happen and happen, those minds said tiredly. It will go on. Now, this minute, they are all here, the young and the old, the man and the woman, gold and flesh and pride and game, all here. Now I can stop the thing. I can, while all are here, turn back to them and give Jennie to them without greed. I can at long last satisfy them.

The pin stopped spinning, and the dagger grew dull, and the room was of a comprehensible dark once more. And she had decided to go out, for the first time since she was ever Jennie, and listen and ask why and get the answers: it was the moment of betrayal.

She would never flee again. Why should she? What had it taught her, to run always before passion? How was she richer? Always she wanted people to give to her of themselves, and always she was the one who was cheated, because she never had anything in return except what was in the bargain, and not always that. Now there would be an end of such cautious reciprocity. Now she would listen and think, and send out shoots of herself like a tree, and let whoever could reach her boughs then perch upon them. She would ask nothing.

All this happened to Jennie in a flash of a flash, so that she hardly faltered as she walked toward the door, eager to reach the patio before the words there went on and she might be missing some of them. She felt noble, plainly. It was miraculous, and so made her somewhat giddy.

She held out her hand and touched the door knob, and then was Jennie again, shaken and laughing to have come so near forgetting it.

She shook herself. In the dim room she picked up the little jewel case and felt that the cap was straight upon her soft hair. She breathed carefully, like a woman.who has nearly died, and the fine familiar scorn of all the world flowed with nourishment and comfort through her once again, and the old excitement. She was Jennie. She was free, out of the pool of words. She would be gone . . .

And when would she return? Why should she, ever? Who next would know her?

Afterword

THE REASON I wrote this book is that two men I dearly loved told me to. One said, "You can do it, and you should." The other said, "You must." So I did, to please them.

Pascal Covici, who ended his long life as one of the last of the "true breed" of editors, started it in Chicago as part-owner of one of those mysteriously potent bookstores that happen in places like Paris and Budapest, and even in Los Angeles when someone like Jake Zeitlin is there . . . or in any smaller town where eager impatient minds must seek out good talk. In Covici's correctly shabby, dusty rendezvous, stripling giants like Theodore Dreiser and Ben Hecht decided the future of the world. Then Pat moved on to New York, to be half of what soon became a prestigious publishing firm, Covici-Friede.

Donald Friede was a well-heeled international roamer in search of cultural reassurance. At one point in his adolescence his mother sent him to a psychiatric-vocational counsellor. The famous doctor, after long talks with Donald, who said later that they were mostly about why *Nicholas Nickleby* was his favorite book, told her that the boy should become either an art dealer or a publisher. So at twenty-one, after going to Harvard, Princeton, and Yale in one year, he was installed as a vice-president in the Horace Liveright kingdom, where he tried hard for a while to be useful about emptying wastebaskets. (He once said mildly, "It is very hard to be a rich Jewish boy. It is harder to be a rich Jewish office boy. But it is perhaps hardest to be a fat rich Jewish office boy.")

In a few years Covici-Friede published a lot a high-class prize-winners and some flops. Then the two parted, thanks perhaps to the current Depression, but with genuine respect and affection.

Covici went on to be editor at Viking and Friede paced restlessly through the Western cultural scene, in Paris and Hollywood and New York.

Both men were attractive and exciting, with varying but always good tastes in books, words, typography, women, paintings, wines. For a time Donald and I were married and Pat was my editor. Both stayed my friends: in Pat's case my mentor and in Donald's the guardian angel of our two daughters. And somewhere they told me, *told me,* to write a novel.

I said, "But I am not a novelist, Some people are and some. . . . I've been reading novels all my life, and I don't want to try to write one." Obviously I had little chance to escape their professional and financial pressures, no matter how subtly or bluntly applied, so I sat down and wrote *Not Now but* Now. It was something I "could and should and must do. . . ."

I decided to make up the whole thing and tell it through a person as totally as possible unlike myself, both physically and morally. I knew I could tell dreams and spin yarns, although always I must depend on some of my own experience. I did finish the book and send it on to a delighted Pat, while Donald congratulated me on a "perfect vehicle" for some movie star he was then promoting.

The "novel" got good reviews, but was a commercial turnip. Pat kept on being my gentle editor, but Donald gave up any dreams of my ever writing a best-seller.

As for the book itself, I was never interested in it, once done, and still feel that North Point Press may be zany to reprint it. But perhaps it was written, no matter how doggedly, a little ahead of its time. To my mind it is really not a novel at all, although Covici was determined to call it that. It is a string of short stories, tied together more or less artfully by a time-trick. The female Jennie appears everywhere, often with heedless cruelty or deliberate destruction to her docile associates, and then slips away in her little snakeskin shoes. . . .

Of course I had to borrow from my own life, since I do not often remember any other, so that it was I who met the undertaker from Lausanne, and so on. The conservation of energy is almost as grave a problem as the Eternal Bitch and the liberation of women, whatever they all may be.

So I'd been told to write a novel and I did my honest best. I still love the two autocratic rascals who thus commanded me, and I hope the present publishers are justified in their stubborn belief that this is indeed a *book,* anyway. All I can do is keep on trying to write a good and pleasing sentence, even if nobody tells me to.

M. F. K. Fisher

Not Now but Now

A NOVEL BY
M.F.K. Fisher